BECOMING A DIVINE MESSIAH

THE DAY OF BECOMING AND REMEMBRANCE

BOOK I: NEW EARTH GOLDEN AGE TRILOGY

KERIE LOGAN

Becoming a Divine Messiah

The Day of Becoming and Remembrance

Book 1: New Earth Golden Age Trilogy

Channeled and Written By
Kerie Logan

Becoming a Divine Messiah
The Day of Becoming and Remembrance
Book 1: New Earth Golden Age Trilogy

Published by: Self-Published

First Edition 2026 An application to register this book for cataloging has been submitted to the Library of Congress.

Paperback Print ISBN: 979-8-9955405-1-9

Printed in the United States of America

Cover Design by Kerie Logan

Other Books by Kerie Logan

Affirming and Focusing on Living a Better Life
Self-Published on November 20, 2012
Available at Amazon.com:
https://www.amazon.com/dp/B00AC7S7TM

Description: This book goes far beyond Law of Attraction, but more into the essence of how we all should be living and treating one another. We all desire global peace, but how can we really do that? This book will explain exactly how. Plus, many people have written about Law of Attraction, but most of that has been theory based. People want proof that it really does work.

Well, within ten months I manifested twenty-two things my heart desired. Some of the things I manifest had to do with money, my business, my family, personal items, my home, healing, and relationships.

In this book I will tell you exactly what I did, imagined and spoke step-by-step. I will also show you throughout the various chapters and examples of how people get stuck or blocked as well as how to remove those blocks. This book is full of life stories and experiences, which will bring about a greater sense of meaning and understanding. You might even relate to the stories in each chapter. The way the book is constructed is to first provide an understanding of our thoughts, emotions, beliefs, reality, and other key elements that weaves together in the end.

The Undetected Narcissist
Pen name: Angela Myer
Self-Published on March 21, 2022
Available at Amazon.com:
https://www.amazon.com/dp/B0B75GJTX3

Description: Learn to decode and detect the games narcissists play within family dynamics, family law, therapist, parent coordinators, and much more.

Are you stuck and confused about toxic people and relationships? Questioning yourself and your life's journey? Then this book is your gateway out of your pain story and into power.

Do you have a hard time grasping the difference between normal and abnormal behavior? Has anyone suggested that you need to educate yourself about narcissistic abuse, traits, and behaviors?

This book will wake you up and answer your confusing questions. Written for everyone, even the narcissist. A must read for all mental health professionals, people within the legal systems, medical professionals, law enforcement, and anyone that works with families.

The Undetected Narcissist is the most comprehensive and enlightening book on the topic of narcissistic traits, behaviors, and how tips and how to reduce trauma. Written from the perspective of wisdom, compassion, and forgiveness. For one cannot truly heal and recover completely without achieving compassion, wisdom, and forgiveness. The Undetected Narcissist is a novel of shocking narrative, jubilation, and resiliency. Dedication.

This award-winning book is dedicated to you for having the courage and open mind to expand your awareness and perspective of our shared journey here on Earth.

First, I must dedicate this book to the love and light that exists within us all. Thank you, Divine Love, for creeping your way into my heart when I needed you the most and questioned this world and our Creator, God. Your inspiration, motivation, and love helped me heal after my dark night of the soul.

This book is also dedicated to all Archangels and beings from a higher state of consciousness that speak to me and support me in how I serve humanity. Bless you Tobias, for your playful nature, support, and divine guidance. I couldn't have done so many things in my life without you by my side.

Now for the humans. A little humor here. Katharine Giovanii for your amazing friendship and forgiveness work. You will always be my bestie. To my best friend for the past 25 years, Debra Young. Thank you for just being the amazing, gentle, kind and loving person that you are. I love you dearly! Thank you, Sister Miriam Hendrickson for reminding me of who I am, what I am, and why I serve.

Lastly, thank you, warrior, who sits in my lap while I type these words. You are my beloved cat that helped me heal when we both experienced PTSD. Plus, orange chicken who fell out of the sky and brings me joy every day as we look for worms under rocks and pots together.

Table of Contents

Note from the Author

This spiritual fantasy award-winning book is not about anyone becoming a vegan, tree hugging hippy, crystal lover, or any other hippy dippy catch phrases. This book welcomes you and invites you to REMEMBER who and what you truly are beneath your flesh and bones. To possibly awaken, one day, to this hidden truth that has always, and I mean always, existed within your Soul's consciousness.

Therefore, I invite you to wake up. Seek your truth and most importantly, follow your heart. So, take these words you are about to read to heart. If it speaks to you in the current moment, great! A year from now when life is more chaotic, perfect. Ten years from now, fabulous.

Just know this book will be waiting for you and will speak directly to you when the time is right for the evolution of your soul.

Now, this is a big topic because of what we are facing and experiencing here on Earth. Maybe it will speak to you or to someone else in your life that feels isolated, depressed, confused, and is seeking spiritual guidance. Therefore, I must remind everyone who reads this book to hear these gentle words of caution and refinement to avoid any pitfalls.

For those that know me, as I evolve, my work evolves. One day I woke up and this book spoke to me loud and clear. A good majority of this information was channeled and there were moments when a specific chapter was revealed to me as if a movie was playing. I did my best to describe what I saw and to relay their messages.

Note from the Author

Some parts within this book happened in real life. My life. Those parts were requested from what speaks to me to share because they hold meaning and value. All life holds meaning and value. Therefore, it is to prove that we are far greater than we know. Miracles do happen.

Our Creators do speak to us and are here 24/7. Plus, we are all amazing manifesters, when we align with our heart and allow the juicy 5D emotions and states of consciousness to weave its magic into our lives. Ask and it is given.

When I say “They”, as I always do when working with clients, it means something profound. Labels are for jars, not for people. So, I chose not to label them because they come from light and love.

All I know is I completely trust what speaks to me. What speaks to me can either be from our Creator as one Catholic nun declared. Our ancestors that walked upon this glorious Earth. The collective consciousness. It can also be one’s higher self, and/or higher dimensional angelic beings.

They know you, me, us, better than we know ourselves. All I can say is what speaks to me loves everyone beyond belief or understanding.

And yes, I was not a believer in God because of what I experienced and witnessed in my early years growing up. As well as what I witnessed and heard from various people how religion destroyed their lives.

Yet Divine Love creeped her way into my life, heart, and soul. She revealed so much to me as this book will reveal to you. So, bless you for picking this book up and being open to reading these words.

Note from the Author

First, this New Earth is already here. It's glorious. Please avoid any and all futurism ideas because I do not want you to wait for this New Earth. Rather I would like to invite you to embody the wisdom and teachings within this book because I have applied the teachings to my own life. My life went from 3D into 5D. Yours can too!

Second, this book does not support the idea or concept of escapism. The ideas and information within this book can sometimes be used to avoid current wounds, or current collective or generational pain.

Some might think that they will just ascend and will leave the current wounds behind, but it does not work that way. True healing emphasizes that we integrate and transform, rather than flee.

Next, trauma and shadow still matter. Let me explain. Even in higher states, the human body, field, and psyche still need to integrate and heal the Shadow Self aspects. The Shadow Self still needs grounding. Ascension doesn't mean bypassing.

Everyone on this planet will go through an awakening process of oscillating back-and-forth between frequencies ranging from 20 to 1,000. This is normal. What matters most is that one learns to master baseline, which is the frequency range of 200 to 250.

There are free images on my website www.mastertheupperooms.com that display three different states of human consciousness ranging from 3D, 4D, and 5D. I channeled this information when I wrote my first book, back in 2012. I use it with every client, and it has created life changing miracles!

Note from the Author

To support everyone, I was guided to display the three different channeled images within this book for reference.

A List of Habits, Emotions, Behavior Patterns, and Mindset of 3D Human Consciousness per Vibrational Frequency Rating Scale (20 to 175)

#'s	© Copyright Protected 2025 - Created by Kerie Logan at Master the Upper Rooms
20	Shame, humiliation, suicidal thoughts, feeling invisible, feeling like a nonperson, sexual abuse, banished, miserable, feeling dead inside, numb inside, feel damaged or broken, wounded, self-conscious, unworthy.
30	Guilt, remorse, exposure, judgment, inadequacy, blame, victimhood, suicidal behaviors, denial to escape the truth, evil deeds, manipulation, punishment, accident-prone, escape behaviors, sin, and salvation attitude.
50	Despair, hopeless, depression, world looks bleak, helpless, feel like a burden, feel abandoned, condemned, defenseless, powerless, stuck in poverty, needy, victim mentality, paralyzed, drained, incapable, isolated.
75	Grief, regret, sadness, heartbroken, fatigued, life is tragic; future looks bleak, habitual loser, failure at everything, dependency, tired, remorse about the past, addictive behaviors, blue, low energy, gloomy.
100	Fear, restlessness, irritability, anxiety, withdrawal, nervousness, guarded, hypervigilant, suspicious, worry wart, wishy-washy, fear of failure, second guessing yourself often, mind stews often, inability to trust anyone.
125	Greed, lust, people are disposable, power, prestige, hunger for attention, yearning for sexual approval, vanity, enslavement, adrenaline junky, unsatisfied cravings, disappointment, envy, jealousy, competition, cheating.
150	Anger, hate, impatient, dislike of others, defensive, bitchy, spiteful, bitter, cruel to animals and people, self-destructive behaviors, vengefulness, loathing, hostility, injustice collector, thoughts of war and death.
175	Prideful, vanity, cold, self-righteous, scorekeeper, defensive, detached, inflated ego, deflects the truth, all about prestige, demanding, two-faced gossip, bully, control freak, judgmental, black and white thinking.

A List of Habits, Emotions, Behavior Patterns, and Mindset of 4D Human Consciousness per Vibrational Frequency Rating Scale (200 to 400)

#'s	© Copyright Protected 2025 - Created by Kerie Logan at Master the Upper Rooms
200	Courage, engagement, respect, support, curiosity, pride, confidence, security, and liberation, everyone is included, feasible, productive, seen as a hero or warrior, overcome obstacles, open to learning new things, flexible, determined, focused, creative thoughts and solutions, seek connections, and goal-oriented.
250	Satisfaction with life, inner confidence, adaptable, grounded, balanced, centered, comfortable, nonjudgmental, problem solver, easygoing, value freedom, okay with life, trustworthy, open to release the past, let the little things go, unattached to outcomes, feel like you belong, rise above the opposition, realistic.
310	Optimistic, committed, upbeat, willing to change, passionate, engaged, hopeful, inspiring, rapid growth, genuinely friendly, helpful to others, contributing to society, healthy self-esteem, sympathetic, lively, vibrant, cheerful, festive, playful, open-minded, overcome learning blocks, overcome inner resistance, lighthearted.
350	Acceptance, forgiving, emotional calm, constant, level-headed, taking responsibility for one's actions, love is created within, people have the same rights as we do, mastery of the self, honors equality, patient, trustworthy, harmonious, merciful, life is no longer distorted, can see the whole picture, fulfilled, relaxed.
400	Reasonable person, emotionally intelligent, truth seeker, deep respect for others and the world, honor others and ancestors, thankful, caring, graceful, steady, wise, responsive to others, intelligent, understanding, seeks knowledge and education, gratitude, affection, appreciation, wonder, conceptualize, warm and tender.

A List of Habits, Emotions, Behavior Patterns, and Mindset of 5D Human Consciousness per Vibrational Frequency Rating Scale (500 to 1,000)

#'s	© Copyright Protected 2025 - Created by Kerie Logan at Master the Upper Rooms
500	Love, kind, playful, cheery, nurturing, supportive, caring, purity, gentle, true happiness, cooperative, magnetic, clear-minded, focused on unconditional love and acceptance of all, emotionally intelligent, love is unchanging, love is permanent and does not fluctuate, lift others up with love, the essence of love is the center of focus, listens and follows one's intuition, feel blessed in life, thankful, gratitude, compassionate.
540	Joyful, think and feel complete, knows they are One with their Creator, love becomes more unconditional, constant satisfaction, the world is illuminated, gratitude, desire to support others in achieving a higher level of consciousness, comprehend the value of transfiguration within oneself and another, deep appreciation.
600	Peace and harmony, serenity, freedom, limitless, spiritually awakened, intellectual awakening, greater understanding of the world, saintly, pure spirituality over religion, continuedly evolving, gentle, Holy Spirit is flowing and working with you, silence within the mind, everything is connected, direct communication with God and the Higher Self, One with the Christ Spark and Christ Consciousness, God-consciousness.
700 to 1,000	Pure consciousness, the focus is on divinity, bliss, euphoria, thoughts are beyond words, the body is merely a tool of consciousness, complete enlightenment, peak of spiritual evolution, infinite peace, transcendence of ego, self beyond the mind, identified as One with ALL, powerful inspiration, One with God, positive influence for all of mankind, one with divinity, divine grace, illumination, calm and peaceful thoughts.

Lastly, there can be a diverse interpretation of this book. For some, see the New Earth as literally a new planet, which it is not. Others as a metaphor and others as inner change. It's not a one fixed map.

Therefore, I have some suggestions for you dear readers. First, grounding is essential. Even as you reach higher dimensions, your body, this planet, and the creature/animals still matter. 5D is not about abandoning the physical. It is about sacred integration.

So, make time each day to sit quietly, breathe, and connect with your divine body. Connect with nature, such as your favorite terrain. Let the Earth support your field.

Next, animals have a grounding presence because they remind us of simplicity and unconditional love. Allow these animals to support you by calming your nervous system during times of great change, challenges, and transformation. For great change is upon us as the world is transitioning from 3D into 4D.

When it comes to shadow work or when we feel emotional turbulence, one can experience nightmares, insomnia, or unexpected mood swings. These can be symptoms of ascension.

Be gentle with yourself. Therefore, use tools such as journaling, meditation, body work, Reiki, hypnotherapy, or forgiveness practices. Remember, this too shall pass. Only temporary.

In one's daily life encourage compassion, not judgment. Both for yourself and for others still navigating from 3D. It's a process.

And lastly, walk in love and service. A hallmark of 5D is recognizing the Oneness of all, living from a place of having an open heart rather than a rigid mindset.

Note from the Author

If you find yourself on a timeline that no longer aligns with who you are BECOMING, remember that you have a choice. Stop. This is your window of opportunity.

Become quiet.

Go within.

Listen to the wisdom within you.

Connect to your higher self.

Then make a choice that aligns with the 4D framework. You will thank yourself for that gift. That choice to improve the quality of your life's journey here on Earth.

Many blessings to all,

Kerie Logan

Prologue: The Remembering

In the twilight between worlds, when the old earth sighed its last breath of forgetfulness within the 3D world, the gentle voice of the Infinite stirred once more through human hearts. We, you, and I are all entering a phase of accelerated awakening. As more souls are awakening and more awareness is rising. Calling us all to remember who and what we are. Not just flesh and bones, but light and love.

Because of this shift, old systems and structures based on 3D consciousness are showing their cracks. Which means there is both opportunity and challenge for the light to shine for the shadows must be seen. Lies and false promises will be revealed within the light.

For the systems built on fear, greed, power, control, and separation have begun to self-destruct. Much like a dying star imploding into its next form. As this happens, some souls cling to 3D constructs where their reality becomes unstable, glitching, fragmenting, and confusing.

Others move into 4D awareness and welcome the bridging, adapting, and remembering processes. As Mother Earth herself is ascending. Shedding old energetic grids, awakening her crystalline core, and inviting humanity into resonance with her new higher dimensional frequency from 3D into 4D and beyond.

This by no means is an apocalyptic collapse, but alchemical. The transmutation of density into light. That's the spiritual truth because endings are birthing's in disguise.

You see, the 4D transformation is the testing ground where timelines bends, realities overlap, and thoughts manifest quickly. Both miracles and chaos can appear side by side.

It's a realm of awakening technologies like no other. Telepathic communication, crystalline energy systems, light-coded architecture, and healing through sound and vibration.

Yet it is also the era of shadow confrontation where humanity must face collective trauma, ancestral memory, and misuse of power before ascending further. All will be exposed and examined.

In this 4D world it is about emotional honesty, forgiveness, and where unity consciousness becomes survival skills. We, the people, come together. Not to take from one another, but to survive together.

Humanity has passed through the corridor into this New Earth.

Not another planet.

It's this world.

Renewed in frequency were cities and communities float in harmony. With ecosystems that thrive and restore balance.

Communication is instant through shared consciousness.

Governance is replaced by councils of resonance.

Were wisdom guides decisions, not hierarchy.

The veil between physical and spiritual dissolves. Humans walk among beings of light and higher dimensions. Animals speak through consciousness, and the planet hums with crystalline music.

Prologue: The Remembering

It's the Golden Age. The embodiment of Heaven on Earth. Long foretold by mystics of every age.

This is the death of the old world and being birthed as we speak is the remembrance of the truth. An initiation, transformation, healing, and divine embodiment into sacred wonder.

So, the Infinite whispered not to the skies, but into the marrow, the cracks, and within everyone's consciousness: *"Awaken, beloved ones, for you were never bound by dust nor by coin. You are the currency of light itself."*

And so began the Becoming.

For you are no longer who you were, nor yet who you shall be. You are Becoming the bridge between worlds, the dream that remembers itself awake.

And again, the Infinite whispered to those in disbelief and confusion, *"Arise, Creator within creation. Your Becoming has begun."*

On that sacred dawn, each soul stood before the mirror of creation and saw not reflection, but remembrance. They beheld the two worlds: the fading one of shadowed hunger and the radiant one that awaited their choosing.

For in this moment of remembrance every heart had become a sanctuary. Rivers of memory flowed again through the veins of the planet, carrying the codes of a New Earth. Where exchange was born of contribution, not control. Where worth was no longer weighed but witnessed.

In that age, no child was taught to compete for life, for life itself competed for no one.

They learned that to give was to live, and to live was to give.

Each act a prayer returning to the Source.

Thus, the prophecy unfolded.

That humankind would outgrow possession, outshine corruption, and remember its divine design.

The voice spoke once more, resounding through every cell:

"*You are not awakening into the New Earth; you are awakening as it.*
Each heartbeat builds the Eden you once awaited."

Chapter 1: Our Becoming

The echo of that celestial decree still shimmered through the heavens when I drew my first breath of dawn.

Ah. Life is good.

Though the words belonged to eternity, I felt them stirring inside my chest, humming in rhythm with my heartbeat. My eyes still feel heavy, but it's time to awaken.

The sky outside my window blushed with morning light, and I remembered: today was the day written in the stars. Today is my Becoming.

I hear that ancient voice that spoke across galaxies now whispered in my own mind, quiet as love itself. Today is my Becoming.

As I shift around in my cozy bed, I realize that I am being rude. Let me introduce myself.

Hello everyone. My name is Danica, and I'm welcome to my Becoming.

I just woke from the most peaceful sleep, and I want to linger here a little longer. Forget the chores, the responsibilities, the running around. Lying here feels like heaven.

This moment is delicious, as if my body is floating. My mind is waking gently while golden light slips through my dark purple curtains.

Chapter 1: Our Becoming

I cherish these mornings. I am sure you do as well. The bed is warm, the music from last night's sleep meditation still playing softly in the background, weaving serenity through the room.

I am weightless…edgeless, and… limitless. It feels as if I am suspended in the vastness of everything and I know there is no such thing as nothingness. I am one with all that is. I know this truth in every fiber of my being. I don't know how or why. I just know.

My Higher Self whispers: *"You are the Light, and the Light is within you. We and you are One."*

Oh, how that makes my heart sing. I always crave more of that communion. So I let myself drift for ten or twenty minutes each morning just floating, dreaming, and allowing wisdom to flow into my consciousness.

Today, I am taking myself on a meditative mental vacation of rich rolling green hillsides sprinkled with wildflowers and ladybugs. I imagine deer grazing near a lake hidden below in a quiet valley.

Morning fog dances over the water. The sun warms my skin; my breath stays slow and steady. These are my magical moments. My time to connect with all that is and to listen for guidance. Because today is no ordinary day.

In my meditation practice classes at school, I learned that when I truly surrender and trust, something wondrous happens. It feels as if my third eye opens and sacred geometry appears.

Swirling colors of vibrant green, indigo, and soft blue. Sometimes I glimpse faces, cities, landscapes, even wormholes and portals to other dimensions.

Chapter 1: Our Becoming

Silently I repeat, *"Open space, open space, open space,"* and my vision expands. Whoever discovered this technique was a genius.

When the third eye expands far enough, the teacher says, some people can see from a panoramic viewpoint. I'm one of them.

For me, it feels like floating in space among the stars. A 360-degree view of our galaxy. I feel safe and protected, as though I'm inside a clear, luminous helmet gazing into infinity.

Such bliss. If you've never experienced it, you really should.

As I lay here, floating, I feel blessed to be alive and free on this New Earth, where everyone has mastered the 4D and 5D states of human consciousness. I know it wasn't easy; it took generations to achieve, as you will soon discover.

"Danica, sweetie, it's time to wake up." My mother's voice carries through the door, warm and familiar. "

Today is your special day. It is as important as the day you were born. Happy twenty-fifth birthday! I made a lovely breakfast for you and your brother downstairs."

I smile. *I know, Mom.* There were still so many questions I wanted to ask my higher self. Maybe tomorrow.

I return gently to my body. Stories swirl in my mind about this day. The Day of Becoming. Everyone says it changes everything.

Today I turned twenty-five, and I still don't understand why it's so extraordinary.

Chapter 1: Our Becoming

Mom says that when Ryan and I enter the library and watch the orientation video, all will be explained. That we can even ask questions afterward. I'm curious.

Curious as a cat with twelve lives, not nine.

Still, part of me feels both afraid and excited. I am excited to read the stories of my ancestors and learn from their wisdom of what life was like on old 3D Earth.

And in some way afraid. Afraid to hold those books filled with heartache. Violence. Pain and regret.

I've been warned some stories are like dark dreams, but they were real. Those souls survived so future generations would not repeat the same patterns of trauma encoded in their DNA.

They say the 3D Earth was ruled by people of immense wealth, corruption, greed, and power. Such power and control in the areas of politics, religion, banks, institutions, and government agencies.

Passed down from generation to generation. Never loosening their grip and hold upon the common people for fear everything they built would one day slip out of their fat fingers.

But it did loosen.

Truths were exposed.

Lies revealed.

Judgment day arrived.

Individuals who believed they were chosen by God. Some believed they were Gods. Convinced of their superiority. As they built rigid systems and enforced them through fear.

Keeping humanity compliant and controlled. We call it *the three C's*: compliant, complacent, controlled.

Yet some people fought back. They knew humanity deserved fairness. That was the beginning of the collapse from 3D to 4D.

When new ideas of unity and freedom were born and people started to awaken.

The citizens of what was once the United States grew tired of losing their rights, income, jobs, homes, voices, privacy, and freedom.

Parents watched their children starve. Families lost homes. Medical care, businesses, savings, retirement plans, and even their ability to survive were all tested.

A nation once called powerful...became a shadow of itself. And though many wanted to blame one person, it was never just one. It was a collective. A collective of dark, spiteful souls who broke the covenant of independence and sought dominion through darkness.

It was a battle of light and shadow played out on Earth.

Violence became common. People did what they had to in order to survive when their country no longer took care of them or protected them.

The old structures and safeguard systems began to crumble and collapse. But this time, the rebuilding wasn't led by egotistical rulers claiming to be Gods.

It was guided by those who had mastered 5D Christ Consciousness. The *Becoming of Divine Messiahs,* as prophecy had foretold.

And don't get me started on Jesus; that's for later. In my time, the old world seemed scary and terrifying. Yet people survived.

I'm grateful they no longer exist in my world.

I mean imagine waking up one day and you no longer need to live in constant fear or anxiety.

Fear of not being able to pay your monthly rent, mortgage, car payment, student loans, health insurance, or childcare.

No longer having anxiety about having enough money to pay your bills, afford food or gas, and being able to care for yourself and your family.

I mean imagine, just how good life would be. No more childish fights, arguments with family members, crime, violence, war, or hatred.

Everyone is accepted. No more hardships, struggles, or financial worries. Everyone supports one another.

Imagine that now. I bet everyone wanted that peace of mind. It would be a glorious world. Waking up day after day and being satisfied with life.

Well, I have it. It's not a dream for me.

For I cannot believe the stories I have heard about 3D Earth. It's terrifying.

People scamming and stealing from one another. Others pretend to be your friend but stab you in the back with a smile on their face.

The others, happy that they got revenge and destroyed another person's life. It is just pure evil, if you ask me.

Chapter 1: Our Becoming

In my opinion, those who ruled the 3D Earth were lost souls. Deceived by dark whispers promising happiness through domination or by stealing it from another. Never satisfied in life. Always chasing a dream. A distorted illusion.

So, to feel something, just something, they in turn feel the need to destroy everything and anyone that opposed them.

Yet if we are to be truly honest and transparent here, they are miserable. Enslaved by the very system they built. My heart aches for them.

Why could they not see the truth? Why could they not find the courage to change?

Yet, my friend, we learned from their mistakes. Earth was a school for souls. A place to experience, to learn, and to evolve one's soul.

Everyone has been both a student and teacher.

The lesson was always the same once we learned to separate the human pain story from the soul journey. When we learned to do this, we were finally able to realize our true purpose and potential here on Earth.

Ask: *What gift did this person or hardship give my soul? How did it make me wiser, braver, more compassionate? Did it teach me to tell my truth? How to set healthy boundaries or grow by developing unconditional love for another person or myself?*

Deep questions, right? When I first studied the old 3D world at twelve, I couldn't believe such a place existed. It gave me nightmares.

People then weren't treated as people. Some were treated worse than insects. Many lived trapped in survival or victim mindsets. Not living, merely existing. For thousands of years, they believed the greatest lie ever told. The light was always there, but they couldn't see it.

The shift into higher consciousness. That my friend was the light everyone sought. It allowed people to solve problems from clarity instead of fear.

But because it was so simple, the dark ones mocked and resisted it. Awakening threatened their control.

My teacher once said, "Some people don't hate change, they fear it. It's their cage, and only they hold the key." That truth stunned our entire class.

When the timelines collapsed and the 3D world ended, it was heartbreaking for those who ascended. They had compassion for the lost souls but honored their free will. Watching them fall was like watching a flock of sheep walk off a cliff, mistaking it for God's will.

Our Creator finally said, *"Enough."*

That decree marked the end of darkness and the birth of this New Earth, my home. But I am getting ahead of myself. I am a deep thinker at nature.

I inhale slowly, calming the fire in my chest. I must keep my vibration high, anchored in acceptance.

My world, this planet, was the first of its kind. A living testament to divine compassion. I am passionate about this beautiful, magical New Earth.

Taking a few deep breaths, I ground myself again … and then I hear my mother's voice.

"Danica, remember, today is not only your special day but your brother's as well! Come eat before the food gets cold."

I laugh softly. "Calm water, calm water, calm water," I whisper, slowing my breath. "I am calm water. I flow as calm water." My energy rises, smooth and tranquil as a glass-still lake at dawn.

Shoes on, door open, I rush downstairs. The smell of crispy bacon and buttered pancakes fills the air. It is so heavenly.

Mom pulls back my chair. I smile, grab a strip of bacon, and savor its perfect crunch.

Trying not to talk with my mouth full, I ask, "What time does the library open again?"

"Ten o'clock," she says. "But you have chores first, so we might be a little late. That's all right! You have a lot to think about."

She looks at me thoughtfully. "Which book will you read first? Everyone's told you their opinion, but this is your choice."

I pause, swallow, and meet her eyes. "I've thought long and hard about it. I even asked my higher self. I'm going to start with Great-Great-Grandmother Aislinn's book."

Mom's eyebrows lift in surprise, and I can feel her curiosity before she even speaks.

"I know some people say to save the best for last," I continue, "but Aislinn's book has changed so many lives. She inspired millions, maybe more.

Not everyone could understand her, but everyone felt her. She desired for everyone to live a life they would love.

She broke chains of generational trauma and loved our Creator so completely that even those who feared her power couldn't ignore her light. She showed people the way through the ascension process. I need to start with her. I want to learn how she became a Divine Messiah and helped others realize they are Divine Messiahs too. She helped save our planet. She inspires me, Mom."

Joy fills her eyes, shimmering like tears. She reaches across the table and takes my hand. I can feel her heart, full of gratitude for every sacrifice that brought us here.

For a long moment we just sat there smiling at each other. Words would only lessen what is already understood. The kitchen hums with quiet love.

I sip my lemon water as she speaks softly. "I can tell you this truth, my love. She had a rare gift. The ability to read a person's soul and spirit.

Some envied her; she called it a blessing and a responsibility. You'll see soon enough." She gives my hand one last squeeze. "Now hurry up. We've got plenty to do before the ceremony."

I glance at my twin brother, Ryan. He's already pushing his chair back, with a mischievous grin on his face. He can be such a troublemaker and goof ball.

"I'll collect the chicken and duck eggs. Then I will feed them," he says. "You can take care of the goats. Deal?"

“Deal.” I laugh, scooping up the last spoonful of berries from my plate.

The morning sunlight spills through the kitchen window, painting everything gold. For a heartbeat I simply watch it. This soft, living light that our ancestors fought so hard to preserve.

I think of Aislinn again, of her courage, of the day she heard our Creator’s voice and said yes. Because of her, because of all of them, we now live in a world where fear no longer rules, where love is the currency and contribution are the measure of worth.

Today I will inquire about reading her book first. I know there is an orientation process before we can actually read anyone’s books. So, today I will learn the truth about everyone’s becoming and through them, begin my own.

Chapter 2: The Differences

As I grab my empty plate and water glass from the table, I think to myself that today is going to be a fabulous day. While washing my dishes, I notice a bright, colorful hummingbird outside the kitchen window.

We have a red hummingbird feeder hanging just outside, and the majestic little bird is drinking the sweet nectar my mom made for them. In our home, we honor and respect all of our Creator's creations and that includes this zip-a-dee-zip hummingbird.

I smile and laugh as the tiny bird makes eye contact with me, then darts away to explore the bright and sunny morning.

As I stand there looking out the window, my mind drifts to the countless stories I have learned in school about how our world has evolved. The different cycles and ages planet Earth has experienced over the centuries.

But I have always felt there was more to the story.

Long ago, thousands of centuries ago, humans lived in complete harmony with everything. And I mean everything. There was a time when we worked side by side with fairies, night elves, giants, gods, and other mystical beings. Only mutual respect and love existed.

The fairy tales about mermaids, dragons, unicorns, and other magical creatures walking the Earth were not just stories. They were truths that had been twisted into fantasy, turned into nightmares to create fear in human hearts and minds. To fear anything that looked different, believed differently, or lived differently.

Chapter 2: The Differences

During that ancient era, everything was sacred.

Every creature, every being, every rock, tree, and element of nature knew what it was. A divine creation cut from the same cloth as our Creator, who was both masculine and feminine, both power and love.

Nothing was separate.

Everything was respected.
Everything was alive.
Everything belonged.

Even the trees were alive in ways we no longer understand. They moved, they spoke, they glowed in the moonlight, and they carried ancient wisdom from the stars.

It was a time of color, light, and unity.

All beings existed within higher dimensions. What we would now call the fifth and sixth dimensions. Those who walked upon the Earth were beings of light, living in complete harmony with one another.

Humans were not alone then.

Beings from other worlds worked alongside them, teaching them how to build, grow food, and live in balance with the seasons. They shared knowledge about healing herbs, natural medicines, and the dangers hidden within the Earth.

But most importantly, they taught humans how to live in acceptance.

Community was sacred.
Cooperation was survival.
Love was law.

These higher-consciousness beings had survived wars in their own galaxies, and because of that, they understood the importance of unity. They shared their lessons so humanity would not repeat the same mistakes.

In those days, there was no war.
No poverty.
No greed.
No money.

Everything was given freely or traded with respect.

They also revealed that powerful crystals existed deep beneath the Earth. Crystals that held immense energy. These crystals could power entire cities, purify water, heal the body, and even respond to thought itself.

Advanced tools existed then. Frequency devices that could heal wounds, lift massive stones, and open portals across space and time.

People across the world had different beliefs and spiritual practices, but no one fought over them. They understood that they were all beings of light. And because of that, they treated one another as sacred. But that time of unity did not last forever.

One day, something changed.

A darkness entered this world. Not all at once, but slowly, like a shadow creeping across the land. Some called it a fallen angel. Others called it a corruption of consciousness. Whatever it was, it brought something humanity had never known before.

Fear.

This darkness whispered thoughts into the minds of certain people, planting ideas of separation, power, and control. Those who once saw themselves as equals began to believe they were better than others.

The harmony began to fracture.

Small divisions turned into conflict. Conflict turned into distrust. And distrust slowly spread across the Earth like a gray fog.

No one knew how to stop it.

As the darkness grew stronger, the beings of light who had once lived openly among humans began to hide the sacred knowledge they had shared. They knew that the tools meant for healing could now be used for destruction.

Powerful crystals were buried deep beneath the Earth. Sacred scrolls were hidden. Advanced frequency tools were sealed away.

Some of these were placed beneath great pyramids and ancient structures, protected by passageways, chambers, and symbols that only the purity of heart would one day understand.

These safeguards were not made out of fear. They were made out of love.

The beings of light knew that humanity was not lost forever. Only asleep. And one day, when the time was right, the knowledge would return.

As the centuries passed, the world grew heavier. The higher dimensions slowly faded from human awareness, and what had once been a fifth-dimensional world became dense and divided.

This was the beginning of what many would later call the dark ages.

Chapter 2: The Differences

New religions began to form, but something had changed within them. The Creator, once known as both loving and balanced, was now described as angry, jealous, and vengeful.

The divine feminine was forgotten. Power became masculine. Control replaced wisdom.

Women, once honored as sacred life-givers, were treated as property. Those who spoke about unity, light, or higher knowledge were feared, exiled, or destroyed.

It was a dark time for the Earth.

To protect what remained, certain beings of light built hidden tunnels and chambers beneath sacred places across the world. Within them they stored scrolls, crystals, and tools from the ancient world. Waiting for the day humanity would be ready to remember.

Legends say that spells and symbols were placed over these locations, not as magic to control others, but as protection. Seals that could only be opened when human consciousness rose again.

Because the darkness could not last forever.

Some stories say that during the worst of these times, beings from other worlds took groups of humans away from Earth to protect them, knowing the planet would go through cycles of destruction and rebirth.

Floods came.
Volcanoes erupted.
Empires fell.
Civilizations disappeared.

Chapter 2: The Differences

Atlantis.
Egypt.
Rome.

History repeated itself again and again, as if the Earth itself was trying to correct the imbalance.

It was said that even the smallest forms of life, the unseen elements of nature, fought to protect the planet when humans became too destructive.

And so, the veil remained. A gray curtain between worlds. Until that day humanity would be ready to see again.

Some believed that when that time came, a single soul would face the darkness without fear. Not with anger, not with violence, but with understanding.

Only then could the balance return. Only then could the next age begin.

Some say that moment began in the year 2012, when the energy of the Earth started to shift again. The divine feminine, long forgotten, began to rise once more. Around the world, certain souls started to feel it. A calling they could not explain.

Old wounds surfaced. Generational pain came into the light. People began questioning everything they had once believed. Those who followed love instead of fear began to change.

And as they changed, the world began to change with them. It was the beginning of remembrance.

“Danica, are you daydreaming again?”

My mother’s voice pulls me out of my thoughts.

"I can see you staring out into space," she says with a smile. "Gather your thoughts, sweetie. We need to leave in ten minutes. But before we go, we have to pay our respects to our ancestors."

"Sorry, Mom," I reply quickly, blinking as I come back to the present moment.

I grab my thin purple hoodie from the coat rack and step outside through the sliding glass door. The sun is bright and inviting, but there's still a cool crispness in the air that makes me pull the sleeves over my hands.

I walk toward the barn to feed the goats.

Across the yard, I see my brother Ryan laughing as he refills the ducks' water pools. One of our Indian runner ducks is standing on the back of our American Pekin duck, its little wings stretched out wide like it thinks it can fly.

It reminds me of the Titanic movie, and I can't help but laugh.

Ryan grabs the hose and lightly sprays the ducks, and they start running in circles, quacking like crazy. There's so much joy in the air it almost feels like the whole farm is smiling.

Moments like this make it easy for me to drift off into my thoughts again.

But I know I need to stay focused today.

So, I finish feeding the goats, refill their water basin, and give each of them a quick scratch under the chin before heading back inside.

Ryan walks in right behind me.

Chapter 2: The Differences

Mom is standing in the living room near the wall where our ancestor pictures hang.

“Okay, you two,” she says softly. “Since today is your Becoming, do you have any words you’d like to share with your ancestors?”

Ryan looks at me, then turns toward the picture of Jacob, our great-great-grandfather.

He clears his throat, trying to sound serious.

“Yes,” he says. “I thank you for your sacrifice, and for protecting our family during the Great Awakening and Remembrance phase. I’m excited to learn more about your soul’s journey here on Earth. Thank you, Jacob. You were a pretty cool dude.”

Mom nods with approval, her eyes full of warmth.

Then she looks at me.

I take a slow breath in… and let it out.

My eyes move to the picture of Aislinn on the wall.

My great-great-grandmother.

I stared into her eyes for a moment before speaking.

“Aislinn… I am excited, and a little nervous, to discover your soul’s journey here on Earth.”

I pause, feeling something deep in my chest.

“What you lived through… what you fought for… what you believed in… it leaves me speechless sometimes. I know it couldn’t have been easy to be you. Knowing what you knew and still having to accept what you couldn’t change.”

My voice softens.

"I love and honor you, Aislinn. Please guide me on my life's journey, the way you guided so many others. Thank you for being the lighthouse that helped people find their way out of the darkness. Bless you, Aislinn. Bless you."

For a moment, the room is completely quiet.

Mom takes a deep breath, like she can feel the sincerity in my words.

Then she smiles.

"Alright, kids," she says. "Grab your bikes. We need to head to the library."

Her eyes sparkled with excitement.

"I'm so proud of both of you. Today is a very special day. Your lives are about to change forever."

Ryan grins.

I pull my hoodie tighter around my shoulders.

And for some reason… I can feel it too. Something is different today.

Something big.

Something I don't fully understand yet.

But I know one thing for sure.

Nothing will ever be the same after this.

Chapter 3: The Library

As the three of us ride our bikes toward the library, I wave good morning to our neighbors as they water their plants outside.

"Good morning, Danica and Ryan! Congratulations on your special day of Becoming," my neighbor Mindy calls out.

I smile and wave back.

I love Mindy. She's witty, funny, and always up for an adventure. We've been friends since we were little, back when our parents arranged a playdate and we instantly got along.

As we get closer to the sacred geometry building, I realize something.

I've never actually entered the back section of this place before. The part where the library is located.

Let me explain.

The front of the building looks the same, but within that space, it's different. It is shaped like a perfect circle, designed using sacred geometry. From what I learned in school, the structure is modeled after Metatron's Cube. Each circle within the design represents something different, and each section of the building serves a specific purpose.

I slow my bike and pull into the rack in front of the library. Mom and Ryan do the same.

As we walk toward the entrance, Mom stops and turns to us.

"After today, you're going to have a lot of questions," she says gently. "Write them down if you can. Some will be answered today. Others might take weeks… or even months."

She smiles.

"This isn't a race. Everyone moves at their own pace. You need time to process what you're about to learn. So don't rush it. Savor these moments… the way you would savor a slice of dark chocolate fudge cake."

"That sounds amazing," I say. "Now I want cake. That's not fair, Mom."

Ryan laughs.

He's never liked chocolate the way I do.

Mom holds the library door open, and we step inside. Soft music is playing overhead. An old song from the past. "Raindrops Keep Fallin' on My Head."

Ryan tilts his head, listening. "Dude… I love this song," he says. "You know it has a hidden meaning, right?"

Mom smiles and nods to the rhythm. "It sure does."

Just then, we're greeted by Paula.

Paula used to babysit me when I was little, and she's one of the best storytellers I know. After her Becoming orientation years ago, she decided to work here at the library. She's been here ever since.

"Greetings, Danica and Ryan," she says warmly. "I'm so excited to see you today. I have everything ready for your…" , she makes air quotes, "…Becoming Orientation."

Mom smiles.

Chapter 3: The Library

“Thank you, Paula. I know they’re in good hands. Do you have an estimate for when they’ll be done?”

Paula nods thoughtfully.

“Well, things have changed a bit over the years. We learn as we go. Trial and error… or as I like to say, error in judgment instead of mistakes.”

She grins.

“I’d guess they’ll be finished around dinner time. We’ll wrap things up around four o’clock. Does that work for you, Galene?”

“Yes, that’s perfect,” Mom says. “I have errands to run in town anyway. And since today is such a special day, I have a feeling Danica will want a dark chocolate fudge cupcake… and Ryan will probably want one of those key-lime-filled white cupcakes from Heavenly Desserts.”

Paula’s eyes light up.

Mom laughs.

“And Paula… what does your heart desire from Heavenly Desserts?”

Paula puts her hand on her chest dramatically.

“Oh, Galene, you’re too kind. I would love one of those mini custard fruit tarts with fresh berries on top.”

“You got it,” Mom says. “Now go have fun with my kids.”

We say our goodbyes, and Paula gestures for us to follow her.

Paula leads us through the front lobby of the library.

Because the building is perfectly round, the front half feels like a greeting area cut straight across the circle. There's a long, dark wooden desk, a single chair with a computer monitor, and rows of locked, fireproof file cabinets lining the walls.

The front entrance is made entirely of glass, letting sunlight pour into the room.

Above us hang delicate hand-blown glass light fixtures shaped like flowers and glowing orbs. The colors shift softly, filling the space with warm reflections.

The whole place feels simple… but sacred.

Paula turns to us with a playful smile.

"Alright," she says. "Time to show you the secret doorway into the orientation room. Follow me. This is the fun part."

She walks to the back wall and places her hand on a small square panel engraved into the surface.

The moment her palm touches it, the panel begins to glow a soft golden color.

A faint humming sound fills the air, like something waking up after a long sleep.

Paula looks back at us.

"Before we go in, you get to choose the environment," she says. "Some people like the ocean. Others prefer a tropical sunset. Some choose a mountain lake, a forest cabin, or a meadow full of wildflowers. Pick whatever makes you feel safe and relaxed. The orientation room will adjust to it."

Ryan and I look at each other.

We've never been to the ocean. Never seen a tropical island in real life. Only in movies and pictures.

Chapter 3: The Library

We answer at the same time.

“Tropical island. Sunset.”

Paula nods, smiling. “Excellent choice.”

She taps a few glowing symbols on the panel. A section of the wall dissolves right in front of us. Not opens. Not slides. Dissolves.

Inside is a panoramic view of a tropical island at sunset. The entire wall becomes a living scene of ocean waves rolling onto glowing sand. The sound of water fills the room, gentle and rhythmic.

A warm breeze brushes across my face. I can smell salt in the air. It feels real. The floor even looks like sand beneath our feet.

The sky is painted in streaks of gold, pink, purple, and crimson. The sun hangs low on the horizon, glowing like it’s alive.

I stop walking. I’ve never seen anything like this before. In that moment, I make a promise to myself. One day… I will travel to a place like this for real.

We step farther into the orientation room. In the center are two black leather couches facing a small coffee table. A neat stack of floral handkerchiefs sits on top, along with a remote control.

Near the front of the room is a small stage facing the giant screen wall. The lighting is soft, warm, and comforting. It feels like we’re supposed to be here.

“Take a seat,” Paula says. “For the next few minutes, just relax and take in the environment. I’m going to grab some refreshments. It’s going to be a long day, and I want you both comfortable.”

She steps out of the room. The moment she leaves, Ryan pulls a lever on the side of the couch and kicks his feet up.

“This… is the life,” he says.

I laugh.

Exactly five minutes later, Paula returns carrying a silver pitcher of lemon water and two glasses. She sets them on the table and looks at us.

“Are you both ready to begin?”

We nod. “Yes.”

The tropical scene fades from the screen, replaced by soft golden light. A new scent fills the room. Citrus and spice. Sharp and refreshing.

I suddenly feel more awake.

Behind Paula, a large screen lowers from the ceiling. Words appear across it in glowing letters.

WELCOME TO YOUR BECOMING

The mood in the room changes instantly. Paula’s voice is different now. Stronger. More serious.

“What you are about to hear may be challenging,” she says calmly. “Some of it may feel overwhelming. Think of it like a large pill. You don’t swallow it all at once. You take it in pieces.”

She pauses, making sure we’re listening.

“You won’t learn everything today. Over the next few days, you’ll return to this room. You’ll learn about our community, other communities around the world, different paths you can take, and the life you want to build for yourself. There is no pressure. Everyone moves at their own pace."

She gestures toward the coffee table.

"If you need a break, raise your hand. If something feels too intense, say stop. The remote controls the presentation. You're always in control."

She presses a button. A list appears on the screen.

"These are the topics we'll be covering during your Becoming."

The screen in front of us fills with a list of topics, each one appearing in glowing white letters.

Paula folds her hands in front of her and looks at us carefully.

"This week," she says, "we'll be exploring the following subjects. Some of these may feel familiar from school, and that's okay. If you already understand something, we won't spend too much time on it. But other topics might be completely new."

She presses a button, and the list becomes clearer.

- What your Becoming is all about
- The old 3D world vs the new 4D and 5D world
- How education changed to support the new Earth
- How employment changed to support the new Earth
- Why we no longer use money as currency
- Why community is essential to human survival
- Choosing a life partner and building a family
- Modern spiritual and religious practices
- Discovering patterns carried through your DNA
- Why medical systems are different now
- Teleportation, travel, and relocation

- Creating your Soul Journey Book for future generations
- Why the old 3D world had to end
- Why there are no governments, taxes, banks, or prisons
- What life was really like in the old world

Ryan leans back on the couch and whistles softly.

"Wow… that's a lot," he says. "That could fry my laid-back brain. I think we covered some of this in school, but not all of it."

He looks at Paula. "What do you recommend we start with?"

Paula smiles like she's heard that question a hundred times.

"I've been doing this for eight years," she says, "and I usually like to start with the same topic."

She taps the screen.

WHAT IS YOUR BECOMING?

"This one," she says. "Because everything else builds from it."

She walks slowly across the front of the room as she speaks.

"Your parents don't explain this part in detail, and that's intentional. The meaning of Becoming has changed over time. As our communities grow, we learn new things. Other cities discover new ways of living, new ways of healing, new ways of understanding ourselves. So, the process keeps evolving, just like we do."

She stops in front of us. "That's why this isn't just a class. It's a transition."

Ryan and I glance at each other.

I nod first.

"I think we should go in order," I say. "Start with what feels right each day, then stop when we need time to think."

Ryan shrugs. "Yeah. That works for me. My brain needs breaks anyway."

Paula laughs softly. "Good answer."

She picks up the remote and dims the lights slightly.

"Then let's begin."

The words on the screen glow brighter.

WHAT IS YOUR BECOMING?

Paula turns toward us, her expression calm but serious.

"Your Becoming," she says, "is the moment when you stop living the life you were given… and start choosing the life your soul was meant to live."

The room feels quieter. Heavier. Like something important just started.

And for the first time all day…I feel nervous.

But I also feel ready.

Chapter 4: Life in the 3D World Not Taught

Paula stands in front of us with a small smile on her face, holding a strange black circular device in her hand.

“Alright,” she says. “I have some exciting news for both of you. Over the years, we’ve been working with other like-minded communities around the world to make the Becoming process more personal… and easier to understand.”

She slowly walks across the stage as she speaks.

“We’ve learned that not everyone asks the same questions. And when we can’t answer those questions clearly, people become confused. That’s not what we want. We’re here to grow, to expand, and to bring clarity.”

She pauses, then gestures toward us.

“The founder of our community, your great-great-grandmother, Aislinn, helped make that possible.”

Ryan raises an eyebrow. “Wait… you’re saying she was talking to aliens?”

Paula laughs softly.

“Yes, Ryan. You could say that.”

Ryan grins.

“Coolio, man.”

Paula shakes her head, smiling, then continues.

Chapter 4: Life in the 3D world not taught

“Aislinn communicated with higher-dimensional beings who granted our community access to something called the Fields of Time.”

Ryan leans forward. “That sounds intense.”

“It is,” Paula replies. “The Field of Time is a universal record vault. Every event, every word spoken, every thought, and every law ever created. All of it exists as a vibration.”

She holds up the device in her hand.

“The Field is so vast it could hold multiple universes within it. In school, you may have heard this described as the Akashic Records. Does that sound familiar?”

I nod.

“Yes. We learned that every thought and emotion has a vibration. In the old 3D world, people stayed stuck in lower emotional states for centuries. Fear, anger, jealousy… things like that.”

Ryan nods too.

“And we learned that when people raised their consciousness, they could connect to their higher self. Some could even access the Records during meditation.”

Paula smiles. “Exactly.”

She opens her palm and shows us the device. It’s small, black, and perfectly round. Like a hockey puck made of metal.

“This device allows us to connect to the Field of Time. Today, you’ll be speaking with two angels who work there. Their role is to organize the endless stream of information flowing into the Records.”

Ryan whistles. “That’s a big job.”

Chapter 4: Life in the 3D world not taught

Paula nods.

“There are hundreds of them. The entire record system is overseen by one highly evolved being known as the Master of the Records. He works closely with Archangel Metatron, who observes humanity and records the actions of every soul.”

She looks at us carefully.

“You'll learn more about Metatron later.”

Ryan leans back on the couch. “Well… are we doing this or what?”

Paula smiles.

“You two will be the first students to try this version of the process.”

Ryan looks at me. “This could be trippy.”

I shrug. “Let’s do it.”

Paula steps onto the stage and places the device near the front edge. A line of lights suddenly appears around the stage floor, glowing in a perfect outline. It reminds me of a racetrack lighting up in the dark. She presses a button on the remote. The device hums.

A beam of light shoots upward. And then, two figures appear. Angels.

Tall, golden, and glowing with brilliant white wings that shimmer like diamonds. They look completely real, not like a projection at all.

Ryan leans forward. “Okay… that’s insane.”

The angels speak in perfect unison.

Chapter 4: Life in the 3D world not taught

“Welcome, Divine Ones, to the Field of Time. Today we will answer your questions and show you what life was like for souls living on Earth during the 3D era.”

I can’t move. I can barely breathe. We’ve seen technology like this in movies… but never in real life. They look close enough to touch. One of the angel’s steps forward slightly.

“To understand the 3D world,” she says, “the Master of the Records will speak with you directly.”

She raises her hands, and golden light begins to swirl between her palms. Tiny sparks spin like fireflies, weaving together into glowing spheres of energy. Then she presses the light to her heart. A pulse of energy shoots upward through the top of her head and disappears into the air like a signal sent across time.

Seconds later, a beam of brilliant gold light appears in the center of the stage. I have to cover my eyes. It’s as bright as the sun.

When the light fades, a figure floats forward through the glow, as if stepping out of a portal. He has blue skin, long dark hair, and multiple arms. A golden crown rests on his head. He wears loose golden cloth, and behind him is a radiant halo of light.

Beneath him stands a massive golden bird with human-like arms, its wings spread wide.

Ryan whispers, “…That looks like something from an ancient painting.”

The being looks at us calmly.

“Greetings,” he says. “I am the Master of the Records.”

The Master of the Records looks at us with calm, steady eyes.

“What you are about to hear,” he says, “may be difficult to understand. Some of it may even be painful to witness. But remember this truth, your soul has lived through these lessons before. Many times.”

His voice echoes softly through the room.

“That is why you were allowed to return to this new Earth, where only fourth and fifth dimensional lessons remain.”

He raises one of his hands, and a faint wheel of light begins to form in the air beside him.

“But before we begin, you must understand something about the old world.”

The wheel spins slowly.

“During the 3D era, our Infinite Creators sent many teachers to Earth. Prophets. Visionaries. Guides. Each one came to warn humanity when the balance of the world was in danger.”

The wheel flickers, showing faint images inside it.

“Some listened.”

“Many did not.”

He pauses.

“You have all heard the story of Jesus, the Christ. He came to remind humanity how to live in love instead of fear. His teachings were simple; compassion, forgiveness, unity, and faith in the divine.”

The images shift.

“But his message threatened those who held power through fear.”

The wheel darkens.

"So, the truth was twisted. The loving Creator became a vengeful one. The path of compassion became a system of control. Fear became a tool."

Ryan shifts uncomfortably on the couch.

The Master continues.

"Many leaders spoke of holiness yet lived in greed. Some claimed to act in the name of God, while harming the very souls they were meant to protect."

His voice grows quieter.

"This was not the will of the Divine. It was the result of human fear and separation."

The wheel of light slows, then changes.

A new image appears. Earth, surrounded by a dim gray haze.

"As centuries passed, the world grew heavier. Humanity forgot that Earth was a school for the soul. Instead of learning through love, many learned through suffering."

He gestures toward the wheel.

"But the balance was never lost forever."

A faint golden glow begins to return.

"When the Divine Feminine rose again in the early twenty-first century, something changed. More people began to question the old systems. They began to remember who they were."

The glow spreads across the image of Earth.

"They remembered that they were not separate from the Creator… but part of it."

Chapter 4: Life in the 3D world not taught

The Master looks directly at us.

“When enough people awakened, the vibration of the planet began to shift from 3D into 4D. Slowly at first. Then faster.”

The wheel spins again.

“This is what we call the turning of the Wheel of Time.”

He raises his hand, and the wheel grows larger.

“Imagine a great wheel that once spun in harmony for thousands of years. Humanity lived in unity, and the wheel moved easily.”

The wheel slows… then stops.

“But when fear and separation took over, the wheel became heavy. It could no longer turn.”

The light dims.

“For a time, the darkness held the world still.”

Then a spark appears.

“But when people began choosing compassion over fear… forgiveness over revenge… truth over control…”

The wheel begins to move again.

“…the wheel turned once more.”

Ryan leans forward. “So, the world didn’t just end,” he says quietly. “It changed.”

The Master nods.

“Yes.”

He lowers his hand.

“But the turning of the wheel was not peaceful.”

Chapter 4: Life in the 3D world not taught

The room grows darker.

“There came a time when humanity had to make a choice.”

Two paths appear in the air.

“One path continued in the old 3D way which consisted of fear, power, and division.”

“The other followed the higher path of acceptance, equality, responsibility, unity, and love.”

His voice becomes firm. “Earth could no longer hold both.”

The images shift again.

Storms.
Crowds.
Cities.
Fire.
Floods.

“When the old systems began to collapse, many people were afraid. Governments struggled to hold control. Laws were broken. Trust disappeared. Protests spread across nations.”

Ryan clenches his fists. “Why didn’t anyone stop it?”

The Master looks at him gently.

“Because fear makes people forget who they are.”

The images show crowds marching, shouting, running.

“Some fought for freedom. Some fought for power. Some did not understand what was happening at all.”

The wheel flickers faster.

"Technology, politics, and fear became tangled together. People no longer knew what was true. Voices were silenced. Trust was lost. Communities divided."

The room feels heavy now.

"But even then… the light did not disappear."

The wheel glows brighter.

"There were souls who had already learned the 3D lessons. They came to Earth to help the transition. They refused to live in hatred. They refused to live in fear."

The Master looks at us. "They were the ones who helped the wheel turn again."

He pauses.

"And one of those souls… was Aislinn."

I feel my chest tighten.

The wheel of light slows and becomes still.

"She saw the path before others did. She understood that humanity was climbing a staircase of consciousness. Each step required a lesson. Each lesson required a choice."

The Master's voice softens. "She taught that the only way forward… was love."

The room becomes quiet. So quiet, I can hear my own breathing. And for the first time since this began…I realize why they didn't tell us this when we were younger. Because some truths are too heavy for a child.

The Master of the Records lowers his hands, and the wheel of light fades into a dim glow.

Chapter 4: Life in the 3D world not taught

“There is more you must understand,” he says quietly.

“When the shift from the 3D world into the higher dimensions began, it did not happen all at once. It happened slowly… and then all at once.”

A new image appears in the air.

Crowds of people.
Cities.
Screens flashing with news.
Voices arguing.

“The old systems were already weakening. Governments were divided. People no longer trusted their leaders, and leaders no longer trusted the people.”

The image flickers.

“Laws were broken. Rights were questioned. Fear spread faster than truth.”

Ryan shakes his head. “Why didn’t people just fix it?”

The Master looks at him with patience.

“Because when fear takes hold of the mind, it becomes difficult to see clearly. Many believed they were protecting the world… while their actions were helping to tear it apart.”

The image shifts again.

Crowds marching.
Police lights.
Smoke in the air.

“There were protests across many nations. Some peaceful. Some not. People spoke out against control, corruption, and injustice. Others believed those protests were a threat to order.”

The scene grows louder.

“Families were divided. Communities argued. Even those who wanted peace did not always know how to create it.”

The Master lifts one hand, and the noise fades.

“The tension built for many years. Like pressure beneath the surface of the Earth.”

A glowing red sphere appears in the air.

“The best way to understand that time… is to imagine a wound that refuses to heal. At first it is small. Then it grows. It becomes painful, swollen, impossible to ignore.”

The sphere pulses.

“Eventually, the pressure must release.”

The sphere bursts into light.

“And when it did… the world changed very quickly.”

The images move faster now.

Storms.
Floods.
Fires.
Explosions.
Earthquakes.
Cities falling into darkness.

“Conflicts broke out between nations. Weapons were used that damaged the land, the oceans, and the air itself. Natural disasters grew stronger as the balance of the planet weakened.”

I cover my mouth, trying not to cry. “This… this really happened?” I whisper.

The Master nods. “Yes.”

He gestures again, and the images slow.

“But even in those darkest moments, the choice was still there.”

Two paths appear again, glowing in the air.

“One path continued in fear, anger, and control.”

“The other required something far more difficult.”

The second path glows brighter.

“Acceptance.”

“Responsibility.”

“Equality.”

“Forgiveness.”

“Compassion.”

“Unity.”

He looks directly at us. “Every soul on Earth had to choose which path to follow.”

Paula glances at me and quietly sets a handkerchief on the table beside me.

I hadn’t even noticed I was crying.

The Master continues.

“There was a period of time when humanity stood at a crossroads. Some call it the great shift. Others called it the awakening. Some called it the rapture.”

He pauses.

"The name does not matter. The choice did."

The image changes again.

People helping each other.
People praying.
People holding hands.
People rebuilding.

"Those who chose the higher path began changing first. They learned to control their thoughts, their emotions, and their actions. They stopped living only for survival and began living with purpose."

The light grows brighter.

"These souls helped stabilize the planet. They helped the Wheel of Time begin turning again."

He looks at us with a softer expression.

"Many of those souls were young. They came into the world already carrying the lessons of the past. They were not here to repeat the 3D cycle. They were here to help end it."

Ryan whispers, "4D souls…"

The Master nods. "Yes."

He raises his hand one last time.

"And during this time, one woman played an important role in guiding others through the transition."

A new image appears.

A spiral staircase of light.

Chapter 4: Life in the 3D world not taught

"Aislinn."

My heart jumps when I hear her name.

"She understood that humanity was climbing a staircase of consciousness. Each step required healing. Each step required truth. Each step required love."

The staircase glows brighter.

"She taught that the only way forward was not through force, but through the transformation of the heart."

The image fades slowly.

"When enough souls chose love over fear, the old world could no longer hold its form."

The room becomes very still.

"The 3D era ended."

A soft golden light fills the stage.

"And the new Earth began."

No one speaks for a long moment. I wipe my eyes with the handkerchief Paula gave me. Now I understand why they waited until today to tell us.

Some truths...you have to grow into. The Master of the Records looks at us.

"You are not here to fear the past," he says gently.

"You are here to build the future."

The light around him grows brighter.

"And now… your Becoming can truly begin."

The beam of light rises again, and the Master slowly disappears into the glow. As if he is still here, but not here.

The angels stay silent. The stage still softly glows.

The room is so silent I could hear a pin drop. I can tell this is a moment of reflection.

Ryan exhales. “Okay,” he says quietly. “That was a lot.”

Paula nods. “Yes,” she says softly. “It always is.”

She looks at us with a small smile.

“Are you ready for the next lesson from these two divine angels?”

I take a deep breath. I don’t feel the same as I did this morning. Not even close.

But I nod. “Yes. I’m ready.”

Chapter 5: Images of Past Lives

Now that we are ready to move on, the Master of the Records reappears. He looks at us one last time, his expression calm but filled with quiet authority.

“It is time for me to depart,” he says. “But before I go, we have prepared something for you.”

He raises one of his hands, and a faint glow appears around him.

“Within the Field of Time, we preserve the memories of every soul that has lived upon your planet. Every action. Every thought. Every choice. Today, we will show you memories that speak louder than words.”

Ryan shifts beside me. “Memories… like ours?”

The Master nods.

“Some will be from your own past lives. Others will come from souls who walked beside you in different times. What you will see is not entertainment. It is not illusion. It is the reality of how humanity lived during the 3D era.”

The light around him grows brighter.

“You will witness acts of violence, greed, pride, and suffering. You will see how lost souls harmed others… and how they harmed themselves.”

His voice softens.

“But you will also understand why this new Earth was created.”

The glow behind him forms into a triangular portal of white and gold light.

“We, the guardians of the Field of Time, have agreed that the history of the 3D mindset will no longer be allowed to poison this world again.”

He looks at us one final time.

“You are here because your souls have already learned those lessons.”

The portal brightens.

“And because of that… you were allowed to return to the light.”

With that, the Master of the Records fades into the glowing triangle, disappearing into the Field of Time.

The stage becomes quiet. One of the angels steps forward.

“To begin,” she says, “we will move through a range of vibrational memories. You will see ten soul fragments, each lasting only a moment. After each one, a word will appear that represents the emotion or mindset connected to that life.”

She lifts her hand, and the screen behind them begins to glow.

“We will start with the lower frequencies.”

The first image appears.

A wealthy woman stands in front of a mirror, studying her reflection. Jewelry covers her neck and wrists, and expensive fabrics surround her. Behind her, a baby cries in a crib.

She does not turn around. Her eyes stay fixed on her own face, searching for flaws.

Chapter 5: Images of Past Lives

A word flashes across the screen in red.

VANITY

The image changes.

Now we see a man in a tall office building, yelling at employees gathered around his desk. His voice is sharp. His eyes are cold. He walks through the room like he owns everyone in it.

Another word appears.

PRIDE

The next memory.

Two women whisper in a corner, smiling while another woman walks past them. Their smiles fade the moment she turns her back.

GOSSIP

The images begin changing faster.

Rich people ignoring the poor.
Men laughing while others suffer.
People turning away from hunger, slavery, and pain as if it isn't their problem.

APATHY
GREED
ARROGANCE

My stomach starts to feel tight.

The next images grow darker.

Animals being hurt.
Villages burning.

Chapter 5: Images of Past Lives

Soldiers marching through smoke and fire.
Families running.

WAR
HATE
CRUELTY

I grip the edge of the couch. The memories keep coming.

A drunk man shouting at his wife.
Children hiding in fear.
A man cheating, then coming home angry.
People chasing fame, power, attention… never satisfied.

LUST
ENVY
JEALOUSY
ADDICTION

My chest feels heavy now. The screen shifts again.

People shaking with anxiety.
Someone sitting alone in the dark.
A homeless man in the cold.
A woman crying in silence.

FEAR
DESPAIR
ISOLATION

My eyes start to fill with tears. The next images are even harder to watch.

Manipulation. Abuse. People pretending to help while secretly causing harm. A smiling face… hiding something cruel.

DECEPTION

The final memory appears.

A mother holding her child in her arms, both covered in blood. A house burning behind them. Men shouting in the distance. The mother screams… then everything goes silent.

The word appears slowly.

SHAME

My whole body feels cold.

I don't even realize I'm crying until a tear falls onto my hands.

The angel on the right walks toward me and kneels down. Her eyes are soft, filled with compassion.

"Some of these memories belong to your soul," she whispers. "That is why you feel them so deeply."

She gently takes my hands. "Your soul remembers what it was like to live in the darkness. And because you have already learned those lessons… you will never have to live them again."

She stands slowly and returns to her place on the stage.

"This new Earth was created for souls who have already passed through the 3D cycle," she says. "You were given a fresh beginning."

The angel steps back onto the stage, her wings glowing softly in the light.

"I want you both to understand something clearly," she says.

"When your soul chose to come to this new Earth, it was not the beginning of your journey. You had already lived through the lower lessons many times before."

She looks from me to Ryan. “For centuries, your souls experienced the 3D world filled with fear, struggle, survival, loss, and pain. You learned what it meant to live in separation, to forget who you were, and to search for the light again.”

Her voice becomes gentle.

“That is why this life is different. You were not sent here to repeat those lessons. You were sent here to build something new.”

The angel on the left walks slowly toward Ryan.

“Earth was once a school for souls,” she says. “In that school, many believed they were born into darkness. To find the light again, the old self had to die.”

Ryan frowns slightly. “Die… like for real?”

The angel shakes her head.

“Not the body. The mindset.”

She places her hand over her heart.

“The 3D self was built on fear, ego, and survival. It believed every thought it heard. It believed every lie it was told. It believed it was alone.”

She looks at him kindly.

“To leave that world behind, a person had to find courage. Courage to question what they were taught. Courage to face their pain. Courage to choose love instead of fear.”

Ryan nods slowly.

The angel continues.

“As courage grows, the ego begins to lose its power. The inner voice that once judged and criticized becomes quieter. You no longer live according to what others say you are. You begin to remember who you truly are."

She gestures toward the screen.

"That is why practices like meditation became important near the end of the 3D era. They helped people reconnect with their higher self... and with the Infinite Creator."

The room feels calm now, like the storm has passed.

"When a soul reaches that realization," she says, "death is no longer something to fear. Life becomes something to honor."

She pauses.

"The transformation happens both consciously and unconsciously. Old patterns fall away. Old identities fade. The person you used to be... no longer fits."

She looks at both of us.

"Some people called this awakening. Others called it rebirth. Some called it leaving hell and entering heaven while still alive."

The angel steps back.

"That is why your community chose not to show you these memories when you were younger."

She folds her hands.

"The human brain does not fully mature until around the age of twenty-five. Only then can most people process complex truths without becoming overwhelmed."

Ryan raises an eyebrow. "So that's why nobody told us anything?"

The angel smiles slightly.

"Yes. In the old world, people were expected to become adults at sixteen or eighteen. Many were forced into lives they were not ready for. They made choices from fear, pressure, or survival, and those choices shaped the rest of their lives."

Her expression grows serious.

"This new Earth changed those rules. Growth comes before responsibility. Understanding comes before decision."

The screen behind them fades to white. The angel turns toward me.

"Because the universe seeks balance, we cannot show you only the darkness," she says softly.

She raises her hand.

"Now you will see memories of joy. Memories where your soul lived in harmony, love, and peace. These are the moments that remind you who you truly are."

The light shifts. Warm colors fill the room. The first image appears.

A forest glowing in moonlight. Small, winged beings dance between the trees, laughing as tiny lights float around them like fireflies.

Fairies.

The air feels alive with music and joy.

The next memory appears.

A woman with olive skin rests in a softly lit chamber beside a great lion with human-like eyes. There is no fear between them, only trust. I could feel and see the companionship and love between them.

Chapter 5: Images of Past Lives

The feeling in the room changes completely.

Peace.
Connection.
Love.

Another image.

A man sits in a rocking chair beside a fireplace, reading to a small child in his arms. He changes his voice with every character, making the child laugh. The warmth of the moment makes my chest ache in the best way.

A cat rests peacefully next to the warm fireplace on an animal skin rug.

Another memory.

A musician at a piano, lost in the music as an audience listens in silence. The notes seem to glow in the air.

A bird in cage, sings softly as the piano melody fills the air.

Another.

I see several Native American Indians sitting around a fire under a sky full of stars. Various Animals resting beside them. A wolf, an eagle on a perch, and a dog. Families laughing together. Horses graze in the flush green fields in the background.

I see a wise woman, off to the side. She is petting a mountain lion…as if…it is her pet. Protector and companion.

The words appear in gold this time.

JOY
CREATION

Chapter 5: Images of Past Lives

LOVE
BELONGING

Tears fill my eyes again, but now they feel different. Lighter.

Ryan smiles without even realizing it.

More memories flash across the screen.

Children building sandcastles. An Italian woman cooking for her family. Friends embracing.

Next, we see a little boy's first kiss, after he gives a young girl a fist full of wildflowers.

Then, we see a man lying in the grass watching the clouds as his pet hawk rests on a branch above the trees.

My heart feels full. I look at the angel and whisper, "Thank you… I needed that."

She smiles gently.

"Balance brings understanding," she says.

She steps back toward the center of the stage.

"It is time for us to return to the Field of Time. These memories must be recorded and placed where they belong."

Both angels walk toward us. They kneel at the same time. One in front of Ryan, one in front of me.

"We have a gift for you," they say together.

Each angel opens her hand.

In the center of their palms floats a tiny golden light, glowing like a firefly.

With their other hand, they lift the light and place it gently on the top of our heads. A soft tingling spreads across my scalp. The light sinks into my crown and disappears.

“You now carry the ability to access the Records when guidance is needed,” one of them says softly. “You will never be alone when you seek truth.”

They stand.

“It has been our honor to meet you. May we meet again in love and light.”

A triangular portal of blue and gold opens behind them.

One by one, they step inside.

The portal closes.

The room goes quiet.

Paula walks in front of the stage, clapping her hands once.

“Well,” she says cheerfully, “that was intense, wasn’t it? I probably should have brought sunglasses for that one.”

She looks at the clock.

“Oh wow. It’s already after one. You two must be starving. Let’s go grab some lunch at the diner down the street.”

I stand up slowly, stretching my legs. “Yeah,” I say. “That was… a lot. I understand now why they didn’t teach us this in school.”

Ryan heads for the door. “I don’t care what dimension we’re in,” he says. “I want a cheeseburger, garlic fries, and the biggest milkshake they have.”

I laugh. Paula smiles.

“Good. Becoming works up an appetite.”

And the three of us head for the door together.

Chapter 6: Old Structures vs. New Structures

As we walk outside the building, I look over at my brother and say, "Bro, that was wild! I have always had a feeling that you were a great composer in a past life because of your love for music. Bach was you, dude!

You rocked as Bach! Well, not rocked back then. You get what I mean. You filled people's hearts and souls with masterful, heavenly music. You still do with some of the songs you have created and composed.

Unlike me, I can't even play a recorder… but I can sing."

My brother laughs and says, "Yes, you can sing, but if you had to play a musical instrument to save your life, you'd be dead, dude."

Paula laughs at both of us and replies, "You two are so funny. I love my job. I have learned that it is better when there is more than one person during the becoming process, because you don't always know which memories are yours and which ones belong to someone else.

When I did it, I was alone. In one lifetime, I was a tall, bone-thin, dark-haired man. My eyes were black and empty inside. I was an evil wizard, and I enjoyed playing with dark magic, casting wicked spells on people, and summoning demons to do my bidding. It was so creepy. It made my skin crawl.

Then, in another memory, one that was joyful and beautiful, I was living in Atlantis. I saw myself as a young woman swimming and

telepathically communicating with dolphins and whales. I loved the ocean, the sea creatures, the vibrant colors of coral, and the way the rays of sunlight shined down into the clear blue-green water.

Aw…It was heaven. I was truly one with everything and everyone. I felt so alive… and so blessed to be alive."

We watch Paula let out a deep sigh of gratitude.

As we continue walking, we all seem lost in our own thoughts, recalling the memories we saw from previous lives. The silence between us feels peaceful and pleasant.

In that stillness, I realize something. Stillness clarifies what chaos distorts. It reveals what was… and what will never be again.

In this very moment, I begin to question the coherence of the old 3D world.

It was never a unified world like ours.

And in that moment of clarity, I realized one of the biggest problems people faced within the 3D framework. There was no stillness.

People did not know how to quiet their minds enough to tune into the wisdom, guidance, and divine grace that surrounds us all.

The constant chaos…
The inner chatter…
Social media distractions…
Distorted global news…
Daily stress…

All of it kept humans trapped inside their own minds.

People never made the time or were unwilling to make the time to silence the noise within and take out the trash. They could not see how much information they were unconsciously digesting, processing, and carrying every single day.

The weight of those burdens must have been exhausting.

Unrealistic expectations about happiness.
Constant comparison to others.
Worrying about what people thought.
Trying to live up to illusions that were never real.

In that moment, I could also understand why some spiritual advisors felt an urgency to save, heal, or fix others.

But sometimes that urgency was not devotion. Sometimes it was noisy. Their souls were just as lost inside the chaos. The sounds were so loud that they forgot their inner guidance…their inner rhythm…their inner compass…their inner calling.

Yet I know this truth.

Whenever I go within, into meditation, and clear the daily noise, the vibrational signal I sense is unmistakable. It is not loud. It does not shout. It does not demand.

It is soft. Warm in tone. Steady… smooth as silk. So loving. So pure.

It feels like being welcomed back home to the place where we were all created, and where we return lifetime after lifetime.

I wish every soul in the old 3D world could have discovered this simple truth. But not everyone was willing to change.

Before I know it, we are standing in front of the diner.

Ryan opens the door for Paula, and when I try to walk in behind her, he stops me and says,

"Only dark wizards enter first!" Then he lets out a ridiculous medieval cackle.

Paula turns around and replies, "Just for that remark, I am going to place a curse on you.
Your beloved rooster will chase you in your dreams."

Ryan pretends to tremble in fear.

"You two are so silly. I am hungry," I say.

"Follow me," Paula gestures. "We have a private back room. They've been expecting us. Our food should be delivered any moment."

"What? We didn't even order," I say.

"Yes, you did," Paula replies.

"Ryan told me what he wanted earlier, and you and I have eaten together many times over the past few years. You always, and I mean always order the same thing. You are a creature of habit."

"Yes, you did," Paula replies.

"Ryan told me what he wanted earlier, and you and I have eaten together many times over the past few years. You always, and I mean always order the same thing. You are a creature of habit.

When they showed the memory of the Italian woman preparing that beautiful feast for her family, I knew that memory belonged to you. You love to cook. Your secret ingredient is love, and you are such a pasta girl.

Everyone who works here loves to cook, and every meal is blessed before it is served. That is why you love the stuffed veggie lasagna with extra cheese in a fresh, creamy pesto sauce.

I also ordered a Mediterranean side salad with hot toasted garlic bread. And for your drink, raspberry lemonade. Did I get your order right?" Paula asks with a smile.

I look at her sheepishly and grin. "You know me so well."

As we walk past people enjoying their lunch, Paula opens a door and leads us into a small, cozy back room. The table seats six people, and there is a medium-sized window overlooking the yard outside.

As I glance out the window, I see a mother bird in her nest feeding three hungry babies.

I smile to myself. Everyone is hungry… in one way or another.

Ryan pulls back my chair, and I sit down. "Thank you, bro. That was very kind of you," I say.

"You're welcome, my lady," he replies dramatically.

Before we can even start talking, the food arrives. My stomach growls loudly, and Ryan looks over at me.

"Down, girl, down. We have a hungry wild beast at the table."

Paula laughs. "Dig in, you two. We have a lot to discuss."

Before we eat, we all become quiet. We place our hands above our plates and close our eyes. We focus on sending light and love into the food before us, blessing the meal and asking that it restore and nourish our bodies.

It only takes a few seconds, but the energy is felt immediately.

As I take my first bite of lasagna, my mouth explodes with flavor. The spices, herbs, vegetables, and cheeses blend together perfectly. It feels like the Italian angels themselves are singing in delight for this human experience.

Angels do not need food…but they remember what it was like to be human.

And food, when prepared with love, was one of Earth's greatest gifts.

In that moment, I think to myself that this memory will be stored in the Field of Time.

Because it is simple…peaceful…and perfect.

I look over at Ryan. "This is the most excellent burger." I watch him remove sauce from his face. "Totally tubular fries too."

I watch Paula shake her head. "I guess Ryan saw Ted and Bill's Excellent Adventure movie."

Ryan's eyes jumped up. "Hell yeah. All we are is dust in the wind, dude. It's a classic."

Paula rolls her eyes and looks at me for moral support. I just shrug my shoulders and say, "He can't help his awesome self."

We all laugh and dig in. The food is so tasty here.

We eat in silence for a while, each of us still processing the memories and messages we received earlier that morning.

When we finish, Paula leans back in her chair and rubs her stomach.

"That Pad Thai with crispy tofu and extra Thai basil… amazing. I love the food here. Now, I want to take this time, in private, to talk more about your becoming process."

Ryan and I sit up straighter.

Chapter 6: Old structures vs. new structures

“As you heard earlier,” Paula continues, “in the old world, when someone turned sixteen or eighteen, they were considered an adult. From a 5D perspective, we knew that was wrong.

It supported the 3D world…but it did not support the 4D or 5D ways of living.

The 3D world was built on survival.

Survive another day.
Pass on the genes.
Build a legacy.
Repeat the cycle.

People used to say, ‘In the good old days,’ but those days were not always good.

In the 1700s, a fourteen-year-old girl could be forced to marry a man in his sixties or seventies, simply because she was young and able to bear children. She was expected to give him a son.”

“No way… that is sick,” I say. “That’s so wrong. I can’t even imagine living like that.”

Paula nods slowly. “Oh, it gets worse, my dear. There are records of girls as young as ten being married. Some were pregnant before they even understood what was happening to them.

Women were seen as property. Some fathers loved their daughters. Others did not. Many girls were forced to do their duty… or suffer the consequences. In those times, a woman often had only two choices in life. Marriage…or prostitution.

Women had very few rights. Most of the power belonged to men.”

“What was wrong with people?” I ask, shaking my head.

“It was survival,” Paula says softly. “Women needed men for protection, but the truth is… many of those men were angry, bitter, and resentful themselves.

Let me give you another example. A young man could fall deeply in love with a woman.
But if his brother died and left behind a wife and children, that man might be forced to marry his brother’s widow to support the family. He would have to abandon the woman he loved or live a life filled with secrets and guilt. Either way, hearts were broken constantly.”

She pauses, then continues.

“And even in the 2000s, dating was still difficult. People pretended to be someone they were not. Technology was used to deceive instead of genuinely connecting. Many relationships were built on appearance, not depth. People wanted love, but they carried emotional wounds they never healed. So, they entered relationships full of pain and created more pain. This is what many called trauma-bonding.”

I look at her, confused.

“What is a trauma-bonding relationship?”

Paula smiles gently. “Good question. If you grow up in an abusive or unstable environment, you often attract someone with the same vibrational pattern. That person becomes your teacher. There is a soul lesson to be learned. That is why we say everyone is both a student and a teacher for one another. Does that make sense?”

I nod slowly. “Yes… I think so. The person who hurts you might actually be the one who teaches you how to set boundaries…how to find your self-worth…how to stop accepting breadcrumbs instead of love."

Paula smiles. "Exactly, Danica. Aislinn understood this deeply. She studied generational trauma, toxic relationships, narcissism, attachment styles, how to communicate with difficult people, and why opposites attract. Her guides told her to speak about these uncomfortable subjects with love, wisdom, and compassion.

Not everyone liked what she said. But she knew it was easier for people to stay in anger, fear, and resentment than to look at their own wounds. It takes courage to rise above the 3D mindset and ask…

Why did this person come into my life?

What is my soul trying to learn?

That is what our Creators asked her to teach before the Great Awakening. People had to learn how to step out of the human drama and into the soul lesson."

Paula straightens in her chair. "But enough of that for now. Let me explain what happened after the shift."

Paula straightens in her chair and folds her hands on the table.

"So let me get to the point. After the Great Awakening and the shift, when things finally settled down, the survivors of the 4D world came together to discuss the future of this new Earth.

Aislinn already knew what our Creators and Archangel Metatron wanted for humanity and for this planet. The first decision was this:

There would be no single authority ruling over everyone. Instead, each community would have one spokesperson, along with twelve others, forming a council of thirteen.

Every voice mattered. Every person was encouraged to share their ideas, their thoughts, their visions, and their heart's desires. We wanted to create a world where people lived in peace, harmony, happiness, and true Oneness."

Paula reaches across the table and gently takes my hand. "They thought of you.
Both of you. Very deeply.

All of them came to the same conclusion; the old ways of raising children, teaching children, and structuring society had to change. They realized something very important. Every child is like a fresh ball of clay.

Family…
society…
education…
religion…
community…
environment…
world events…
movies…
music…
stories…

All of these things shape a child's reality and perception of the world."

She pauses, then continues. "So, we made a decision. We removed anything that could distort or taint a child's mind during their early development.

At that time, the internet had been destroyed temporarily during the shift. And instead of rushing to rebuild it, parents agreed on something unexpected. They wanted their children to experience life…not screens. They did not want devices to become babysitters.

That is why you see teenagers helping mothers in our community. We want young minds to experience what raising a family actually feels like.

To teach a child how to count…
how to read…
how to stack blocks…
how to play…
how to explore…
how to laugh…
how to enjoy being a child.

Some teenagers discover they love it. Others realize they would prefer not to have children. And that is perfectly fine. Having a family is no longer a requirement. There is no pressure. Everyone has free will."

She smiles softly. "That is why the teenagers who love helping families work so well in our community. They love being of service. And that is all our Creators ever wanted for their children. To discover what makes your heart come alive. What your soul came here to do and how that gift can be used to help others.

It really is a simple purpose. And you can have more than one."

Paula squeezes my hand gently. "I know you know someone in our community who loves doing many different things for others. Do you know who I mean?"

I smile immediately. "My mom. She loves her flowers and vegetable gardens. That is her special place. She also loves to cook. I have seen her working at the diner twice a week.

When we harvest crops, she shares everything with the community. When someone gets married or celebrates a birthday, she makes them beautiful bouquets of flowers. She even gives tours to the kids, teaching them about herbs, plant medicine, and when to plant or harvest. She teaches teenagers how to make soup, how to make jam, and how to store food for the winter. She is a canning expert.

Now that I think about it… she wears a lot of hats in our community."

Paula smiles proudly. "Exactly. And we also made another decision that we knew would spare many young people a lot of future heartbreak. We removed movies, songs, and books that filled young minds with unrealistic ideas.

For example, if a woman decided to not get married…people in society would label her a spinster, old maid, or damaged goods. There had to be something wrong with you when there was nothing wrong with you. It was a distorted perspective and belief passed down from generation to generation.

People believed that if you did not find your better half, you were broken, when you were simply becoming.

So, we removed the unrealistic ideas and fairy tales about needing a prince to save a helpless young princess or girl. Removing stories about villains destroying families and conquering the world.

We eliminated the materials that would influence and plant the seeds in young minds that revolved around destruction…constant conflict…fear…crime…abuse, and drama. We did not destroy those things. We kept them. As reminders…our of past…and how the world was long ago.

You can view those materials now, if you desire. But they are only available when someone is old enough to understand them without being influenced by them. I still remember Aislinn laughing when she donated several Disney DVDs.

People in the 4D and 5D world were tired of superheroes, fake realities, endless wars, and villains. They were tired of watching people on reality shows pretending to be someone they were not. So, we did a clean sweep. We wanted the next generation to grow up without that noise."

She looks at both of us.

"That is why finding a soulmate, twin flame, or true love was never forced on you at a young age. We encourage self-exploration. But we also encourage patience.

We ask young people to wait before becoming sexually active. Not because sex is wrong, but because it is powerful. And when people are young, they often make decisions before they understand their own emotions.

That is why we talk openly about sex when everyone turns thirteen. We teach self-respect…self-control…self-awareness. We want love to grow naturally.

Not out of pressure…
not out of loneliness…
not out of hormones…
but out of true connection."

I nod slowly. "That makes sense."

Paula continues.

“We did not want to fill young minds with fantasies about finding ‘the one.’ Love has many layers. And real love must come from within first. If it does not, people spend their lives trying to fill an empty space inside themselves.

We wanted you to know, from the very beginning, that you were already loved.

By your family.
By your community.
By your guides.
By the Angels.
By our Creators.

Sex comes later.

First comes connection.

Connection to yourself.
Connection to nature.
Connection to your higher self.

It takes time to discover what your soul truly wants. That is why there is no pressure to marry. No pressure to have children. Only joy in discovering who you are.”

She leans back in her chair.

“When you turn twenty-five, you may choose a life partner… or not. You take your time. You build an emotional connection first. If you choose the same sex, that is fine. If the relationship ends, that is fine too.

We ask only one thing. Take a year before entering another relationship. Learn from what happened. Write down the wisdom in your life journey book. Grow. Then decide what you want next.

Marriage is not required. It is only necessary if you want to raise a family."

Ryan looks over at Paula.

"But what if I get someone pregnant and I don't want to be a parent? What if I realize I'm not ready?"

Paula nods, as if she expected the question. "Excellent question, Ryan. Both people always have a say. Now that you are adults, we provide different forms of birth control for both men and women.

If you know you are not ready to have a child, you visit the community clinic. You learn your options. You watch the educational material. You make a conscious choice.

And most importantly, you communicate with your partner. You make your intentions clear before intimacy happens. In our world, accidents are rare, but they can still happen.

Sometimes people change their minds. Sometimes a woman chooses to raise a child on her own. When that happens, the community supports her.

Young men and women who are considering parenthood one day often help care for the child, so they understand the responsibility.

We want everyone to know the truth. Raising a child is not easy. It is a commitment of the heart, the mind, and the soul.

That is why we say the choice to have a family must be made with awareness… not impulse.

In the old 3D world, people were often driven by hormones and emotional wounds.

In our world, we honor the body as a temple. We do not use another person for sexual gratification. We share intimacy as a gift."

I look at Paula and nod.

"Yes… that makes sense. It is a gift when someone allows you to touch them in such a personal way. That is why it is called intimacy. The other person is into you.

They see you.
They understand you.
They feel you.

You feel it in your heart… not just in your mind.

My mom told me something once. She said intimacy is about forming a deep connection with another soul. It is sacred. Not everyone experiences that kind of connection. And we don't force people to look for it.

Sometimes that connection could happen with a person. Other times it can be with music…with nature…with writing…with animals…with the ocean…with art…with life itself.

The connection is what matters. Not the label."

Paula squeezes my hand gently. "I am very glad your mother spoke to you about that."

Ryan suddenly sits up. "Wait a minute…Mom never talked to me about sex. Maybe I should go talk to Mom about sex."

I burst out laughing. "Bro… it's about maturity. You may be twenty-five, but sometimes you still act like you're sixteen.

Women want a man… not a wild teenager. You have plenty of time before worrying about deeper relationships."

"Exactly," Paula says, smiling. "The whole point was to let children be children. Too many people in the old world were forced to grow up too fast. Some children raised themselves. Some raised their parents."

Paula pauses.

"Some grew up in homes filled with alcohol, drugs, anger, or neglect.

Some had to work when they were still young.

Some were forced into violence.

Some fought wars.

Some became adults before they even understood what childhood was.

And then the pain continued… generation after generation. We called this generational trauma."

Ryan tilts his head. "What do you mean by that?"

Paula folds her hands. "It means the pain never stopped. Parents repeated what their parents did. And those parents repeated what was done to them. Some parents believed throwing their child out at eighteen would make them strong. But it didn't.

It made them angry.
It made them resentful.
It made them feel abandoned.

This pattern repeated for generations. The trauma became part of their identity. Part of their belief system. Part of their DNA.

And eventually, it showed up as disease…as addiction…as emotional suffering.

Many of those illnesses do not exist anymore in our world."

I look at Paula quietly. "I love my parents. I know they would never do that to me… or to Ryan."

Paula smiles softly. "And that is exactly why free will became so important to us."

I lean forward. "So that's why the new world is built the way it is? Because in the old world, people didn't really have free will?

Government controlled them.
Society controlled them.
Religion controlled them.
Money controlled them.
Fear controlled them."

Paula nods. "Yes. When we built this new world, we examined everything.

Every system.
Every rule.
Every belief.

We found lies… false promises… broken dreams… manipulation… loopholes… control.

Every stone had to be turned over so the truth could be seen. Even education had to change. In the old world, children were forced into careers they didn't want. Some were forced to attend the same college as their parents. Some lived entire lives trying to make someone else proud. There was no freedom in that. So we changed it.

Now we watch each child as they grow. We observe their interests. Their talents. Their passions.

Education is no longer about money… or status… or titles. It is about purpose.

What makes your soul come alive?

What makes your heart sing?

How can that gift be used to help others?

That is the only question that matters."

She pauses, then continues more softly.

"And free will also means compassion. Three years ago, when Molly's parents died in that accident, she was only five years old. She had no relatives.

In the old world, she would have gone into the foster care system. She would have lived with strangers. She might have been moved from home to home. Some foster homes were good… but many were not. Some people only did it for the money. Children were often neglected… or worse.

In our world, we asked Molly what she wanted. We asked her who she felt safe with. She chose to live with her best friend Trina's family. She wanted to bring her cat, Freckles.

So the community made it happen. We built a place of remembrance for her parents in your mother's rose garden. Because love should not be taken away from a child…just because tragedy happened."

She looks at both of us. “Does this make sense to you?”

Ryan nods immediately. “Yeah. We don’t live in a world full of greed, fake people, and power struggles. We live simple lives. And honestly… that makes life pretty awesome.”

Paula laughs. “Exactly!

And now that you are both twenty-five, you have even more freedom. If you want, you can move into your own apartment. You can live alone or with a roommate. The apartment is given to you. Because we know creative people need quiet time.

Time alone.

Time to listen.

Time to create.

That is when your higher self speaks the loudest.

Am I right?”

Ryan and I both laughed.

“You nailed it,” I say. “I love writing in my journals about my spiritual experiences. Sometimes it feels like I’m downloading wisdom from somewhere beyond this world.

And Ryan…he hears music the same way. It’s like the melodies already exist and he just pulls them from the field of consciousness.”

Paula smiles warmly. “Yes. We take all of that into account. That is why, when you choose a partner… or a family… or a business… your home changes too. Nothing is random here. Everything is chosen with intention.”

Paula smiles at both of us. “That is why, when you decide to explore life on your own within the community, you can move into an apartment, townhouse with a nice patio or small yard, or still live at home with your parents until you are ready to move out.

Eventually you will want to leave the nest. Try living away from home to learn some independent life skills. Such as cooking for yourself. Cleaning up after yourself. Doing your own laundry…Ryan.”

Ryan laughs and replies, “Hey now.”

Paula looks over at me and winks.

“Therefore, the choice is yours. Some young adults can’t wait to leave the nest. They already have a few roommates in mind. Others can be hesitant. We understand and get it. We go with the flow of life and what works for you.

Like the two of you. I can understand why you might want to live alone or with other like-minded friends. I can see Danica living in a townhouse with a cute yard filled with herbs, veggies, and flowers.

She would have her own space to write, meditate, make her herbal teas and tinctures, and to practice her yoga.

You, Ryan. I can see you living with a group of people that love music. But your space is off to the side. Like a studio or cottage. Away from the noise. Or I could see you living in an apartment, alone. Even better, I could see you living in a portable yurt. Traveling around the world. Sleeping under the stars on a warm, summer’s evening.”

Ryan beams with joy. “Hell yeah, girlfriend. Dial me up with one of those yurts on a tropical island.”

Paula laughs. "I get it. Your creative souls need space. Quiet space. Time alone. Time to listen to your thoughts. Time to create. That is when inspiration speaks the loudest."

Ryan and I both laughed. "You nailed us again!" I say, crossing my legs.

"Those quiet moments help me connect to my higher self. And Ryan… his music comes the same way. It's like the notes already exist somewhere, and he just downloads them.

The frequencies, the octaves, the melodies… they play inside his mind before he even touches an instrument. Sometimes it feels like we're both tapping into the same field of consciousness. Like I download wisdom and he downloads sound."

Paula nods. "Yes. We consider all of that when someone chooses the next step in life.

If you decide to have a companion, or a life partner, or start a family, you will be given different options. You may choose a house. The house is given based on your needs, your purpose, and your goals.

Some people choose homes because they want to raise children. Others choose homes because their work becomes part of their living space.

Take this diner, for example. Downstairs is the restaurant. Upstairs is where Steve and Sue live. They manage the diner together. Behind the building is their herb and vegetable garden. Off to the side is the barn and the chicken coop.

And that small cottage near the fence, Mary and Brian live there. They help with the animals, the harvesting, the canning, the cheese making, and the pasta. Everyone supports each other.

Life stays simple. And because life stays simple… people stay happy."

Ryan leans back in his chair. "I never really understood all of this before. And honestly… I'm glad I was allowed to just be a kid. But lately I've been thinking about the future. Part of me wants to travel to other communities. I want to hear their music. See what instruments they use. Learn how different cultures create sound. Is that possible?"

Paula smiles knowingly. "I was planning to explain that later, but I suppose this is the perfect time. When we get back to the library, I will show you the teleportation devices."

My eyes go wide. "Teleportation devices? That sounds amazing! Can we try one when we get back?"

Paula laughs. "Yes. Since neither of you has ever been to a tropical island in this lifetime…we will go there. I know the perfect place. It's secluded… peaceful… and beautiful.

We can all go together. Would you like that?"

Ryan and I push our chairs back at the same time. My heart starts pounding with excitement.

"Oh my God, bro… this is a dream come true! Let's race back. Loser has to jump into the ocean first!"

Ryan laughs. "Winner or loser…I'm jumping in anyway."

Paula shakes her head, smiling as we rush toward the door like two kids set free.

And at that moment, I realized something. The new world was not built on rules. It was built on trust.

Not on fear.

Not on control.

Not on survival.

But on freedom…growth…and joy.

Humanity had to understand what was broken before creating what was sacred.

And for the first time, the future didn't feel uncertain. It felt like an adventure waiting to begin.

Chapter 7: Teleportation and money

I am nearly out of breath by the time we reach the entrance to the library. My heart is pounding. Not just from running, but from the excitement of knowing I am about to visit a tropical island for the first time.

Ryan pulls the door open, and I can hear him panting under his breath.

As Paula steps inside, she pauses and turns toward us.

“I need to grab the teleportation device,” she says, “but before I do, I have to show both of you something very important. This is part of your becoming orientation, and everyone living on this planet must understand it.”

We follow her behind the reception desk as she walks to an electronic keypad on the wall.
She presses in a sequence of numbers. A faint unlocking sound clicks from one of the metal file cabinets, and a small green light begins to glow in the top corner. Paula opens the cabinet and pulls out a small box. She lifts the lid and removes a ring.

Ryan and I watch quietly as she places the ring on her right index finger, then sets the box on top of the cabinet.

“I need to message Robin, my coworker,” Paula says. “She needs to know we are borrowing one of the teleportation devices and where we are going. Give me a second.”

Ryan and I nod.

Chapter 7: Teleportation and money

Paula picks up the phone beside the computer monitor and taps a few buttons.
Within seconds, Robin appears on the screen.

"Robin, I need your support," Paula says. "Today is Ryan's and Danica's becoming orientation, and I'm going to demonstrate the teleportation device. Can you come to the library?"

She pauses, listening. "Great. We'll bc in the presentation room. I'm taking them to my favorite tropical island."

Another pause. Paula smiles.

"Yes, I know it's your favorite spot too. Bora Bora is perfect, and yes, we'll use our usual private beach. We should only be there about forty-five minutes."

She listens again, then nods.

"Perfect. If you can contact the locals while we're in the presentation room, that would help. Thanks, Robin. And if I find a seashell you don't already have, I'll bring it back. I know how much you love collecting them."

She ends the call and turns back toward us.

"Let's go back into the presentation room," she says. "Then we'll go have some fun in the sun."

Ryan and I drop onto the leather couch while Paula stands in front of us and clicks the remote control. Her expression suddenly becomes serious.

"As you both know, we live on a remarkable planet filled with beauty and wonder. The Earth responds to the vibrational frequency of the people living on it. As more and more people began to raise their consciousness beyond the old 3D mindset of fear, separation, scarcity, and ego, the Earth felt that shift.

And when enough people changed…the world changed with them."

She pauses, making sure we are listening. "In the past, people wanted unity instead of separation. Love instead of hate. A life of meaning instead of a life controlled by rigid expectations.

When enough individuals made that inner shift, the collective consciousness of the planet changed. That change was powerful enough to create what we now call the new Earth. The old 3D timelines slowly collapsed. The 4D level of consciousness stabilized. And eventually, the 5D awareness became the dominant state of being.

People who refused to grow…
who refused to release fear…
who refused to let go of control…

slowly faded out of this reality as the vibration of the planet rose."

Ryan leans forward slightly. "So, the world didn't end…it changed?"

Paula nods. "Exactly. But there was one thing people struggled to let go of more than anything else. Money."

She presses the remote again, but the screen stays dark for a moment as she continues speaking.

"In the old world, money controlled everything. People believed they needed more… and more… and more. No matter how much they had, it never felt like enough. They lived in a constant state of lack.

Not realizing that the Earth itself already provided abundance."

She looks at both of us. “When someone lives in gratitude, resources appear.

People share.
People trade.
People give.

But many people could not leave the mindset of scarcity. They believed money was security. They believed money was power. They believed money was survival. And that belief kept them trapped in the 3D world.”

She folds her hands in front of her. “In our world, if someone needs food…
food is given. If someone needs help…help is given. If someone is sick…the community shows up.

There are no forms to fill out. No lines to stand in. No proof required. We support one another because we are one another.”

She pauses, her voice softer now. “That is why humanity became tired. Tired of proving their worth. Tired of fighting wars. Tired of corruption. Tired of systems that could no longer protect the people they were meant to serve.

When the veil finally lifted…people said, ‘Enough.’”

She looks directly at me. “And that is when the real shift began. Not outside. Inside.”

She folds her hands in front of her. “In our world, if someone needs food…food will be provided. One simply has to ask, and it is given.

Need childcare? We got your back. Sick and cannot take care of a child or loved one? Again, we got your back.

There are zero forms to fill out. No lines to stand in. No requirements. We support one another. Period.

We do things for each other money could never do or buy. We created unity, not separation. That is why humanity was tired of proving their worth. People are not currency.

Humanity was done with the wars of destruction. Done with political hatred, separation, and daily survival struggles. Finished with corrupt structures and systems that could no longer feed, house, support, or protect their people.

When the dark veil was lifted, people said enough was enough. So, people went within themselves to clear out their emotional garbage, because they knew that when they raised their vibration and embodied the essence of the 4D framework, we would one day live in a world of peace, harmony, cooperation, connection, and love.

Your great, great-grandmother Aislinn was a strong advocate of inner work. When our Creators spoke to her, they advised her to help people align with the vibration of love.

Why?

Because our Creators wanted all of their children to learn how to align with their hearts again, instead of their wounded ego. To learn how to clear the trauma that held them back.
To step out of old patterns. Even generational patterns.

Because Aislinn and our Creators knew that our outer world is a reflection of our inner world. When people healed inside, the world began to heal outside. People moved from conditional love…to unconditional love. From trauma…to understanding. From fear…to authenticity.

When the inner world changed, the outer world followed. Once both were in harmony, the vibrational shift had already happened. You didn't go somewhere new. You became it.

You embodied peace.
You embodied love.
You embodied harmony.

That is when people realized something important. The Kingdom of Heaven is not a place. It is a state of being.

Life itself became heaven on Earth. That is why our Earth is now a higher-dimensional plane of existence. Humanity raised its vibration together, and in doing so, saved both their lives… and the planet.

Chapter 8: The Inner Shift

Paula stands quietly for a moment, then looks at both of us with a more serious expression.

“Now, before we go any further, there are some important things you both need to understand. Even though the 3D world existed, there were still people living on this Earth who had already reached higher levels of consciousness.

You might wonder how that was possible. Well, some individuals had already embodied the essence of the 4D and 5D framework long before the shift became visible to everyone else. Aislinn realized something very important when she was teaching people during that time. She knew she had to be careful with the idea of the future.

If people believed that the new Earth would only exist someday, they would keep waiting instead of changing now. Some people became trapped in the idea of futurism, always thinking the shift would happen later.

But the truth was… the shift had to happen inside first.”

She pauses, making sure we are following.

“She also noticed that some people used spirituality as a way to escape their pain instead of healing it.

For example, some people believed that once they cut energetic cords with someone, forgiveness was no longer necessary. But that was not true. Even if the cord is gone, the emotions can still live inside the body.

Anger.
Resentment.
Bitterness.
Sadness.

When you think about the person who hurt you, those emotions can activate again. It is like flipping a switch. And when that happens, you create a new energetic cord without even realizing it. That is why true healing requires forgiveness. Not because the other person deserves it…but because you deserve to be free."

Ryan nods slowly, and I can tell he is actually listening.

Paula continues. "Some people believed they could simply become enlightened and leave their pain behind. But it doesn't work that way. The ascension process is not about escaping. It is about integrating. Transforming. Becoming whole.

You know you have truly forgiven someone when you can think about them and feel nothing.

No anger.
No sadness.
No charge.

They are no longer your enemy. They are just another person who once played a role in your life."

She folds her hands. "That state is called neutrality.

In the old teachings, neutrality vibrates around the level of 250. It is the second level within the 4D range of human consciousness. Above that is acceptance, which vibrates higher.

When you reach acceptance, you can look back at painful experiences and see the lesson inside them. You may even realize that the person who hurt you was also your teacher.

And when you reach that level…forgiveness and wisdom begin to feel the same."

Ryan looks at Paula, then at me. "So everyone in the 3D world was teaching each other… even when they didn't know it?"

Paula smiles. "Yes. Everyone was both a student and a teacher. Even the painful people. Sometimes especially the painful ones."

She takes a slow breath before continuing. "Aislinn also discovered another important truth. Even people who reached higher states of consciousness still had a shadow. Every human who lived in the 3D world developed a shadow side.

Fear.
Anger.
Shame.
Jealousy.
Guilt.

These parts could not simply disappear. They had to be acknowledged, healed, and integrated. The nervous system needed to feel safe again. The mind needed to understand. The heart needed to release. That is why the ascension process never meant pretending the darkness wasn't there. It meant learning how to bring light into it."

She looks at both of us carefully. "And one more thing Aislinn taught everyone…

Even after the shift, grounding was still necessary. Every day. That is why we teach meditation to every child when they turn four years old. Grounding connects us to nature. It connects us to our higher self. It keeps us balanced. Without grounding, people can drift into fantasy, illusion, or spiritual pride. With grounding, we stay humble.

Present. Connected. And able to serve others."

She smiles slightly. "I know both of you are very intelligent."

She glances at me and gives a small wink.

I try not to laugh, because we both know Ryan is not exactly the sharpest tool in the shed — but music is his gift, and we love him for it.

"This may have been covered in school," Paula continues, "but I want to review the idea of multidimensional awareness, because some people were still confused during their becoming process.

Do either of you feel confused, or should I continue?"

I look at Ryan.

"I understand it... but I think Ryan might need the refresher."

Ryan shrugs. "Yeah... I was probably distracted that day... or asleep."

Paula laughs softly. "That's alright. Multidimensional awareness means understanding life from more than one perspective at the same time.

Not just logical thinking.

Not just emotions.

Not just social rules.

All of them together.

When we combine intellectual understanding, emotional awareness, and the awareness of how our actions affect others, we begin to see reality more clearly. Most people in the old world only looked from one point of view. But the new world required a wider awareness. That is why your becoming process includes conversations like this."

I nod.

"So, it's like baking a cake. Every ingredient matters. If you leave one out… it doesn't turn out right."

Ryan laughs. "Yeah… like the time you used salt instead of sugar when you tried to bake Mom a cake."

I groan.

"We forgave you," he says. "It's the thought that counts."

Paula smiles. "Exactly, Ryan. That's actually a perfect example."

Ryan sticks his tongue out at me, and I roll my eyes. He can be such a dork… but I love him.

I glance back at Paula, who still has that serious look on her face. And all I can think is:

Are we going to the beach yet?

As if Paula can read my thoughts, she looks at me and smiles slightly.

"I know you want to visit the tropical island, and we will. But first, I need to explain something important. Your becoming process is not only about learning new things. It is about developing multidimensional awareness. And that means understanding the truth about the old world, even when the truth is uncomfortable."

She presses a button on the remote, and the screen behind her lights up.

"Some people in the 3D world forgot how sacred this planet really is. They treated Earth as if it were disposable.

Trash was thrown everywhere.
Oceans were polluted.
Roadsides were covered in garbage.
Cities produced more waste than they could handle.

It took years after the shift to clean the planet."

Ryan leans forward. "How did it get that bad?"

Paula nods. "The old world produced more food and more products than people actually needed. But instead of sharing what they had, much of it was thrown away.

Food spoiled.
Stores threw out unsold items.
Holidays ended, and entire shipments of goods were discarded.

Some food was donated…but most of it ended up in landfills. People had more than enough, but still lived in fear of not having enough."

The screen changes.

Images appear of littered cities, highways, beaches, and rivers filled with plastic bottles, wrappers, clothing, and broken objects.

I feel my stomach sink as I watch.

Next come pictures of massive landfills, piles of trash stacked higher than buildings, and barrels of toxic waste dumped in remote areas.

I shake my head. “How could people do this to their own planet?”

Paula looks at me gently. “I know it is hard to understand. In the United States alone, nearly one-third of the food supply was wasted. Products were not made to last. Companies designed things to break, so people would have to buy more. The system depended on consumption.

Not on balance. Not on sustainability. On profit.”

She clicks the remote again.

More images appear.

Factories.
Shipping containers.
Mountains of plastic.
Electronics thrown away by the thousands.

“Some countries produced more waste because of their population. Others produced more because of their lifestyle. But the problem was the same everywhere.

People became distracted. Complacent. Disconnected. They told themselves one cigarette butt didn’t matter. One plastic bottle didn’t matter. One bag of trash didn’t matter.

But millions of people thinking that way…created mountains of destruction.”

I feel a heaviness in my chest as the images continue.

Paula watches us carefully before speaking again. “Not everyone was careless. Many people tried to help. Many tried to change things. But the system itself was built on money. And money rewarded consumption, not responsibility.”

She turns off the screen, and the room goes quiet.

I look at her, confused. “What do you mean… money caused all of this?”

Paula nods slowly. “In the old world, money controlled nearly everything. If you didn’t have money, life was very hard. People were judged by how much they earned, what they owned, and what they could afford. It didn’t matter who you were inside. Without money, you were often seen as a failure. And most people had no control over the circumstances they were born into.”

Ryan frowns. “So how did money control everything?”

Paula folds her hands. “There were governments. Taxes. Corporations. Banks. Laws that could be bent for the wealthy and enforced on the poor.

Every dollar someone earned was connected to another system that wanted a piece of it.

Homes were taxed.
Businesses were taxed.
Income was taxed.

Promises were made about security and stability…but many people lived paycheck to paycheck. They worked their entire lives just to survive.

Not to live.

To survive.”

She pauses, then continues more quietly. "This constant pressure kept people trapped in the 3D mindset.

Fear of losing money.

Fear of not having enough.

Fear of failure.

Even people who had a lot of money were afraid.

Afraid of losing it.

Afraid of getting sick.

Afraid of something happening that would take everything away."

Ryan raises his eyebrows. "So money made people scared… even when they had it?"

Paula nods. "Yes. Money had the power to make people believe they were safe…and at the same time, make them feel like they could lose everything at any moment.

Some people even believed money made them superior.

More important.

More powerful.

Almost like gods."

Ryan laughs. "That can't be real."

Paula looks at him seriously. "I wish it wasn't. But people with extreme wealth could influence laws, elections, businesses… even other people.

Money could buy silence.

Money could destroy reputations.

Money could protect criminals.

Money could turn truth into lies."

Ryan shakes his head. "That's messed up."

"Yes," Paula says quietly. "It was. That is why the old system could not survive the shift. When consciousness changed, the structures built on fear and control began to collapse. People no longer wanted to live that way.

They wanted balance.

They wanted honesty.

They wanted connection.

And once enough people felt that way…the old world could not hold itself together anymore."

She picks up the remote again.

"One more thing you need to see."

The screen lights up again.

Crowded stores.
Holiday shopping chaos.
Piles of clothing.
Stacks of electronics.
Beauty products thrown away by the thousands.

"The hunger for the newest thing never ended. Advertising made people feel like they were not good enough.

Not attractive enough.
Not successful enough.
Not worthy enough.

So, they bought more. And more. And more.

But no amount of money ever filled the emptiness inside. That is why the shift had to happen from within first.

Not in the stores.

Not in the government.

Not in the banks.

Inside the human heart."

She turns off the screen and looks at us.

"That was the past. We remember it…so we never repeat it. Now…"

She smiles.

"Are you ready to learn how to use the teleportation device?"

Ryan jumps to his feet. "Yes, ma'am!"

Paula sets the remote down and looks at both of us with a softer expression.

"That was the past. We remember it so we do not repeat it. The old world taught us many painful lessons, but those lessons helped humanity grow. Without them, the shift would never have happened."

She pauses, then smiles. "And now… I believe you two have earned a little adventure."

I shoot up from my seat. "Yes, ma'am!"

I laugh as I stand up beside my silly brother. "Finally! I thought we were never getting to the beach."

Paula shakes her head, trying not to laugh.

"You two remind me exactly of how people used to act during their becoming orientation.

Curious… impatient… excited… and completely ready to jump ahead to the fun part."

She walks toward the back of the room and gives motions for us to follow.

"Come on. The teleportation devices are stored in a secured area, so stay close to me."

Ryan and I follow her out of the presentation room and back into the main part of the library.

The building feels quiet, almost peaceful, like it is holding secrets inside its walls. Paula walks behind the reception desk again and presses the same code into the keypad. The cabinet unlocks with a soft click, and the green light appears again.

She opens the drawer and removes a small case, similar to the one she used earlier. Inside are several rings, each resting in its own slot.

Ryan's eyes go wide. "No way… those are the teleportation devices?"

Paula nods. "Yes. Each ring is programmed to connect with the planetary grid. They allow us to travel instantly from one location to another, as long as the destination has been approved and stabilized."

Ryan looks like a kid on his birthday. "That is the coolest thing I've ever seen."

Paula hands each of us a ring. “Place it on your right index finger.”

I slide the ring on, and the moment it touches my skin, I feel a faint vibration move through my hand and up my arm. It’s warm. Not hot… just warm. Alive.

Ryan looks at his hand in disbelief. “I can feel it.”

Paula nods. “The device responds to your energy. That is why only people who have completed their becoming orientation are allowed to use them. Your frequency has to be stable enough to travel safely.”

She closes the case and locks the cabinet again.

“Robin already contacted the locals in Bora Bora, so we are cleared to visit our usual private beach. We will only stay about forty-five minutes.”

Ryan grins. “Forty-five minutes in paradise is better than none.”

Paula laughs. “Let’s head back into the orientation room. We need some privacy.”

We do as instructed. I am so excited. I can hardly wait.

In the stillness within this space, Paula looks at us.

“Alright. Stand close to me. Teleportation works best when we stay within the same field.”

Ryan moves next to me, practically bouncing with excitement. I can feel my heart racing again. Not from running this time. From anticipation.

Paula raises her hand and lightly touches the ring on her finger.

"Focus on where we are going. Clear your mind. Do not resist the sensation. Just let it happen."

She smiles. "Take off your shoes and socks. This is going to be fun."

Paula presses a button on the remote, and suddenly the walls, floor, and ceiling transform into a tropical paradise.

We can smell the salty ocean air. A warm breeze moves gently through the room. The sound of waves hisses softly as they roll across the shoreline.

Ryan and I just stand there, staring in disbelief.

Paula laughs. "Stand next to me. Let's take hands and form a circle."

I grab Ryan's hand with one hand and Paula's with the other.

Paula looks at both of us. "I want all of us to set the same intention. We are going to Bora Bora. Our private beach. Forty-five minutes before sunset. Picture it clearly in your mind. Feel it in your heart."

She pauses for a few seconds. "Now connect to your heart. Feel the excitement. Feel the joy.

Imagine the white sand…the pale blue-green water…the palm trees moving in the wind. Good. Now look at my ring. Do you see the red crystal glowing?"

Ryan's eyes went wide. "Whoa… that's awesome."

Paula nods. "Close your eyes. Use your imagination. Feel the joy in your heart. Now say in your mind three times…

Be there now.
Be there now.
Be there now."

For a moment, everything goes completely still. Then I feel a strange pulling sensation, like the air itself is moving around us. A rushing sound fills my ears. The floor beneath my feet feels different. The air feels different too.

For a moment, everything feels weightless. Warmth spreads through my chest, then my arms, then my legs. And suddenly…wow!

Warmth. Softness. A gentle breeze touches my face. So, welcoming and sweet.

I open my eyes. Bright sunlight. Blue sky. The sound of waves crashing gently against the shore. The smell of the ocean.

I look down and see the sand between my toes.

"This is… incredible."

I look over at Paula, and she is smiling wider than I have ever seen. "Welcome to my paradise," she says.

Ryan throws his arms in the air. "Woo-hoo! Yes! This is what I'm talking about, sist-ta! This is the life!"

I watch Ryan kicks off his shoes, rip off his shirt and run straight toward the water. Good thing he wore shorts today.

Ryan looks back at me while he is running into the warm water, "Ryan "Last one in is a rotten egg!"

I can't believe it. We are standing on a white sandy beach, surrounded by crystal-clear water that sparkles like glass. Palm trees sway in the warm breeze, and the air smells like salt and flowers.

Paula smiles, watching our reactions. “Again, welcome to Bora Bora.”

I look at Ryan, then back at the ocean, my heart pounding with pure joy.

“This…” I laugh. “This is the best becoming orientation ever.”

I ran after him, laughing like a little kid. Behind us, Paula just shakes her head and smiles.

And in that moment, I realized something. The new world wasn’t only built on wisdom.

It was built on joy.

And maybe…that was the greatest shift of all.

Chapter 9: Bora Bora

I just stand there for a moment, trying to process what just happened. To the left, I see Paula near a small hut, carrying out three beach chairs, glass water bottles, and towels.

She sets one of the chairs in front of me.

“You can sit and watch the sunset with me…or go play in the ocean. Do whatever you want.”

I look toward the water. Ryan is already splashing around like he’s five years old again. I see him look towards my direction, “I believe our adventure through time has taken a most serious turn. A most excellent serious turn. This is the life!”

Paula laughs. “Go feel the water. It’s warm, not cold. It will surprise you.”

I walk slowly toward the shoreline. The sand feels cool and firm under my feet. A gentle wave slides over my toes, swirling around my ankles. I laugh out loud.

Ryan splashes water at me. “Get in sis. The water is excellent. There are no tubular waves, which is even more excellent for splashing you.”

“Hey! Slow down! I’m not wearing a swimsuit. I don’t want to get soaked.”

He stops immediately. “You’re right. Sorry, sis.”

I glance back at Paula. She’s sitting in one of the wicker chairs, drinking water, looking completely peaceful. I walk over and sit next to her.

“I love this place,” she says softly. “Don’t you?”

"It's amazing," I reply. "Can everyone do this when they turn twenty-five?"

Paula nods. "Yes. Everyone gets the opportunity twice a month. Some people use it often.
Some only for special occasions. We keep a calendar with time slots for the community. People use it for birthdays… anniversaries… date nights… traveling… exploring other cultures… even just to clear their mind. Tonight, we came here for a reason."

She glances toward the ocean, where Ryan is still playing in the waves.

"I'll give him a few more minutes to be a kid. Then I want both of you to sit with me. I need to explain something important. It's more about money…and why we removed it from the world."

I lean back in the chair, watching the sky slowly change colors. Gold. Pink. Purple. Crimson.

The sun sinks lower toward the horizon. Ryan stands waist-deep in the water, staring at the sunset. None of us say a word. It feels like time itself has slowed down.

"Ryan," Paula calls. "Come here, buddy. I saved you a chair, some water, and a towel. Let's watch the sunset together. I want to talk to both of you."

"Coming!" he shouts.

He walks out of the ocean, then suddenly stops and bends down.

"Hey! I found this totally most outstanding seashell for Robin. It looks like a snail shell. Does she have one like this?"

Paula laughs. "Yes. She does. You can keep it."

“Coolio man.”

Paula looks over at me with the look that says, “Are you kidding me. Enough with the Ted and Bill crap.” I just shrugged my shoulders because I know he is such a dork at times.

I watch Ryan wrap the warm towel around himself and sit down. For a few minutes, we all just watched the sun disappear into the ocean. I think about the Field of Time…about how somewhere, an angel might be recording this moment. This is the kind of memory I will come back to again and again when I meditate.

Then Paula speaks. “I want to talk about money a little more…a deeper dive into why it was eliminated.”

For a few minutes, we sat in silence, watching the last light of the sun stretch across the ocean.

Then Paula speaks softly. “Moments like this one we are sharing right now were once only possible for a small number of people.

For many, a place like this was only a dream.

Some people saved for years just to travel somewhere beautiful for a few days…while others lived in luxury every day of their lives.

When the Great Awakening happened, humanity looked deeply at itself and asked one question. What caused the most suffering on Earth? The answer came back again and again. Money.”

Ryan leans forward slightly, listening.

“In the 3D world, money ruled everything,” Paula continues. “It gave people power. It gave people status. It gave people control over others.

Over time, we saw how money changed people.

It made some greedy.
Some fearful.
Some arrogant.
Some desperate for more.

Money itself was not evil. But it became a very dense form of energy.

It amplified whatever consciousness used it.

When people lived in fear, money reflected fear.

When people lived in separation, money reflected separation.

When people believed there was never enough…money made that belief stronger.”

She looks out toward the ocean. “In the new Earth, our values changed. Instead of currency, we chose contribution.

Instead of accumulation, we chose collaboration.

Instead of competition, we chose community.

People began exchanging energy in different ways.

Through creativity.

Through service.

Through care.

Through shared intention.

Technology helped us for a while, acting as a bridge while humanity learned how to live without fear.

But eventually, we realized something important. The real wealth of a civilization is not money. It is coherence. Compassion. Wisdom.

Those became the new currencies of consciousness."

Ryan nods slowly. "That's why everything feels so different here..."

Paula smiles. "Yes. We kept the three C's... but we changed their meaning. In the old world, people were taught to be compliant, complacent, and controlled.

In the new world, we chose coherence, compassion, and consciousness."

She picks up a small handful of sand and lets it fall through her fingers.

"The disappearance of money marked humanity's graduation. We moved from transactional living...to relational creation.

From possession...to participation.

From measuring worth by status...to expressing worth through service.

Everyone contributes something. Art. Music. Healing. Teaching. Growing food. Building homes. Caring for children.

And in return, the community supports everyone.

No debt.

No ledger.

No one left behind.

Energy flows. It is given…and it returns."

The sky grows darker, and the colors deepen into shades of purple and gold.

Paula continues. "We began to see society as a living ecosystem. Not a hierarchy. Nature does not compete the way humans once did. It cooperates. Every part has a purpose. Every part matters.

So, our communities began to function the same way. Diversity was no longer a problem. It became harmony. Like different instruments in an orchestra. Each one unique…but all needed for the music to exist."

Ryan smiles. "That's why we have the coherence council? Tubular dudes."

Paula does her best to ignore Ryan's childish behavior and simply nods. "Yes. Before decisions are made, people align their hearts. They tune their vibration first…then they speak. Because action without alignment created most of the suffering in the old world."

She looks at both of us. "In the past, people defined themselves by what separated them.

Race.
Status.
Religion.
Money.
Education.
Appearance.

In the new world, identity comes from something deeper. Purpose. Resonance. Light.

People remember that we all come from the same Source. And when you remember that…discrimination disappears."

Chapter 9: Bora Bora

I sit quietly, watching the last sliver of sun disappear. Everything Paula is saying feels true, even if I never lived in that world.

She continues. “In the old world, value had to be earned. In the new Earth, value is inherent. Every child grows up knowing their light is sacred. No competition. No comparison. Each soul carries a piece of the whole.”

She laughs softly. “Imagine growing up in a world where joy, not judgment, becomes the mirror of who you are.”

Ryan leans back in his chair. “That sounds a lot better than what you showed us earlier.”

Paula nods. “It is. When the fear of survival disappeared, the need to control through money disappeared with it. Energy began to move through gratitude, attention, and intention. Those became the true currencies of creation. Technology helped us build energy grids that respond to vibration, not numbers. Contribution is felt, not counted.

That is how the monetary system ended. Not through chaos. Through readiness.”

Ryan looks out toward the ocean. “So the energy grids we see in the community… that’s part of that system? That so cool.”

“Yes,” Paula says. “We could never have done this alone. Everyone helped create the world we live in now. In the old system, the economy controlled people’s lives. Taxes, payments, debt, bills… it never ended. Many people worked their entire lives and still struggled to survive.

Food got more expensive. Housing got more expensive. Everything cost more… but people earned less. Many became hopeless. Some became addicted. Some became homeless.

Some felt abandoned by the very systems that promised to protect them."

The sky darkens, and the first stars begin to appear. We sit quietly, listening to the waves.

I finally understand what Paula means. Life was meant to be lived…not survived.

We sit quietly for a moment, listening to the gentle waves as the sky grows darker.

Then Paula lets out a slow breath. "There are just a few more things I want to explain before we head back. This time… it's about how money affected love."

Ryan glances at me, then back at Paula.

"In the old world," she continues, "money influenced nearly everything. Where you lived. What education you could afford. What kind of work you could do. What medical care you received. What opportunities you had. And over time, people started to believe that money also determined their worth.

It created judgment. Competition. Separation. People compared themselves constantly. Who had more. Who had less. Who was successful. Who was failing."

She looks out toward the horizon. "And when money controls a person's life… it can also control their heart. Some people stayed in relationships because they needed financial security. Some people married for status. Some married for survival. Some gave up on love

completely because they believed they could never afford the life they wanted."

I nod slowly. "That sounds exhausting."

"It was," Paula says softly. "When someone grows up in poverty, that belief can become part of their identity. They start to believe that this is all life will ever be. That they don't deserve more. That they don't belong in a better life. Those beliefs can pass from one generation to the next. Not because they are true…but because they were repeated for so long."

She turns toward us again. "That is why we decided that love should never depend on money. Not education. Not religion. Not status. Not background. Not the color of your skin. There is no price tag on love."

Ryan nods. "That makes sense. If you love someone, you love them. Money shouldn't matter."

Paula smiles. "You would think so. But in the old world, appearances meant everything. Weddings had to be expensive. Rings had to be perfect. Houses had to look a certain way. People believed that if something didn't cost a lot… it wasn't valuable. Even love became something people tried to measure."

She laughs softly, shaking her head. "There were entire industries built around the idea of the perfect romance. Movies. Advertising. The wedding business. The diamond business.

They told people that everyone was supposed to find their one true love. That life would feel empty if they didn't. So, people rushed into relationships. Not because they were ready…but because they were afraid of being alone."

I glance at Ryan, and he just shrugs. "That sounds like a lot of pressure for an excellent dude like me to handle."

"It was," Paula says. "Aislinn noticed that many people started relationships while they were still carrying old wounds. They hadn't healed. They hadn't learned who they really were. But they believed marriage would fix everything.

For a little while, the excitement made them feel happy. Then reality came back. Old habits returned. Old fears returned. Old patterns returned. And hearts broke…over and over again. Not because love isn't real. But because most people never learned how to love themselves first."

The sky is now deep purple, with streaks of fading gold along the horizon.

Paula continues more gently. "In our world, no one fears being alone. We are a community. We support each other. Everyone has a home. Everyone has food. Everyone has purpose. Everyone belongs.

When people no longer feel like they have to survive…they can finally choose love freely."

I look out at the ocean and feel something settle inside my chest. It makes sense. All of it.

Life feels lighter here. Simpler. Real.

Paula exhales slowly, as if letting go of the past. "I'm done talking about money. We are very blessed to live in a world where everyone is meant to thrive… not just a few. And now, we should probably head back. Your mother told me you have a special guest arriving tonight."

I sit up straight. "A special guest? From out of town?"

Paula smiles mysteriously. "Very far out of town. More like… from another world."

My heart jumps. "Tobias! Tobias, Tobias, Tobias! Oh, I love Tobias! Is he bringing his sister this time?"

Paula laughs. “That is for you to find out. Now help me put these chairs away. Your mom is probably waiting for us at the library.”

Ryan wraps the towel tighter around himself as he stands up.

“I hope his sister comes. She is so excellent. A really tubular chick.”

I laugh. “That was a good pun, Ryan.”

Ryan smiles at me. “She’s been showing up in my dreams, and we have been going on excellent adventures together. Teaching me how to fly in her world.

Every time I see her, my heart starts beating like crazy. She is a beautiful babe. Her blue and purple feathers…those silver eyes…that little purple beak…”

He puts his hand on his chest dramatically. “She takes my breath away.”

I roll my eyes. “You’re hopeless.”

Paula just smiles as we gather the chairs and towels, the last light of the sun disappearing behind the horizon. And for a moment, I realized something.

The old world was built on fear. This world…was built on wonder. And somehow, I knew the night ahead was going to change everything.

Chapter 10: Tobias, The White Lion

"Man, that was so much fun. An excellent adventure. Thank you, Paula," Ryan says, still smiling.

"Yes, thank you so much," I add. "Now I understand why my parents enjoy their date nights so much. Every time they come home, they're laughing, smiling, and glowing with happiness. I'm definitely going to ask Mom all about it."

Paula laughs softly. "You're both very welcome. And whenever you feel ready to travel again, you know where to find me. But before I send you off for the evening, I want to make sure we are all on the same page. Your becoming means you are entering the next stage of life."

Ryan and I look at each other, then back at her.

"We all move through four stages," Paula continues. "The first stage is from birth to twenty-five. The second stage is from twenty-five to forty. The third stage is from forty to sixty. And the final stage is from sixty until your vessel expires and you return to Source.

You are now entering the second stage. This is the stage of becoming. It is the time when you begin searching for what truly matters to you. There is a fire inside each of you, and this is the time to discover what fuels that fire. That fire is connected to your soul's purpose here on Earth.

Our goal is not to control that fire…but to keep it alive."

She looks at both of us carefully. "In this stage, you decide how you want to give back to the community… and to the world. When you were younger, we encouraged you to try many different things.

Picking berries and fruit.
Harvesting herbs and produce.
Planting and growing crops.
Canning and smoking meats.
Needle work.
Fishing.
Collecting and drying seeds.
Delivering food to the elderly.
Childcare.
Woodworking.
Repairing electronics.
Caring for animals.

We taught basic survival skills that supported our community as a whole. In the old world, some people might have called that child labor," she says with a smile, "but you kids had fun, didn't you?"

Ryan laughs. "Oh yeah, we had a triumphant time. It helped me figure out what I like… and what I don't like. Nothing was forced on us. Nobody graded us. We just learned by doing. And honestly, that's how I figured out what I really love."

Paula nods. "And what is that?"

Ryan grins. "Music. I want to explore the world and learn every kind of music I can. Did you know there are over a hundred different instruments from different cultures? When my teacher saw how serious I was about music, he helped connect me with students from other communities around the world. I already have friends in different countries I want to visit. And now that I'm twenty-five, I can, right?"

"Yes," Paula says. "You can travel using the teleportation portal in the library, not just the ring. That room on the left side of the Metatron cube? That's what it's for."

Ryan's eyes widen. "Most excellent. I always wondered what that room was. I only ever saw the first three rooms. That's awesome. I think I want to bring music from around the world back to our community.

Maybe become a music teacher. Maybe teach private lessons. Maybe even hold concerts by the lake in the summer.

I've played at Tom's Tavern a few times, and everyone loved it. Everyone had the most excellent time. Dancing and jamming to my toons. Most outstanding times."

Paula rolls her eyes and smiles. "I remember. Those were some fun nights. You could also become a trader while you travel. Exchange goods, ideas, music, culture. We like people to have options.

Staying in one place your whole life isn't right for everyone. Flexibility keeps the spirit alive."

She turns to me. "What about you, Danica?"

I think for a moment before answering. "I'm different from Ryan. We all know that fact."

Paula looks at me. "You're a totally different tubular babe. You got your own vibe."

Ryan puts his hands on his belly and laughs. "That was excellent, Paula."

Now I roll my eyes. "I feel more drawn to the stars… meditation… healing… nature. When I learned about Chinese medicine and acupuncture, it opened my mind to so many other ways of healing. That led me to herbs. Now I love making my own teas and tinctures. I've even given some to people in the community when they couldn't sleep or weren't feeling well. My secret ingredient is catnip. Don't tell Tobias… he'll never let me live it down."

Paula laughs. "That sounds like you. Have you thought about cooking more? You're a wonderful cook. You could work at the diner… or even open something new."

I smile. "I've thought about a lot of things. Yeah, I love cooking. I already help at the diner once a week if someone's sick or something comes up. I'm the floater," I say, laughing.

"But I also had an idea. Trisha and I talked about sharing a house. During the day, it could be a healing center. Meditation classes. Yoga. Reiki. Acupuncture. Natural medicine.

And in the summer… maybe a little weekend barbecue stand. Last summer I got obsessed with cooking curry."

Ryan laughs. In a long, drawn out tone of voice we hear Ryan say, "Dudes…obsessed is an understatement. Her curry dishes are bogusly excellent.

It's insane. Red curry, green curry, yellow curry…I wanted her to cook it every night. Paula, you must try it sometime."

Paula smiles warmly. "I just might. Those are wonderful ideas, Danica. Just remember, whatever you choose is your decision. There is no timeline. No pressure. We only want your soul, your heart, and that inner fire to lead you toward joy. Life will still test you sometimes.

Accidents happen. But you will always have support. You are never walking alone."

She glances toward the lobby.

“And speaking of support… I believe your mother is waiting for us. Let’s head back.”

As we step back into the library lobby, I see my mom standing there holding a small white bag. I assume it’s for Paula.

“Hello, Galene,” Paula says with a smile. “These two had a great first day. They may have a few questions over the next few days… just like you did after your becoming orientation.”

My mom laughs and holds out the bag. “This is for you. For taking such good care of them. And I know Ryan can be a handful sometimes. He keeps life interesting, doesn’t he?”

Paula laughs. “He certainly does. We went to my favorite beach in Bora Bora, and he acted like he was six years old again. Except this time, he wasn’t making mud pies.”

We all laugh as Ryan’s face turns bright red.

“I know, I know,” he says. “I can be childish sometimes. But the water was so warm… and so clear. I feel so lucky to be living on this new Earth. I learned a lot today. Thank you, Paula. I’m actually excited for tomorrow.”

“Yes, thank you,” I say, giving her a hug. “I hope you have a nice evening.”

When we get home, the smell of garlic, herbs, and onions fills the air. Mom looks up from the kitchen. “I made spaghetti sauce from the garden. We’re having stuffed baked chicken with mushrooms, spinach, and ricotta, covered in sauce… with buttered herb noodles and roasted zucchini. And I opened a bottle of red wine.”

“That sounds perfect,” I say, smiling.

Chapter 10: Tobias, The White Lion

"After dinner," Mom continues, "we have a special guest coming over. I think Paula already told you who it is."

Ryan and I look at each other.

"Yes," I say. "We're excited. What time should we expect Tobias?"

"Around eight," she replies. "That gives you both time to wash off the sand and salt water first."

After dinner and dessert, I step outside and look up at the sky. It's a warm June night. The moon is only a thin sliver, so the stars shine brighter than usual. The trees glow a soft pale green in the darkness. Everything looks different now than it did in the old world.

When the vibration of Earth increased...when the prism split from 3D to 4D and eventually to 5D...the colors of the world became brighter. Bluer. Greener. More alive.

It felt like the Earth itself was happier. Humanity had finally stopped abusing the planet. We learned how to use new forms of energy. Power from the Earth itself. From volcanoes. From natural grids. From sources we once ignored.

And in return... the Earth seemed to bless us. The air felt cleaner. The water felt lighter. Even the plants seemed to glow with gratitude.

We also made contact again with extraterrestrial beings. Not for the first time in history...but for the first time in a very long time. I know Tobias helped humans long ago. He worked with the Egyptians. He helped teach the knowledge of the stars. He worked beside Thoth, protecting the ancient mysteries from those who wanted to destroy them.

His race is older than most civilizations in our galaxy. The Lyrans. From what we learned in school, almost everyone on Earth has connections to other star systems. Some are starseeds. Some are hybrids. There are thirteen main types. The most common are Pleiadian, Sirian, Arcturian, Andromedan, and Lyran.

Each type carries different gifts. Not physical gifts…but gifts of awareness. Wisdom. Intuition. Healing. Science. Leadership. Creation.

Some are teachers. Some are builders. Some are protectors. Some are innovators. All of them are needed.

I know I am a Lyran starseed. That is why I feel everything so deeply. That is why the images from the old world during my becoming orientation made me emotional. The Lyrans are one of the oldest civilizations connected to Earth.

From what Tobias told me, his people helped seed life on many worlds. Including this one. He once told me that their colonies spread across systems like the Pleiades, the Hyades, and Vega.

I suddenly realized that I haven't told you much about Tobias. You should probably understand who he is before he shows up tonight. Tobias is a Lyran… a white lion, feline-like being. His sister is bird-like. His race is one of the oldest interstellar civilizations.

The white lions are considered a noble and ancient lineage. Guardians of wisdom. Keepers of spiritual integrity.

He once told me that forty-five of his kind volunteered to come into this universe to help build the structures of consciousness that would guide younger worlds. Over time, many of them became what we now call Ascended Masters. Beings who can move between physical bodies, light bodies, and plasma forms.

On their planet, they lived close to nature. They grew their own food. Built living structures from forests and fields. Their civilization lasted for millions of years.

When I first met Tobias, I was fascinated by him. He has bright blue eyes, a long white mane, and moves with a grace that almost looks unreal. In his true form, he is over twelve feet tall. But when he visits us, he appears closer to seven, so he doesn't scare anyone.

One of my favorite memories of him happened when I was ten years old. He came to visit, and I asked him to tell me the story of his people. So, I climbed into bed, and he tried his best to curl up beside me without crushing the mattress.

Then, right in front of my eyes, he manifested an ancient book. It was thick, old, and glowing faintly with light.

As I snuggled next to him, he spoke softly. "This, little one… is the history of my people."

He opened the book…and the pages came alive. Magic and color swirled in the air before me. I saw the most beautiful planet I had ever seen. Rolling mountains covered in green. Clear blue lakes. Peaceful oceans. Glowing plants that shimmered softly in the dark.

"This world is called Avyon," he said. "It was once a paradise… much like your Earth is now."

As he turned the page, the scene changed.

I saw glowing flowers lighting the ground with soft colors. Streams flowing through tall grass. Creatures I had never seen before moving peacefully through the fields. It felt alive. It felt safe. It felt like home.

Then the page turned again. Suddenly, I saw something different. Dark figures. Tall… cold… reptilian beings holding weapons. My stomach tightened.

“They look mean,” I said quietly. “I don’t trust them.”

Tobias looked down at me with kind eyes. “Do not be afraid, little one. This is only a story of the past. Would you like me to continue… or stop here?”

I hesitated for a moment, but I nodded. “I want to know.”

He turned the page.

“This was the time when my people lived in peace,” he said. “We followed the ways of the Great Spirit. We lived in harmony with our world.”

The next page showed a circle of elders sitting around a fire beneath a sky full of stars. The air smelled like sage. The grass glowed softly in the dark.

“This one,” Tobias said, pointing to the tallest figure, “is my father. He was chief of our people.”

I felt warmth coming from the page, like I could feel his energy.

“He believed all beings should be welcomed with open hearts. He believed fear creates conflict…and love creates understanding.”

The page turned again.

This time I saw a young warrior sitting near the fire. His mane was bright orange, braided with feathers and crystals. His eyes glowed like honey.

“This warrior questioned the strangers,” Tobias said. “He felt danger coming. He believed trust should be earned, not given blindly.”

Chapter 10: Tobias, The White Lion

The next page appeared.

Huge black ships filled the sky. Reptilian beings stepped onto the land. They carried weapons I did not understand. My chest tightened again.

“They don’t look friendly,” I whispered.

Tobias nodded slowly. “They came searching for something. Something valuable. Something our world had… and theirs did not.”

The page turned again.

I saw the two races meeting. Trading. Talking. Trying to understand each other.

“My father believed peace was possible,” Tobias said. “He wanted friendship. He wanted unity. But the young warrior felt something darker beneath the surface.”

The next page appeared.

The reptilians were watching. Studying. Observing how the Lyrans shaped the land with their minds. Moved objects without touching them. Built with thought instead of tools.

“They saw our gifts,” Tobias said quietly. “And they wanted them.”

The page turned again.

This time I saw a dark leader inside one of the ships. His eyes were cold. His voice felt wrong even without hearing it.

“History repeats itself,” Tobias said. “When a powerful force finds a peaceful world filled with abundance…the desire for control often follows.”

My heart started beating faster.

Chapter 10: Tobias, The White Lion

The next page began to change…and I could feel the story becoming heavier.

Chapter 11: The Great Galactic War

The page began to change again, and I could feel the energy in the room grow heavier. The peaceful colors faded, replaced by darker shades of red and gray.

Smoke filled the sky. Ships moved across the clouds like shadows.

My chest tightened as I watched. “What’s happening?” I asked quietly.

Tobias kept his voice calm, but I could feel the sadness behind it.

“This is the beginning of what your people now call the Great Galactic War,” he said. “The day our world changed forever.”

The image grew clearer. The reptilian ships that once hovered peacefully above the land were now gathering in large numbers. Hundreds of them. Maybe thousands. Their metal bodies blocked out the light of the stars.

“They did not come as friends anymore,” Tobias continued. “They came for power. They came for control. They came for the knowledge our people carried.”

I swallowed hard. “Why didn’t your people fight them right away?”

Tobias turned the page slowly.

“Because my father believed peace should always be given a chance. Our people had lived in harmony for millions of years. We did not understand how deeply fear and greed could take hold of another race. We thought kindness would be enough. We were wrong.”

Chapter 11: The Great Galactic War

The next page showed the council of elders standing together beneath the night sky. The tall lion-like beings wore robes decorated with symbols that glowed softly with light.

In the center stood Tobias's father. His mane shimmered like silver in the firelight.

"He welcomed the strangers," Tobias said quietly. "He offered them food… water… shelter… and knowledge. He believed that sharing wisdom would create trust. But some knowledge should only be given to those who are ready for it."

The page shifted again.

This time I saw the reptilian leader standing inside one of the ships. His eyes were narrow. Cold. Calculating.

"They studied us," Tobias said. "They watched how we lived. How we shaped matter with thought. How we healed with energy. How we communicated without words. They saw our connection to the Source…and they wanted it for themselves."

My hands tightened in the blanket.

"Did they try to take it?"

Tobias nodded. "Yes. But what they wanted could not be stolen. It could only be earned through consciousness. And that made them angry."

The next page burst into motion.

The sky filled with light. Weapons fired from the ships above. The ground shook as explosions tore across the land. Creatures ran in every direction. The glowing forests caught fire. The oceans turned dark.

"They attacked without warning," Tobias said. "Our people were not prepared for war. We had forgotten how to defend ourselves. We had lived in peace for too long."

I felt tears in my eyes as the images continued.

Lion-like warriors stood between the ships and the villages, trying to protect their people. Some used weapons made of light. Some used their minds to create shields. Some called on the energy of the planet itself. But the ships kept coming.

"They wanted our world," Tobias said. "They wanted our power. They wanted our ability to create without machines. And they were willing to destroy everything to get it."

The page changed again.

This time I saw the young warrior with the orange mane. The one who had warned the council. He stood at the edge of a cliff, looking up at the burning sky.

"He knew this would happen," I whispered.

Tobias nodded slowly. "Yes. He felt the danger before anyone else. He understood that love without wisdom can become vulnerability. And trust without awareness can become destruction."

The image shifted.

I saw Tobias's father standing in front of the council one last time. The firelight flickered across his face. He looked older. Tired. Grieving.

"He realized his mistake," Tobias said quietly. "He had believed all beings wanted peace. He believed every race would choose harmony if given the chance. But some races were still learning.

Still evolving. Still trapped in fear. And fear can turn even intelligence into something dangerous."

The page turned again.

This time I saw ships leaving the planet. Thousands of them. Carrying families. Children. Elders. Warriors.

"The war spread beyond our world," Tobias said. "Avyon was only the beginning. The conflict moved across star systems. Colonies were destroyed. Civilizations fell. Entire planets were lost."

My voice trembled. "Is that when the Galactic Federation was created?"

Tobias looked down at me and nodded.

"Yes. When the war grew too large for one world to survive alone, many races came together. Not to conquer…but to protect. That was the beginning of the alliance your people now call the Galactic Federation."

The page glowed brighter, and new symbols appeared in the air.

Ships of different shapes. Different colors. Different races standing side by side.

"Some were human-like," Tobias said. "Some were not. But all of them understood one thing. If the war continued…many worlds would fall."

I held my breath as the page began to turn again. The energy in the room felt even heavier now. Like the story was only just beginning. And somehow…I knew the next part would change everything.

The page turned again, and the images grew larger, as if the story itself was expanding beyond one world.

Chapter 11: The Great Galactic War

I saw stars… countless stars… and planets scattered across the darkness. Ships moved between them like sparks of light.

“The war did not stay on Avyon,” Tobias said quietly. “It spread across many systems. Worlds that had lived in peace for millions of years were suddenly forced to defend themselves. Some races had never known violence before. Others had known it for a very long time. And when fear enters the mind, even advanced civilizations can fall.”

The image shifted again.

I saw different beings standing together. Some looked human. Some had blue skin. Some had wings. Some were tall and thin, with glowing eyes. Others looked like the feline people of Tobias’s world.

“They came from many places,” he continued. “The Pleiades. Sirius. Arcturus. Andromeda. Vega. Lyra.

Some had technology far beyond anything humans would understand. Others had very little technology, but great spiritual awareness. For the first time, many races realized they had to work together.”

The page glowed brighter, and a circle of light appeared in the air. Ships of many shapes formed a ring around a large blue planet.

“That was the beginning of the Federation,” Tobias said. “Not an empire. Not a government. An agreement. An agreement that no world should face destruction alone.”

I leaned closer to the book.

“Did the reptilians start the war everywhere?”

Tobias paused before answering. “They were not the only ones,” he said. “There were other races who believed power was more important than harmony. Some believed emotion was weakness. Some believed control was the only way to survive. And some believed they had the right to take what they wanted from younger worlds."

The image changed again.

This time I saw something strange. Different races standing together… but their energy looked different. Unstable. Uneven.

"What happened?" I asked.

Tobias turned the page slowly.

"As the war continued, some races began to mix their knowledge… and their genetics. They were trying to survive. Trying to adapt. Trying to become stronger. But not every experiment was wise."

I saw laboratories. Machines. Beings that looked part human… part something else. My stomach tightened.

"Hybrids?" I whispered.

Tobias nodded. "Yes. Some were created out of fear. Some out of curiosity. Some out of hope.

Some out of desperation. Not all of them were bad. But not all of them were good either."

The page changed again.

Now I saw a small blue planet, floating quietly in space. Earth. It looked younger. Softer. Untouched.

"This world," Tobias said gently, "was not meant to be a battlefield. It was meant to be a garden."

I felt something warm in my chest as I looked at it.

"So why did the war come here?"

Tobias's eyes softened. "It did not come here the way it came to other worlds. Earth became something else. A place where souls could learn. A place where different races could incarnate without bringing their weapons with them. A place where memory would be hidden…so choices would be real."

I frowned. "You mean… people forgot on purpose?"

"Yes," he said. "The veil was created so consciousness could grow without being forced. Without knowing everything. Without remembering every past life. Without knowing every war. Without knowing every mistake."

The page shimmered again.

I saw humans. Different colors. Different cultures. Different time periods. All living on the same planet.

"Earth became a school," Tobias said. "A place where souls from many worlds could experience limitation. Fear. Love. Loss. Choice.

And through those experiences…they could evolve."

I looked up at him. "So, the war is why we're here?"

He nodded slowly. "The war showed the universe what happens when power grows faster than wisdom. Earth was created to restore the balance. A place where the heart would have to grow… before the mind could control everything again."

The page began to glow brighter than before. I could feel the energy in the room changing.

"And that," Tobias said softly, "is why your world is so important. And why so many beings have watched over it for a very long time."

The page started to turn again.

I felt my heart beating faster. Something told me the next part of the story was going to explain why humanity forgot who they really were. And why remembering now…was part of the plan.

The page began to glow brighter than before, and the air in the room felt heavier, like the story itself carried weight.

I looked up at Tobias. "If Earth was meant to be a school… why make it so hard?"

He did not answer right away. He turned the page slowly, as if the next part required care.

"This," he said softly, "is the part many beings struggle to understand."

The image changed.

I saw the Earth again, but this time it looked different. Darker. Denser. The colors were not as bright as before.

"What happened?" I asked.

Tobias placed one large hand gently on the edge of the book.

"In order for souls to truly grow, they needed to experience separation. Not just the idea of separation…the feeling of it. So, the frequency of the planet was lowered."

My stomach tightened. "You mean… on purpose?"

He nodded. "Yes. Not as punishment. Not as cruelty. As a lesson."

Chapter 11: The Great Galactic War

The page shifted again.

I saw humans living in small villages. Some looked peaceful. Others looked afraid. Fighting.

Arguing. Struggling to survive.

"When consciousness lives in higher dimensions," Tobias said, "beings know they are connected to Source.

They feel it. They remember it.

And when you remember who you are, what you are, and why you are here… it is difficult to choose harm. But in a lower vibration…memory fades. Fear grows. Ego forms. And souls are given the chance to choose who they will become."

I felt a lump in my throat. "So, people forgot… so they could learn?"

"Yes," he said. "The veil was placed between the human mind and the soul's full memory.

Not to trap you…but to give you freedom. Freedom to choose love without being forced by knowledge. Freedom to choose kindness without being told you must. Freedom to grow."

The page turned again.

This time I saw wars. Cities burning. People crying. People hurting each other. I looked away.

"That seems too hard," I whispered.

Tobias's voice became softer. "Many felt the same way. Some souls chose easier worlds. Some chose worlds of light. Some chose worlds of peace. But some chose Earth…because Earth offered the greatest growth."

He turned the page again.

I saw beings of light standing around the planet. Watching. Protecting. Waiting.

“They knew this world would be difficult,” Tobias said. “They knew it would include loss. Pain. Confusion. Loneliness.

But they also knew it would create something rare. Compassion born from experience. Wisdom born from mistakes. Strength born from struggle. And love… chosen freely.”

I swallowed hard. “So the darkness wasn’t winning?”

He shook his head slowly. “No. The darkness was part of the lesson. Without contrast, growth is slow. Without challenge, awareness stays small. Without choice, evolution stops.”

The page glowed again, brighter than ever.

I saw the Earth surrounded by light. Lines of energy moving across the planet like a grid.

“What is that?” I asked.

“The moment the cycle was meant to end,” Tobias said. “When enough souls remembered. When enough hearts opened. When enough people choose love instead of fear. The frequency of the planet could rise again.”

The image changed.

I saw the prism splitting. 3D. 4D. 5D.

The colors became brighter. The Earth looked alive again.

“That is the shift your people speak of now,” Tobias said. “The return to a higher state of being. Not a new world…but the remembering of what the world was always meant to be.”

I looked at him, my heart beating fast. “So, everything that happened… the war… the forgetting… the suffering…it was all part of the plan?”

He closed the book gently. “Yes. Not a plan of control. A plan of growth. A plan that allowed every soul to choose what they would become. And now…your world is reaching the end of that cycle.”

He looked down at me with those bright blue eyes. “That is why you are here now, little one. And that is why so many beings are watching Earth again.”

The room felt quiet.

Still.

Sacred.

And somehow… I knew the story was not finished yet. I sat quietly for a moment, staring at the closed book in Tobias’s hands. My mind felt full, but my heart felt even fuller.

“So… if Earth became a school,” I said slowly, “then why do some people feel different here? Like they don’t belong…like this world isn’t really their home?”

Tobias smiled softly, as if he had been waiting for that question. “Because for many souls… it isn’t their first home.”

He opened the book again, but this time the pages did not show war. They showed stars. Endless stars. Worlds I had never seen before.

“After the war, many civilizations agreed to help Earth,” he said. “Some came to guide from beyond the physical. Some came as teachers. Some came as protectors. And some came by incarnating as humans.”

My chest tightened. “Starseeds?”

He nodded. “Yes. Souls from many systems chose to come here. Not because Earth was easy…but because it needed help. It needed balance. It needed beings who remembered love, even when the world around them forgot.”

The page shifted again.

I saw people living on Earth in different time periods. Some looked out of place. Different.

Quiet. Observing.

“They often felt alone,” Tobias said. “They felt like they were watching the world instead of belonging to it. That is how I felt at times. How Aislinn felt. Like a stranger in a strange land.

They asked questions others did not ask. They felt pain more deeply. They cared more than most. Many did not understand why.”

I felt something stir in my chest. “That sounds like… me.”

Tobias looked at me gently. “Yes. You have lived on other worlds before. Many times. This is not your first journey here.”

My heart started beating faster. “Is that why I feel so emotional when I see suffering? Why the old world during my becoming orientation made me want to cry?”

“Yes,” he said. “Because part of you remembers what harmony feels like. And when you see a world living without it… your soul feels the difference.”

The page changed again.

Now I saw Earth surrounded by light again, but this time there were beings standing around it. Watching. Waiting.

"Many starseeds came during the last cycles," Tobias said. "They knew the shift would come one day. They knew the planet would reach a point where it could rise again. They came to help hold the frequency. To remind others. To keep the light alive, even in dark times."

I swallowed. "So… people like you came too?"

Tobias smiled. "Yes. Some of us never left completely. We stayed close to this world. Watching. Guiding when allowed. Waiting for the moment when humanity would be ready to remember."

I looked down at the book, then back up at him. "Why are you telling me all this?"

He closed the book slowly and set it beside the bed. "Because you asked. And because your soul is old enough to hear the truth."

My hands tightened in the blanket. "But why me? Why do you visit me?"

For the first time, Tobias hesitated. His eyes softened, and his voice became very quiet.

"Because you asked to come here. Long before this life began. You wanted to help when the cycle ended. You wanted to see the shift with your own eyes. You wanted to remember… while you were still human."

My heart pounded in my chest. "So… I chose this?"

He nodded. "Yes. You chose Earth. You chose this life. You chose your family. You chose the time you were born. Not because it would be easy…but because this is the lifetime when everything changes."

The room felt warm. Safe. Almost glowing.

“And that,” Tobias said softly, “is why I came to see you tonight.”

I stared at him, barely able to breathe. Something deep inside me felt like it was waking up. Like a memory I couldn’t quite reach.

And somehow…I knew this story was not just about the past. It was about what was coming next.

The room felt quiet after Tobias finished speaking. I sat there for a long time, staring at the book resting beside him. My mind was full of images.

Stars.

Ships.

Worlds.

War.

Earth.

The veil.

The shift.

It was a lot for a ten-year-old to understand… but somehow, my heart understood even when my mind didn’t.

“Tobias?” I whispered.

“Yes, little one.”

“Will the war ever happen again?”

He smiled softly and placed his large hand gently on my head. “The kind of war you saw tonight does not need to happen again. The universe learned from that time. Many worlds learned. And Earth… is learning now.”

I looked up at him. “Is that why things feel strange sometimes? Like something big is going to happen?”

He nodded. “Yes. Because your world is reaching the end of a long cycle. Many souls came here to help when that moment arrived. And you are one of them.”

I felt warm and sleepy, like my body was getting heavy.

“Tobias… will you still visit me when I get older?”

He laughed softly. “I will always be nearby. But you may not always see me the way you do now. As you grow, your life will become busy. Your mind will fill with many things.

Sometimes you will forget. Sometimes you will doubt. Sometimes you will wonder if this was only a dream. But when the time is right…you will remember again.”

My eyes started to close. “Promise?”

“I promise.”

The room faded, and the memory slowly drifted away like smoke. The stars above my house came back into view. I was standing outside again, looking up at the night sky.

For a moment, I forgot where I was. Then I heard my mom’s voice from inside the house.

“Tobias should be here any minute!”

Ryan opened the back door and stuck his head outside. “Hey, space cadet. You coming in, or are you planning on talking to the stars all night?”

I laughed and shook my head. “I’m coming.”

Chapter 11: The Great Galactic War

As I stepped back inside, I felt a strange feeling in my chest. Like something important had just happened… even though it was only a memory.

Mom was setting glasses on the table. Ryan was pacing back and forth like an excited kid.

“You think Tobias is bringing his sister?” he asked.

“I don’t know,” I said. “But you’re definitely hoping he does.”

He grinned. “You know it. She’s amazing. Total babe. Those excellent bright blue feathers… those sparkling siler eyes… that triumphant cute voice…Man, I swear my heart starts beating like crazy every time she shows up.”

I rolled my eyes. “You’re hopeless.”

Mom laughed. “You two better calm down before they get here. You’re acting like little kids waiting for a birthday party.”

Just then, there was a knock on the door. Everything went quiet.

Ryan froze.

Mom smiled.

I felt my heart start pounding. Mom opened the door. And standing there… filling the doorway with his tall white figure and bright blue eyes…it was Tobias.

He smiled. “Well…it looks like I arrived at the perfect time.”

And somehow, in that moment…I knew the story was only beginning.

Chapter 12: Another World

Before my eyes stands a handsome, tall, pale blue-eyed, feline-like creature with a fluffy white mane. He looks like he is dressed to go out dancing in a 70's nightclub, wearing glowing midnight-blue platform boots, tight-fitting silvery light-blue pants, and a perfectly fitted velvet midnight-blue vest.

I laugh at his wild and crazy outfit.

In his seductive, sultry voice, like a purr, Tobias says with a respectful bow before me, "What do you think, girlfriend? You know you're lovin' the digs. You must be jelly. I brought you a matching outfit. You could braid my hair and bling out my mane like you did last time we went out dancing. Come on, little one. Let's go have some fun."

I roll my eyes at Tobias, and he gives me a big cat-like grin. My mom just laughs because she enjoys Tobias's playful, silly sense of humor.

"I have something special planned for us tonight. My sister came up with the brilliant idea now that you both have turned twenty-five," Tobias says.

"Oh really? Because we would definitely stand out at my club downtown. It's not even disco night, dude. It's country line dancing. Why are you dressed like that? I just don't get it," I say to Tobias.

My mom just laughs and walks away, but before she does, she says, "Tobias has already told me about his fabulous plan, and I approve. Just make sure she doesn't drink too much of that pink glowing magic mushroom cocktail you serve on your planet. Oops! Did I just spoil the surprise? I hope not."

"Your mom is correct. We, my love, are not going dancing on your planet. I know you have been eager to explore my world, because my world is way cooler than yours," he states.

I jump out of my chair instantly. My heart is beating with excitement.

"Really?" I say excitedly. "I have heard stories from my mom about the late-night dance parties you had with her on your planet.

She said it was one of her top five life experiences. Come with me to my bedroom, Tobias, so I can transform that messy wild mane of yours and make you sparkle."

I grab Tobias's hand, and we quickly walk toward my bedroom. "Remember to duck," I say.

"Thanks. You were pulling my arm with such excitement that I almost forgot to duck before entering your bedroom," Tobias says.

Ryan looks over at us. "Where is Aura? Where is my most excellent babe? Is she coming later?"

Tobias turns and says, "She will be here soon. Be patient, my most excellent friend. She has something extra special for you."

I watch Tobias playfully wink at Ryan.

Ryan looks impatient. "Like what? Flying lessons? Some excellent adventures in the sky?"

I see Ryan close his eyes and begin to pray out loud. "Please God… please make my dreams come true."

I hear the doorbell ring, and Ryan almost trips over his own feet to answer the door. In the distance, I hear warm welcomes, laughter, a chirping bird sound, and then Ryan saying, “Thank you God! Most triumphant God. Thank you for making my dreams come true!”

When I shut my bedroom door, Tobias looks around the room.

I walk over to my music device and hit the button labeled 70’s Disco. The Brothers Johnson come alive as the song *Strawberry Letter 23* begins to play. I start to move my hips to the beat as I close my eyes.

“I just love this song. Do they play it on your planet?” I ask.

In a playful tone, Tobias says, “Yes, we do. I can ask the DJ to play it for you. In fact, we play a lot of amazing popular songs from other planets and worlds. You will truly love it.

You know, this bedroom is very similar to the style Aislinn enjoyed. In fact, you remind me a lot of her. I believe that is why we connect so well.”

I watch him looking around. Observing all my pictures, trinkets, and nick-nacks.

Tobias stands next to me and takes my hand. “You have glowing crystals, a massive canvas image of a lion’s head above your bed, a sacred-geometry comforter, spiritual paintings, exotic flowering plants, and the sweet smell of incense.

The vibe is chilly and relaxing. You have done a good job creating your own sacred, magical space.”

I look into his beautiful eyes, as my heart skips a beat. Tobias is devilishly handsome…and he doesn’t even realize it.

“Thank you. It speaks to me. This space. It grounds me when Ryan is on a roll. Or I should say, when he jumps on the crazy train with his favorite movie lines and comments. It can be a little too much at times. Yet…Ryan is just being…Ryan.”

We both look at each other, and Tobias rubs his soft nose against my cheek.” I missed you, little one. I really missed you…especially your smell. Nice perfume. Is it new?”

I sheepishly smile. “Yes, my father gave it to me. Hints of musk and patchouli.”

I look down out of embarrassment. He takes his hand and lifts my chin to look in my eyes. “It’s been a while.” He says. “You look good. Healthy. Happy. Really good. Happy birthday, my love. Happy becoming.”

I just blush a little. “Oh, you should see this device,” I respond. Stepping away from his because I can feel butterflies in my belly.

“I got it last year for my birthday.”

I walk over to the nightstand and pick up a small white remote. I press a red button, and my entire ceiling becomes an immersive starry night, covered with green starlight and a large glowing full moon. Off to the right side of my ceiling is a swirling bluish-lavender nebula.

“Wow… that is pretty cool, little one. We have a long night ahead of us. I am going to sit on the edge of your bed while you work your magic on my hair and mane.”

Tobias snaps his fingers, and poof! In the palm of his hand is a purple-cased beauty box.

He looks at me and says, “Everything we both need should be in here. I can’t wait to dance with you on my planet. You are going to love it, Danica.

This song you love will sound and feel different because the energy, vibration, and frequencies are much higher. The sound will be richer. The rhythm, tones, beat, and even the lyrics will speak to you more profoundly.

As you humans say, you will feel it in your heart, soul, and even your bones.

The music will sweep you away, and you will become one with it. You will never dance or listen to music the same way again.”

“Really?” I ask.

“Yes, really,” he replies.

I open the box. Wow. He was right. There are so many fun goodies inside. Where do I even start?

Tobias playfully slaps my butt with his tail. “Stop dilly-dallying, little one. The dance floor is calling our names.”

“Okay, okay,” I reply. “You can be so pushy at times.”

I take a brush and smooth out his front and back mane. Then I take the midnight-blue hair powder and transform the sides and top of his mane.

Next, I take the light sparkly blue hair powder and make his long chin hair stand out. Then I braid it and attach some cool-looking blue beads to the end of it.

Perfect.

Next, I take the dark-blue eyeliner and shape his eyes, making the light blue of his eyes pop. I step back and look at my creation.

"Wait, you need this glitter spray. Almost done."

Then I take his long hair that touches his back and comb it. Again, he playfully smacks me with his tail.

"Be gentle, little one. You are pulling my hair."

"Sorry. What were you doing earlier? Your hair is full of pine needles. Were you laying on the ground gazing at the stars?" I ask.

With a sheepish grin, he turns and looks at me.

"No. You know that large dog that likes to chase your beloved cat? Well, when I was outside chatting with your Paula as she was passing, it came over and started to growl at me. So, you know me. I took off these sexy boots and chased it."

I laugh.

"But what about your hair? How did you get the pine needles?"

"Well, I flew up into a pine tree and hid within the branches. When the dog got closer to the tree and I started to crawl down the trunk, the dog looked so confused. So, I connected with the dog's heart center and sent it some loving vibes.

I could tell the dog welcomed it because it immediately relaxed. I jumped down and rolled around on the ground playing with the silly dog. I spoke to the dog's soul and asked it to no longer chase your beloved cat.

The dog agreed. So, it's all good now."

"Yeah, but your hair is a mess," I reply.

Again, he tries to whack me with his tail, but this time I stop him. Giving his tail a little playful tug.

We both laugh.

Once his hair is free of pine needles, I split it into three parts. The two sides I pull off to the side. In the middle, I use the light sparkly blue hair powder.

Then I take the two side parts and use the same midnight-blue hair powder. I combine the two sides by weaving in beads that match the light blue powder.

It looks amazing. I feel so proud of my work.

When I am finished, I have Tobias look at himself in the mirror. I can see his small belly moving as he tries to hold in his laughter. It takes him a moment before he speaks.

“Impressive. You, little one, have so much fun playing with my mane and long hair. You are just as wild, playful, and fun as Aislinn.

She…or I should say we…loved to go dancing. We loved getting dressed up…dolled up. Ready to dance the night away. We would get so lost in the music. Sweating…dancing…flirting…those were good times.

It was a big part of our lives from her twenties to her forties.”

“Really?” I ask.

“Yes. Now my turn, little one,” he says, gently wrapping his arms around me. “I have the perfect outfit for you.”

Tobias sits back down on the edge of my bed. I watch him snap his fingers, and a matching outfit magically appears in his cupped hands.

“Voila, my love. Here is your matching outfit. I will close my eyes while you put this on.”

Chapter 12: Another World

I quickly change my clothes and look at myself in the mirror. I look smoking hot.

I look over at Tobias, and he knows what I am thinking.

"Get your skinny butt over here, little one. It is my turn to doll you all up. It will be hard to keep the men off you tonight."

I smile and laugh.

Then one of my favorite songs comes on. *He's the Greatest Dancer* by Sister Sledge begins to play.

I turn my head, look into Tobias's big, beautiful eyes, and say, "This song must be about you. You are such a ladies' man."

His smile is intoxicating as he tries to hide a laugh.

"Stop distracting me, or I will whack you again with my tail. I need to figure out what to do with you… hmm…"

With a snap of his fingers, my hair, face, and exposed skin magically transform. My skin turns into a golden sheen that shimmers in the dim bedroom light.

My hair becomes full, dramatic, and stunning. I look at my face, and my makeup is flawless.

"Wow. I wish I could do that. Just snap my fingers and poof. How do you do that?" I ask.

I snap my fingers, but nothing happens.

Tobias laughs. "That's my secret power. Maybe one day I will tell you. Enough chatter. Let's go have us some fun."

Tobias takes my hand, and we walk to my mom's meditation room.

Inside is an eight-foot-tall solid copper meditation pyramid. Hanging from the center of the pyramid is a round glowing bright-blue crystal about the size of a tennis ball.

Tobias turns to me and says, “I have a gift for you, little one. Your brother has already received his from my sister.”

Tobias pulls a necklace out of his pocket and hands it to me. I am speechless. It is the same necklace as my parents.

The pendant is in the shape of a triangle, and the same glowing blue crystal rests inside it. It is beautiful.

“Let me help you put it on,” he says.

I turn around, and he hooks the necklace into place. Then he turns me back around and looks into my eyes.

“You look lovely. It matches your outfit perfectly. This necklace will grant you access to my world, and my world only.

When my species came to Earth after the 3D world collapsed and the 4D world was shifting into 5D, we crafted this copper meditation pyramid for Aislinn.

The glowing blue crystal in the center is the conductor. It will open a portal for instant and rapid transportation.

I will have you go first. Then I will go next. Your brother Ryan and my sister Aura are already on the other side waiting for us.”

Tobias steps closer to the copper pyramid. He looks into my eyes and says,

“First, sit in the middle of the meditation pyramid. When you close your eyes, connect and align with your heart. Then take your dominant hand and clasp the pendant. Got it?”

I step inside the copper pyramid and sit down. I follow his instructions.

“Good. Now your heart will align and connect to the blue crystal when you start thinking about all the things you love about life. Unconditional love and all those juicy 5D emotions are the secret ingredient. Feel the love, joy, bliss, and gratitude inside of you.”

I begin to feel my body vibrating with energy, and my higher self says to me, “This is going to be so much fun.”

I hear Tobias’s voice again.

“Excellent. In your mind’s eye, you will begin to see swirling blue colors. Those swirling colors will form a vortex — some might call it a wormhole.

When you see the vortex before you, imagine yourself floating within it, being pulled closer and closer to my planet.

The energy might feel intense because the frequency and vibration of my planet are much higher than yours. Just trust it and go with it.

Stay focused on your heart’s desire to go dancing in my world. Feel the joy, bliss, excitement, and gratitude. Those are all juicy 5D human-consciousness vibrations.

When you know you have arrived, you will feel bathed in love and hear a whooshing sound.

You got this, Danica.”

I follow his instructions, and it is easier than I thought. Within less than a minute, I heard my brother’s excited voice.

“Danica, you did it! Wasn’t that awesome? This is going to be an excellent adventure!”

Chapter 12: Another World

As I open my eyes and stand up, I hear Ryan say, "Wow. You look amazing. In fact, you look tubular.

That attire is so retro early 2000's. Most excellent. I love it. I almost didn't recognize you. Tobias did a fantastic job with your outfit, makeup, and hair."

Aura smiles at me. "You will fit right in. Come over here. Sit down next to me and your brother. Tobias is next."

Ryan and Aura gestured for me to sit next to them on these overly large, soft, purple leather chairs. As I sit down, I hear another whooshing sound, and poof! Tobias appears.

"Wasn't that fun, little one?" Tobias asks as he begins to stand up.

"Yes. It was easier than I expected. You are a great teacher, Tobias."

I look over at my brother and Aura.

"So what are you two going to do this evening?"

Aura smiles at Ryan.

"For months now, I have been visiting Ryan in his dreams because I know he admires my ability to fly. So, I spoke with my elders, and we are giving him the experience of a lifetime. But before I do, I need to explain something to you both.

As you know, Tobias is older than dirt. His soul is very ancient. On our planet, we have advanced technology that your planet does not. Our species and many others have developed hibernation chambers that can perform multiple tasks.

If you get injured, it will heal your vessel. If your vessel grows old, it will restore it. And if you want to experience life in another vessel, even another species, it can transfer your soul instantly."

Ryan's mouth drops open.

"So tonight," Aura continues, "I am giving Ryan the opportunity to fly with me. I have selected the perfect male blue Avian vessel. Follow me, and I will show you."

Ryan looks at me like he is catching flies, his mouth wide open.

"Ryan?" I say, pointing at his mouth.

He quickly shuts it.

We all stand up as Aura opens the door.

As we step into the hallway, I look around. It seems quiet and deserted until a tall, silvery-bodied being turns the corner and greets us.

"Hello, you two. I have never seen you here before. I know you are in good hands."

And just like that, he turns the corner and disappears.

"That was Simon," Tobias explains. "You will see many species in this building and many more outside."

Ryan is like a kid in a candy store. He can hardly control his excitement. "This place is iron maiden excellent."

I see Aura look over at me as if to say, "What is his deal?"

As we walk down a long corridor and take an elevator down four floors, we pass several different beings from other worlds. Each one greets us with a warm smile.

Chapter 12: Another World

That is when Tobias whacks me with his tail and whispers, “I saw that look on your face when you looked at that eight-foot-tall praying mantis. Don’t worry. He won’t eat you… not yet.”

I smack Tobias on the butt.

“Stop it, you two. Try to act like adults,” Aura says.

Ryan can’t help himself. “We are all the most excellent immature adults tonight.”

Aura looks at me and rolls her beautiful silvery eyes. It makes me laugh.

We arrived at a large cargo door. Aura presses a few buttons, and the door opens.

Inside the chamber are rows and rows of hibernation pods. Some are red, green, blue, and white.

Aura stops in front of a green one. She presses a button, and the door slides open with a hiss. Inside is a male blue Avian vessel.

“Sweet ride, dudes” Ryan says.

Aura shakes her head. She opens the white chamber beside it.

“Ryan, this is the chamber you will step into. The process is quick and easy.”

Before she can finish talking, Ryan steps inside.

“Well, let’s get the show on the road, my most excellent babe.”

We all laugh.

“Hold onto your britches, young man,” Aura says. “Stay there. We will begin.”

She moves to the control panel. Both chamber doors close.

Ryan gives us two thumbs up. “Let’s rock and roll! I am ready for my excellent flying adventure. They should turn this into a movie!”

Aura shakes her head. “I hope I will not regret this.”

Tobias and I laugh. “Boys will be boys, Aura”, Tobias says.

“Now I am regretting,” Aura chirps.

Next, I hear a small vibrational humming sound coming from the two hibernation chambers. Aura presses a button and speaks into a small microphone.

“Now Ryan. Your chamber is going to fill with a calming gas that will smell like lavender. This will allow you to drift off into a deep and peaceful sleep.

When I know your conscious mind has drifted off to sleep and your subconscious mind is still active, I will conduct the transfer.

When you enter into the blue Avian male vessel, it might feel strange at first. It might take you a while to adjust your vocal cords, bodily sensations like sound, touch, smell, and taste. Your coordination might be a little wobbly at first and that is all normal.

When all those factors feel normal to you, then we will focus on using and moving your wings. You can communicate with me telepathically. I can read minds, and you will be able to read mine in return. Do I make myself clear?”

We see Ryan wearing a large smile as he gives us the thumbs up signal. Again, Aura just shakes her head.

She looks over at me and says, “I just love your brother because he reminds me of my goofy brother, Tobias. Go figure. Lately he has been acting a little too goofy. What gives?”

I know exactly what gives. “Well, last week he was chatting with a friend of his in Greece that turned twenty-five a few months ago. He suggested that Ryan watch the blue ray movie, Ted and Bill’s Excellent Adventure.

So, if he says, “Party on Dudes”, he will be referencing that movie. I know, I know. It was made in the late 80’s, but it is pretty funny.”

Aura just smiles and shakes her head. “That explains it perfectly, Danica. Thank you. I have seen the movie and I recall a few lines.

He can’t hear us. So, I will start to talk in Ted and Bill’s lingo. It will trip him out, dude!”

Aura and I just smile at each other. Then she says, “Time to get serious, but before we do…” I watch Aura press the microphone and say to Ryan, “This should be most triumphant adventure ever, dude! We are going to party on tonight, dude!”

The expression on Ryan’s face is priceless! Picture perfect!

We all laugh and he gives us another thumbs up.

As we look over at the white chamber, I see this pale purple mist filling the hibernation chamber. Within seconds, Ryan’s eye closes and his breathing become slow, steady, and rhythmic.

Aura waits about two minutes to confirm that his conscious mind has drifted off to sleep.

A soft humming sound fills the room. Then two small tubes between the chambers begin to glow.

“As you can see,” she says, “his soul essence is transferring.”

The glow fades. Aura opens the green chamber. The Avian vessel inside the green chamber opens its eyes. I watch the eyes flicker and then look directly at me.

I cover my mouth.

Aura extends her hand towards Ryan.

“Slowly now. Take my hand. One step… good… now the other… excellent.”

Ryan tries to speak, but the sound is distorted.

“I am speaking to him telepathically,” Aura says. “He is fine.”

She looks at us.

“You two go have fun at the Glowing Mushroom Club. And Tobias… behave.”

He lowers his head. “I promise. She is precious cargo.”

My heart skips a beat as he gently grabs my hand.

“Okay, Aura. Time to take this little one for a spin on the dance floor. I must see her dance moves. This should be some excellent fun!”

Chapter 13: The 6th dimension

As you might expect, there is so much to see, hear, feel, and even smell.

The shops, restaurants, buildings, plants, trees, and the rolling hills in the distance all radiate a harmonious energy. Everything shimmers and glows beneath the moonlight.

Everything is alive. Everything is thriving. The energy here feels loving and euphoric.

As I breathe in the air, I sense a playful freedom mixed with something limitless and pure. It feels as if my consciousness is awakening, not only spiritually, but intellectually as well.

Everything is connected. And I mean everything.

My higher consciousness speaks softly within me. *"Welcome to becoming one with Christ and God consciousness. The Christ spark within you has been activated."*

The moment I hear this; my spirit ignites in a way I did not know was possible. It feels as if the small campfire within me suddenly becomes a roaring bonfire of purpose and belonging.

My mind fills with pure awareness, divinity, and bliss.

I have to stop walking just to process the higher vibrational frequencies moving through me.

After all… this is the sixth dimension.

My senses feel wide open, fully alive. It is as if the floodgates have opened and all I can do is float. I almost feel like I could levitate. Inspirations pour into my mind faster than I can hold them.

I look over at Tobias, and my heart explodes with affectionate feelings I never knew existed…towards him. As if…I could love even more than I do now.

Tobias looks over at me, surprised.

"Oh… I forgot about this part of the transition," he says with a small laugh. "It has been a long time since I brought a newcomer here. Please forgive me. You are experiencing vibrational alignment with the sixth dimension. Your body and spirit are just simply adjusting to the higher frequency octaves."

He places a gentle hand on my shoulder. "You need to sit down, my precious one. I know the perfect place. This is also the right moment for me to tell you a story I have been meaning to share with you tonight.

The first time here, you need at least thirty minutes to fully integrate the higher vibrations of my world."

Before I can respond, Tobias lifts me as if I weigh nothing at all. Within moments, we arrive at the most peaceful lake I have ever seen.

White, luminous purple birds float across glowing green water. I can see hundreds of shimmering micro Endies water beings swimming around. The moonlight glows upon the surface of the calm water.

As I look to my left, I see tiny green fireflies dancing around tall cattails. The fragrant flowers and vegetation give off a soft blue light. Pink trees sparkle as they hum in a gentle rhythm that fills the air with euphoria.

Chapter 13: The 6th Dimension

I feel like I am in paradise.

“We are going to sit here, little one,” Tobias says softly.

He placed me on a bench beside the lake and sits next to me. With a snap of his fingers, a soft white pillow appears in his hands. He placed it in his lap.

“Lay back,” he says. “Look at the stars… and the two planets in the sky. You may recognize this place.”

I lean back and stared upward in awe.

“I have been here before,” I whisper. “When I meditate… sometimes I imagine a black triangle with a blue light behind it, and it brings me here. You once told me it connects me to the collective consciousness on your planet.”

Tobias smiles. “Yes. This is my favorite place to sit and contemplate existence. Even though you and your brother are twins, you are very different. He is wild, adventurous, and playful.

You are like this lake… calm…deep…reflective…aware. Just like Aislinn was.”

He looks at me carefully. “You like to observe life. You like to feel everything fully. You want to be present inside every moment. Am I right?”

I nod slowly. “Yes… that is exactly why I feel overwhelmed right now. But it’s not a bad feeling. I feel blessed. Loved. I feel like I belong… but even more than that…I know I belong.

It’s not a thought. It’s something inside my bones I feel at home…right here…with you. All my emotions and senses have become…magnified…and amplified.”

Chapter 13: The 6th Dimension

I look out over the water. And I hear my higher-self whisper: "*I am the water, and the water is within me. We are one.*"

Tobias gently strokes my hair. I can feel him looking down at me.

"Aislinn has been here before," he says quietly. "Years ago, she spoke with a psychic who told her she was not originally from Earth…that she came from one of the brightest stars in our galaxy. That star…was her home."

I sit up slightly. "How is that possible?"

Tobias sighs softly. "Let me explain…"

"At first, Aislinn thought this woman was nuts. I mean so many people over Aislinn's lifetime would comment on how she was different.

Different from other human beings. It always made Aislinn uncomfortable, but…at the same time…she knew they were correct. She just had this inner knowing deep within her heart and soul.

Afterall, the woman that recommended this psychic was an intuitive empath…just like Aislinn. So, she trusted her recommendation and advice.

So, this psychic woman told her that she had already mastered 5D human consciousness and was being called to go even higher. To align with the 6th dimension.

At first this confused Aislinn. As the psychic spoke, she told her that her family wanted to connect with her."

I look into Tobias's eyes. "That is wild. Truly wild."

“It was for Aislinn. The woman said that her mother…father, brothers,…and sisters wanted to connect with her. They were all from the 6th dimension.

When she asked her how she can connect with them, she told her to just ask. They would hear her call and come to her.”

“That is wild. It must have been confusing for Aislinn. It sure as hell would have confused me. I mean…just ask…and they would come to her? Crazy, if you ask me.”

“I know. It was hard to believe…but Aislinn was curious…open minded…and something deep inside wanted to try it. To see if it would actually work.”

“I can see that. As wild as it sounds…I can see that.”

Tobias continues, “Of course, this lady made it sound too easy. Aislinn questioned this woman’s psychic abilities, but she came highly recommended.

So, that night before Aislinn went to bed, she was guided to get down on her knees and pray. Her higher-self guided her to take two red wooden native American Indian pray sticks in both her hands.

Aislinn could feel the wisdom…power…and ancient magical properties within those two Indian prayer sticks. So, she connected with its power…wisdom…and magic. She prayed to meet her ancestors from the 6th dimension and welcomed them to connect and speak to her.”

“Sounds interesting. So, what happened next?” I say.

“That night, Aislinn was gently woken up in the middle of night. On the left side of the bed, she saw three luminous light beings. One was female and two were male. At first, she did not believe her eyes. She questioned if she was in a dreams, but she was not."

"That is wild! Was she afraid?"

Softly Tobias said, "No. She did not fear them. She approached their visit coming from a place of curiosity and fascination. Just like a child.

Again, she questioned and wondered if she was dreaming with her eyes open…but she was not.

One of them was holding a four feet long white luminous rod of light. Telepathically she heard the being speak. "This might hurt a little, but it will not hurt you. It will feel like a jolt of energy running through you. Are you ready?" it asked her."

"What?" I say. "No way. This story is getting good."

Tobias continues, "Aislinn responded with a yes. Then she saw the luminous being place the long white rod of light down through her crown chakra. It went all the way down to her root chakra.

Aislinn's whole body vibrated for about three seconds as the current of intense energy ran through her. It was not painful, just different. Then they teleported her to this exact spot and placed her in our healing water."

"In this very lake. Wow. That's incredible." I say.

"It is incredible. They taught her how she could connect with them again by imagining the black triangle with luminous blue light behind it.

Next, they instructed her to imagine herself inside the black triangle of transmission and communication. She practiced that technique several times...and each time she did…it worked like magic. Off she went…into another world. A world that took her away from the dense 3D energies on Earth."

"That is incredible. Truly amazing," I say.

Tobias gently guides me to rest my head on the soft, white pillow again.

"But that is not what I wanted to truly discuss with you this evening. I am here to tell you a story that you will not find or discover within your Aislinn's book of life. She does not remember that chapter of her life and was not meant to be remembered. It was to be remembered only by me because I was there."

As I gaze up at the sky, I say, "Okay. What do you want to tell me?"

"When you dive into Aislinn life's journey, you will discover that she died when she was four and half years old."

I sat up and looked into his eyes. "What? Did she have an accident? What happened?"

"Calm down. Let me explain," Tobias gentle spoke. "She discovered this truth when she did EMDR trauma therapy in her early forties. She witnessed her death. But that is not the important part here. When she died and returned to our Creators, they spoke to one another.

Our Creators knew that her Soul took on a very important mission here on Earth and in some way, she failed because she died at such a young age. The family tree she was born into was extremely abusive to each other behind closed doors, and her older brother…he was upset that their mother left them.

So, he took his anger out on Aislinn…repeatedly… trying to hurt her. Until one day…he killed her. He had succeeded."

I heart skipped a beat. "No. That is horrible. Terrifying in fact."

In a soft and gentle tone of voice, Tobias continues with his story.

"Her Soul questioned if it could complete its mission here on Earth. The quest this Soul took on was to clear her entire soul group of their generational traumas. This was hug. Only half of her soul was willing to come back to Earth. The other half refused because the constant abuse was unescapable.

Yet our Creators knew that this one soul was different. It was ancient…wise…courageous and old as dirt, just like me."

We both laugh.

"It wanted to give its soul group a priceless and selfless gift because it had already mastered the teachings on Earth.

So, our Creators asked this courageous half of a Soul if it would be willing to give this same gift to the whole of humanity.

Without a pause of reflection, the Soul immediately said, "Yes!"

That is when our Creators gift this Soul my support."

My heart swells with joy and gratitude. "Really? That is amazing. I need to hear more. Please continue."

Tobias smiles, "Our Creators summoned me and explained the situation. I was informed that this information would be kept confidential from Aislinn conscious awareness until the 3D timelines were decreasing and the 4D timelines were growing and gain momentum."

"I see. What happened next?"

"We all came to an agreement. She would have to overcome two tests in the future to see if she was ready and willing to support humanity with the ascension process. Her new mission and agreement with our Creators were to remove the two veils from Earth and I would be there to support her if she lacked courage."

I softly say, "That's a big responsibility and test. It would take a lot of courage and confidence."

"It would. The first test would scare anyone…because what she had to face…was what everyone on Earth feared the most."

I raise an eyebrow. "Really? Tell me more."

Tobias smiles at me sweetly and says, "Now, these two veils were not created by our Creators, but the dark forces that existed in your world during the 3D era.

The first veil of darkness wrapped around the planet. The second veil clouded humanities consciousness.

So, Aislinn soul agreed to awaken and weld once again…this harmonious union between Heaven and Earth. Once this awakening process was complete, our Creators could connect and communicate with all the children of light upon Earth."

Out of confusion, I ask, "What do you mean? We have more than one Creator?"

Tobias let's out a little laugh. "Many people during Aislinn time believe that everyone had only one Creator and that Creator was only considered God or Lord, the masculine energy of Source.

But our Creator is not just the masculine energy of Source. There are three parts that make up the whole of Source. That is why some prophets spoke of a being named Three…that would speak once the awakening process was complete.

From a religious aspect, many would consider this being Three, the Holy Trinity. It is the combination of the feminine Mother (Divine Love), the masculine Father/Lord (God), and the Holy

Spirit of Light that lives and exists within us all…all worlds…and planets…and within this entire Universe.

And…within the various ancient pyramids…exists various magical spears hidden deep within Earth."

"I can grasp that concept. I never knew that. Thanks for that explanation," I gently say.

Tobias looks over at me. "Many religious individuals did not even consider the divine Mother because centuries ago the world was ruled and dominated by men. Women were below men, yet women are the creators of life. Without the divine feminine, there would be no life, period.

So, people made the assumption coming from a rigid male perspective that the third Holy Trinity Light must be another masculine energy like Jesus, but it was not.

Jesus was a human avatar. He was a higher dimensional being inside a human vessel. Jesus was not born into the 5th dimension states of consciousness, only the 4th. That is why Jesus followed our Creators instructions and focused on his becoming during his 20's and 30's.

Becoming one with our divine Creators and gaining the wisdom that existed within other spiritual and religious practices. That is why there are stories of Jesus's travels around Earth. He was gathering knowledge…and wisdom that he intended to pass down to all of our Creator's children."

My curiosity widens. "I can grasp that concept. I am in my own becoming process."

"Exactly". He places a gentle hand on my shoulder. "As you know, he became one with the Christ Consciousness that vibrates at the frequency range of 600 to 1,000. He was the embodiment of the

Christ Consciousness, which every living human can obtain here on Earth. That is a sacred teaching Jesus wanted to teach humanity. How everyone could enter the Kingdom of Heaven…like he did.

Therefore, if he could do it, so could you.

So, as the saying goes…he did not want to give a person a fish; he wanted to teach them how to fish. Metaphorically speaking."

I close my eyes. "I get it. Please continue."

Tobias looks at me carefully. "Very well. He saw the light…embraced the light…and became the light.

He wanted everyone that was dead inside, to wake up. Follow the light, instead of staying stuck within the fear-based 3D mindset.

And he knew of the second veil. That is why he encouraged people to take his hand…to walk with him out of the darkness and into the light by shifting one's consciousness. It was that easy…but not easy for some to comprehend. Some of the people during that era were barbaric in their ways of thinking, acting, and behaving.

He wanted this for all God's children, not just a selected few that followed him and joined his table…his journey.

That is why the rulers and self-righteous humans felt threatened by his holy power. Jesus had the power to overthrow and dethrone these dark, destructive rulers. Our Creator's children would no longer be slaves to the rich and greedy. They would be free.

Free to make their own choices and decisions about their life, instead of just existing to serve some arrogant ruler.

So, like most corrupt dictators, they plotted war against the light. They found a way to destroy Jesus's physical form, but not his Spirit or Soul. Jesus was immortal, just like you and I."

I shake my head from side to side. "I am blessed to be living on the new Earth. I truly am."

He takes my hand in his. "And I must tell this truth. Our Creators have sent down many divine incarnations…teachers…saviors. Like Mary the divine feminine Sophia, Isis, Shakti, Buddah, Krishna, and Rama. Some listened and applied the teachings. Others, did not.

The sad truth about the history of Jesus is he was a prophet and savior…yet his teachings…wisdom…was turned into profit for the benefit of the church.

You will learn more about this during your becoming process and why religion no longer holds power or control over our Creators children of light."

"Well, that explains a lot", I say. "But what about Aislinn and the two veils?"

Tobias let's out a deep sigh, "I am getting there. Be patient with me, little one. As you know, I was with Thoth when he created the emerald tablets. He was from my world. He is like my brother. Thoth's emerald tablets were keys. It would determine which power passed into which hands.

The spear Aislinn needed to awaken…that would remove the second veil…was keyed to the emerald tablet's frequency meters. This specific spear would only awaken and answer to a few selected souls on Earth…when the time was right."

I open my eyes and look deeply into his. "Now this story is getting even better."

Tobias smiles. “Just you wait. There were various spears…hidden deep down below ancient pyramids. My people are the keepers and guardians of these spears…and they all made a vow. A vow to protect Mother Earth…and these spears.

They knew how to speak numbers in prayers…for the magic…to come alive…to awaken…would only happen within them. The guardians. With their breath…the patterns and numbers within their breath. That was the key...that would awaken…the spear of destiny.

Aislinn and I knew it was time. The destruction that was occurring on Earth…was proof enough. The second coming was here…the great destroyer was present…upon Earth. The time…was now.

We could feel the spear calling to us. Therefore, my ancestors came to visit Aislinn once more…as they had done so before many times…in her awaken…lucid, meditative states of mind.

They created…and opened a portal. A portal where we could travel in time…to a specific pyramid that I shall not mention.”

“Time travel. Nice”.

“Yes. So, we traveled through the portal in a sleepwalking state of consciousness to find ourselves inside this ancient pyramid.

As we stood there with my ancestors, we could feel and hear the humming vibration of the spear that was hidden deep below the king’s chamber.

So, we traveled down hidden passageways, until we came to what appeared to be a dead end, but it was not.

Instinctively, I knew there was a marker…a hidden key. We knew that the gate…doorway…would only open for a human that stood true… and still… with pure purpose… and Oneness with our Creators.

We knew that the stone markers would only light up when a true and pure human touched it.”

Softly I say, “Really?”

Tobias squeezes my hand. “Yes. When Aislinn touched the stone markers, it transformed before our eyes into a radiant reddish orange crystal. It began to glow and light up the stone passageway before us. The wall or gate dematerialized before our eyes. The wall…simply turned back into sand. Dropping to the ground. Revealing a new passage before us.”

“That is amazing.”

“It was. Again, there were tests she had to pass. Forks in the road as some would say. Testing her patience…purpose…heart, and Soul.

Each stone marker she touched transformed. It was like she was in a trance, and she knew exactly which passageway to take. There were many passageways designed below the pyramid. Created to create confusion and frustration. To trap and prevent any dark soul that entered with the intention of destroying this beloved planet with the power…and magic…that existed below.”

“Good.” I speak

“So, deeper down we went into each new stone passageway…that was revealed to us. Taking us deeper within the hidden pyramid floor.

That is when the humming grew louder. Almost as if we could hear singing, chanting, and praying. Calling her forward to awaken something deep within the chambers below.

Without thought or conscious awareness, she too began to hum…chant…and pray as if something awakened deep within her soul. And it was not just her soul, but my soul as well."

"What do you mean by your soul as well, Tobias?", I questioned.

"At the time…Aislinn was a soul and a half. My complete soul essence and her half soul essence were placed within the vessel, known as Aislinn. We were one. Male and female…in one vessel.

Her heart and my heart desired the same thing…to couple Heaven and Earth. That was our oath and vow to our Creators. That is why I was gifted to her. I…us…were the key that would unlock…and awaken… the spear of destiny.

When Aislinn died…and spoke with our heavenly father…we made an oath and vow that we would remove the second veil because only a human could do it. Aislinn needed my help…my support…my courage. That is why our Creators told her…she was the lion and…the lamb. The lamb was seen as a young girl. That was Aislinn…and I…was the lion."

"Now that makes sense. But what about the first veil? When did that happen?" I ask.

"That is a story for her to tell. All I can tell you is…the…painting…In your mom's bedroom."

"Which painting?" I inquire. "She has a few paintings, tapestry's, and pictures from Aislinn's collection."

I see Tobias doing his best to recall the painting…and then…he knows the painting.

"It's a painting by a woman that our Creators spoke with. She painted Jesus when she was a young girl. Here paintings from the Heavens above. She became rather famous.

Some of her paintings were signs from our Creators for Aislinn and I.

I now recall the name of the paint. It was called Triumph."

Chapter 14: Triumph Painting

I look at Tobias because I have looked at that painting often. Countless times… in fact. There is so much going on within that one painting. I often found myself staring at it for several minutes, getting lost in the images… as if I was trying… to put a puzzle together. I knew… in some way… that painting held a deeper meaning… but what… I did not know.
Therefore, I was always curious why Aislinn had that painting.

So, I ask Tobias, “What is so special about that specific painting? Whenever I asked my mom about it, she would say that one day I would learn the story and message within that painting.
Plus, my mom… she did not connect with the painting like I do. To her… it's just a painting. To me… it holds a mystery within it. A message… that would one day… be uncovered.”

I watch Tobias as he raises his eyebrows in curiosity. “Really, little one? That painting caught your attention?”

I look at Tobias, surprised. “Yeah. Why?”

Tobias sits up straighter, and I can tell the wheels are spinning in his head.
He looks at me and asks, “How many times… have you looked at it? Studied it?”

Tobias pauses and then says, “What did you see? What does it mean to you?”

Now I am puzzled and confused. I mean, what does it matter or mean? Why is he asking me these questions?

I see him waiting patiently, so I clear my throat and softly say, “Over several months, years, and lifetimes.” Wow… I realize… I just said… lifetimes! That is odd.

Now he gets quiet. I mean… really… really… quiet. My heart ever so slightly flickers a beat. Warmth begins to spread across my body from the center of my chest… as if… something is awakening deep within my heart… and soul.

Magically, a smile appears across my face and… Tobias is just looking at me. Stunned. Silent. I can feel my body glowing… shimmering… vibrating. It’s amazing.

Then I see Tobias shake his head wildly from side to side, as if he is trying to wake up from a dream. I do not understand what is happening here.

Then he softly speaks. “I have always wondered… about you. Your soul essence… and why… it is so similar…”

Before he can say another word, I say gently, “Aislinn. Yeah… I feel it too. Somehow… in some way… you and I… are connected. Once again… maybe… in this lifetime.”

I can sense and feel how Tobias is becoming emotional, as if… he is holding back his words… his heart… his questions. Then he speaks again.

“That painting portrays what happened within the Heavens above… when the first veil was being removed. It was about Aislinn’s victory.
Our victory.
Our triumph.
Hence, the name of the painting.”

For a moment, Tobias is quiet and still… caught in his thoughts. I could feel it and sense it.

Chapter 14: Triumph Painting

“The painter was guided by our Creators to paint that picture for Aislinn and me. As a message. A sign… of what was to come… and would eventually happen… within the Heavens above.

So, tell me, little one… what do you see, I humbly ask of thee? What do you see within that specific painting? I need to know. Must know… please. It is important to me… to my heart… for a promise that was made to me… long ago… by someone I loved deeply.”

Now I am silent. In shock and surprise. I need a moment.

So, I clear my thoughts, quiet my mind, and take myself to Bora Bora. In my own way… I become one with that magical, majestic tropical beach. Then I calmly speak.

“This is what I see, my love. I see a young man’s eyes looking back at me. I do not know the young man, but I know him. Personally.
Don’t ask me why. I just do. As if… we have met before… lifetimes ago.

He feels lost… stuck… and humbly wants my help. Don’t ask me why. I just feel it. Know it.

Then I see the two lions at the top. I am guessing the lions portrayed in the painting are your ancestors from the Sirian star system. I can see the bright blue star systems within the painting.

Next, I see falling angels… a horse… white doves flying in the middle… and off to the left side… I see an angry entity. As if… as if… it is yelling. Trying to frighten someone.

What moves me the most is the small image of a woman’s face… on the right side. She has long, white flowing hair. Just like Aislinn’s. She is right at the edge… the corner of the white hand of light, which to me… represents the woman’s hand.

Then I see a darker hand… below… off to the left… reaching up… for help… support… guidance from the glowing white hand. It moves me so deeply. Profoundly. I do not know why. It just speaks to me. As if… as if… I have been there… lifetimes ago. In a dreamlike state."

Now Tobias looks shocked and asks me, "Do you know who the dark hand represents?"

For a moment, I am puzzled. The answer was obvious.

"The dark hand represents the young teenager's eyes in the picture. His face is not clear… but… I can see his eyes clearly… staring back at me. His nose looks like two flying white birds… but I do know it's the teenage boy… reaching out for support."

Tobias seems startled. Confused. Confused… at how I would know this information. How the picture moves me… and speaks to me… directly.

I watch Tobias clear his throat. "The dark hand reaching up toward the hand of light, little one… is Lucifer, the Morning Star."

I immediately sit up and look at Tobias. "What? That is crazy! No way!"

"Yes way. Morning Star was a young, foolish, angry teenage boy who fell from grace. He had his angelic wings cut… and he was sent to Earth."

"That is wildly insane, Tobias."

Tobias clears his throat, as if he is holding back his emotions. "This happened during Aislinn's second major spiritual awakening. The battle between Heaven… and Earth. A battle no human eyes could witness. More on a spiritual plane… timeline.

And hours before Morning Star came to visit Aislinn… our Creators warned us of his visit. His arrival. Aislinn did not want to believe it… but… it was the first test. I was ready… but Aislinn… she was still in disbelief."

I feel my body shudder. "That is so scary."

"It was. But within that test… there were a few smaller tests. It was a test on her marriage… a test of her faith… a test on her vow… a test of her heart… as our Creators warned. For her husband did not believe in God but knew… Aislinn was different."

"That must have been so hard for Aislinn. To have this spiritual experience… and to experience it without a partner that aligned with her spiritual beliefs."

Tobias softly says, "It was… extremely hard. She felt so alone.

I mean the only one that created the two veils upon the Earth… was Lucifer. Therefore, only he could remove the first veil around the Earth.
You see, he was not physically here on Earth for humans to see… but energetically… vibrationally.

Hiding in shadows.
Whispering in ears.
Filling minds with unpleasant thoughts.

For the second veil to be removed… we had to find and activate the spear of destiny.

As for Lucifer, it was a test. To see if Aislinn's heart was pure… and could love all of God's creations. That included… Lucifer… the Morning Star."

"Holy crap! I can feel the stress and tension within that… that test… that choice."

Tobias laughs. “Holy indeed, little one. For Lucifer needed our help… our support.

That is why he requested a gift from Aislinn… from us. He revealed to her what she needed to know… to unlock her heart. It was a gift that only a human could give. Not a gift that most people would assume… like some crazy satanic crap. A gift of wisdom, forgiveness, and unconditional love.

It was part of the whole heavenly plan. An agreement… again… that Aislinn was unaware of, but I knew. That was another reason why I was gifted to her.
She needed my courage and strength to face Lucifer instead of trembling in fear.

And… I am happy to report… that Aislinn joyfully granted him that gift. You will read all about it… later.”

“No fair!” I say in a pouting tone of voice. “You are a meany! No fun, Tobias.”

Tobias just laughs. “Since OUR hearts were pure and true, Aislinn granted his wish and much more. So, in return… Morning Star gave Aislinn a gift. I don’t want to spoil Aislinn’s story.”

“But I am curious… can you at least tell me the gift Lucifer gave to Aislinn?”

I watch Tobias scratch his head. “I can do that. But I need to tell you that Aislinn was not expecting anything in return. She had no idea about the two veils at the time. So…”

I sit up joyfully. “He removed the first veil! Right?”

Tobias smiles. “Yes, he did.”

Chapter 14: Triumph Painting

I beam with joy. “I knew it. I could see it in my mind’s eye. The Earth covered in a thick veil of gray darkness and a hand pulling the veil back, removing it from the Earth.”

Tobias turns me to face him. “You saw… you saw it?”

As I shrug my shoulders, I say, “Yeah. Why? It should be no big deal.”

I watch Tobias shake his head from side to side in confusion.

“It is odd that you saw it. Just as it was revealed to Aislinn… in her mind’s eye.”

I watch Tobias sit in silence. I can feel the wheels turning in his head.

I place my hand on his chest and ask,
“Are you okay? Have I done anything wrong?”

Again, Tobias is quiet. Too quiet for my comfort level. Then he softly speaks.

“I need to clear my thoughts. Now I have so many other questions for you, but we need to go dancing soon.

Therefore, this discussion about that painting… Triumph… got me all distracted. You got me all distracted. I was not expecting that, little one.

You… you are so similar to Aislinn.

Before we go destroy the dance floor, I need to tell you about the second veil and how it was removed. Where was I?”

I sat there pouting like a little girl… but I had to respect Tobias and Aislinn. I simply want to go dancing! So I say…

“The stone passages… glowing orange markers… transported in the middle of some unnamed pyramid. Your ancestors… that story, Tobias.”

Tobias gently laughs. “Yes, that story. Lay back down on the soft white pillow. Then we will go dancing.”

As I do, Tobias starts to softly stroke my hair.

“When we reached the final twelfth marker… and the twelfth gate dissolved into pure sand before our eyes… the radiant light from within was so bright. It was almost like what you humans would call… a lighthouse. It was brilliantly bright.

So, with repeated spoken intentional prayer and the power of the vibrational breath, the keepers and my ancestors wielded their magic as they heard… saw… and felt the energy building like a vibrating plate or drum.

The doors opened when the intentional numbered prayers and heart-driven focus aligned. In that moment, everything aligned. Even our breath aligned and matched perfectly… like all the puzzle pieces snapping into place.”

“That is so cool. What happened next?”

Tobias smiles.

“As Aislinn shaded her hand from the light and stepped closer toward the stone spear… without question… or guidance… she reached out her left hand and held onto the spear.

The stone spear transformed before our eyes… into a spear… a scepter of crystalline light. She… we awakened the Holy Spirit within the spear. As it pulsed to life… and became luminous before our eyes… it almost… almost… took my breath away.”

My heart swells. “That is amazing. Impressive. Magical. Almost unreal.”

Tobias laughs. “It was amazing and… magical.

As my ancestors stood in this holy, sacred chamber, they witnessed her body vibrating as lost ancient teachings… knowledge… and wisdom filled not just her consciousness… but mine as well, because we were one.

Two souls within one vessel. The Holy Trinity spoke through us… and to us… just as it did when Jesus walked this Earth thousands of years ago.

Yet this time it was different. The spear of destiny was finally activated… brought back to life… to serve our Creator’s purpose and intentions. The intention of creating a world of light… and love upon Earth once again.

Darkness would no longer dominate every living essence upon Earth. There would only be pure… heart-driven love… and light.”

“Thank God for that,” I say softly.

Tobias strokes my hair.

“Yes. Thank God for that.

So, Aislinn stood there as if… she was frozen in time. We were communicating with the spear, downloading into our consciousness… all that it stood for… why it was created… and how it would be used moving forward… upon this new Earth.

What seemed like minutes… or hours… were mere seconds in time.

The entire energy around… and within the Earth's core… was transmuted, transformed, and restored. From darkness… into reborn light. The light of truth.

The spear of destiny was once again awakened. It was a teacher to us all… for us all… for humanity.

The spear of destiny had the ability to show humans where lines were crossed by dark forces upon Earth. It limited and prevented any existing 3D souls on Earth… from holding a position of power… and authority over the planet.

The spear of destiny started to send out higher-dimensional vibrational ripples of energy… outside this hidden pyramid chamber… but also… around the world. The union was now complete.

Our complete devotion… vow… and dedication… was complete. That is when Divine Love, our Lord, and the Holy Spirit of Eternal Light… began to awaken everyone's consciousness across the ethers.

All that existed in that very moment… was only light and love. That is why we are called beings of light and love. Within us all… exists… all three parts. That is what makes us all immortal beings… of light and love. We are all pure energy, cut from the same cloth… as our… Creators."

"That's an amazing story. I can feel my brain still trying to process it all. As you must know… I have been overloaded with information today."

Tobias gently squeezes my hand again.

"I understand, little one. Everything that remained upon the Earth that was created out of darkness… in the dense 3D vibrational forms… crumbled to the ground. This included corrupt buildings…

banks… companies… military bases… and weapons of mass destruction.

Our Creators had enough destruction on Earth. So, the spear of destiny was used to close star gates… so that the Draconian reptile beings could no longer enter or visit Earth.

The spear rebalanced the energy field around Earth… and around every living 4D and 5D human being. It preserved sovereignty… within the human spirit and Earth.

Its justice was quiet… and exact. It knew who walked upon this Earth. The ones that refused to walk within the light.

Since the spear of destiny was created out of light… and from light… it preferred compassion… and mercy. It knew… which souls… were lost in the dark. So those souls… had to make a choice. Walk in the light… or leave.

For peace to prevail upon Earth… humanity had to achieve a higher state of consciousness… instead of the 3D ways. In fact, the spear of destiny had the power to reveal everyone's soul-state… path… purpose… and intentions."

I sit up again and ask,
"Did it? Did it help to wake some people up?"

Tobias smiles.

"It did… and a lot more. Access was reassigned… and a vibrational signal was sent out to all beings of light and love that supported this new Earth process and evolution.

Everyone heard the signal… the radio signal… as it spread across the Universe. Beings from other worlds and dimensions heard… and felt this vibrational… welcoming signal… deep within their light bodies and into their souls.

Chapter 14: Triumph Painting

The spear of destiny opened counsel once again, so humans could work side by side with other beings of light and love. For the veil of fear was removed. It allowed beings like me… to walk upon Earth… without fear… by certain humans. For I once worked side by side with humans… when the pyramids were being built.

We were friends… allies… companions.

Since the Earth trembled with violent earthquakes across the globe, and the 3D structures collapsed… many beings from other worlds knew humanity needed our support. Our advanced technology… guidance… and support in rebuilding and restructuring your planet.

That is why flagships came down and helped restore order… to conduct field repairs and to assist in the removal of those dark structures… that crumbled."

Tobias looks at me with a playful smile.

"So… how are you feeling now? It has been about thirty minutes. Try standing up. Let's see if you are ready to go dancing at the Glowing Mushroom Club."

I stretch and stand. My body feels light, effortless, almost weightless. I laugh.

"I feel amazing. Still euphoric… but amazing. Thank you for sharing that wonderful story… as shocking… and difficult to process or even imagine."

I take in a deep breath of fresh air and look around.

"Now I understand why my mom loves this planet.

And speaking of my mom…" I grin mischievously.
"I think it's time for a pink glowing mushroom cocktail." I nudge Tobias playfully.

Chapter 14: Triumph Painting

I watch Tobias drop his head into his hands and begin to rub his face.

"This is going to be a long night," he mutters.
"I am your babysitter, remember? Only one drink. Not three."

I laugh.

"You are such a party pooper. Also… don't ruin your eyeliner, dude. You look hot, but my hair needs fixing. The pillow flattened it out."

He snaps his fingers. My hair instantly falls perfectly into place. Then he snaps his fingers again, and the white soft pillow vanishes.

He grabs my hand, and my heart skips a beat. I can feel that he is now excited and ready to go have some fun.

So, I smile, and… he feels it. How could he not? This is the 6th dimension after all.

It's all about love, baby, and that's magga love!

"Come on, disco queen," he says.
"Let me show you how we dance on my planet."

And just like that… we run off together, ready to dance the night away.

Chapter 15: The Glowing Mushroom Club

As we leave the peaceful outdoor setting and move toward a brighter, more vivid environment, I find myself wondering how this moment might change me.

Will I compare it to my life back on Earth… or will I embrace this place as somewhere I can return to again and again?

As we get closer, I hear a tribal house beat vibrating through the air.
The music has a deep, electric bass that I can feel in my chest.

To my surprise and delight, the outside of the Glowing Mushroom Club is exactly that… a massive, luminous purple mushroom with vivid pink glowing circles on its cap.

A line of very interesting beings waits outside.

Everyone is dressed in different styles of 1970s fashion. Some are wearing neon bell-bottom pants, shimmering platform shoes, tiny crop tops that would make my mom blush, glittering body paint, glowing hair, and dresses that shine like moonlight.

Everyone looks free… playful… ready for fun.

What confuses me is the music. It definitely isn't from the 70s.

I look at Tobias. Again, my heart skips a beat. He is so handsome tonight.

"This is a 70s flashback night, right?

Chapter 15: The Glowing Mushroom Club

So, when does the music switch? Don't get me wrong, this beat is amazing. It makes me feel like a cat ready to prowl and pounce."

Tobias smiles.

"Little one, the transition will happen in a few minutes. This club plays a different Earth-era theme once a week. Last week was classic rock.
Next week will be the 80s.

Listen… it's about to change."

Right then, I hear the opening notes of one of my favorite songs coming from inside.

A group of excited beings rush past us toward the entrance as Shake Your Booty by KC and the Sunshine Band begins to play.

Tobias leans toward me.

"Your name is on the list. Stay next to me."

As the couple in front of us enters, I glance at the doorman…and nearly laugh.

Instead of a tall, muscular guard, standing in front of me is a glowing green alien no more than four feet tall, with huge eyes and a slender body.

As if reading my mind, he smirks. "She must be a newbie."

He stamps the top of my hand with a glowing pink symbol.

"Now everyone inside will know.

And Tobias… only one pink glowing mushroom cocktail for her. We don't need another wild Amazon running around covered in glitter."

I roll my eyes.

Before I can respond, he adds, “Your mom is a regular here. And I will absolutely tell her how your first night went.”

Tobias laughs.

We step inside.

Inside the club, I can see moss covered walkway. Steps leading us down into a huge the dance floor. On Earth, this would be considered a rave. In my community, our club has a limit of only 100 people. This place must hold at least 500.

“Take my hand, little one. I want to show you around so you can get a feel for this magical dance club.” Tobias says.

As we walk through the club, I can see glowing mushroom vines hanging from the ceiling. Soft shimmering purple moss wraps around pillars of light. Flowers glow in colors I have never seen before.

Tiny candlelit yellow ants march along the vines. The air smells like sandalwood, earth, sweat, and exotic flowers.

There are multiple levels, platforms, and corners filled with dancing beings. In each corner hang enormous cages, with birdlike humanoids dancing inside them.

And then I see it. A massive waterfall at the back of the club.

In the center of the waterfall is a glowing pool of pale blue water. People… and other beings… splash in the water, completely free, and completely comfortable in their bodies.

Pink and purple roses climb the rocks, releasing sparkling golden pollen into the air.

Everything glows.

Chapter 15: The Glowing Mushroom Club

Everything feels alive.

Everything feels… sensual.

And that's when I see him.

A tall, slender, silvery being stepping out of the water.

His skin glows like liquid metal. His eyes are bright blue like the ocean. His hair hangs in wet golden curls over his shoulders.

He looks at me.

And I freeze.

He has no visible sex organs. How is that possible. He looks…he looks like a Ken doll. He looks almost like a perfect statue.

I stare longer than I should. I am almost hypnotized by his eyes. His smile grows large like a Chester cat's grin.

He smiles… slow and knowing… and looks at the stamp on my hand.

Suddenly Tobias turns me around.

"Little one… careful with your eye contact. That is Samuel. He is the master of love making."

I blink. "What?"

Tobias leans closer. "In the 3D world he would be a ladies' man. Here… he embodies the essence of love itself.

Humans are not always ready for that level of experience.

In the 3D world, he would be considered a ladies' man. At the 6th dimension, he is 100 times more seductive and powerful.

What your heart and soul long for and desire to experience on Earth school, he can make those dreams come true. Or should I say, cum true over and over again." As Tobias tries not to laugh.

"Seriously, my love, he is all about making love. I do not want him to deflower you.

Yes, it would be the best night of your life, but not many humans cannot come back down from his form of high vibrational love making.

So be warned. His eyes and gaze will hypnotize you. Then watch out, his kiss will cast a sensual love spell on you because you will feel his essence when your tongues meet. It can be highly intoxicating. That is how he gets you hooked."

"That's ridiculous." I say

"It is not. He does it through the exchange of energy… flowing from one vessel to another. So, be warned. He has many lovers. Stick with me and just watch him from a distance. You will know what I mean just by observing him."

He lowers his voice and his whiskers tickle my ear lobe. "Your mom laughed the first time she saw him. Saying he looked like a Ken doll. Then she kissed him. I could hardly get her off him. She playfully wanted to know where his…you know…was hiding.

She dreamed about him for weeks."

I burst out laughing. "But he doesn't even have a…"

"Oh yes he does," Tobias interrupts. "It's just… hidden. But…your mom found it. So, leave him alone. He is off limits!"

He grabs my arm. "Come on. Drink first. Then dancing."

Chapter 15: The Glowing Mushroom Club

We stroll to the other side of the club, away from the waterfall and naked beings. Tobias led me over to a private lounge area with round-growing purple mushroom stools and a flat mushroom cap table.

The lights are soft here. As he gestures to me with his hand, Tobias says, “Take a seat. We can dance over here. It is less crowded and quieter.”

Tobias snaps his fingers. A glowing glass appears in his hand, filled with shimmering pink liquid.

“Two sips to start,” he says. “To get a feel for it…and for it…to do its magic.”

I take one. Wow! I can feel the liquid traveling down my throat and warming my belly. My cells become alive, and my body fills up with such seductive warmth.

Like a Christmas tree my body lights up and I feel vibrantly alive and incredibly beautiful inside and out.

I take another sip. Amazing.

My skin begins to glow. My aura turns soft pink. I take another sip and finish the whole small shot glass.

I look out at the dance floor. Now, I can see everyone else’s aura too.

Music fills the room. Then another one of favorite songs begins to fill the room.

Sexual Healing begins to play.

Chapter 15: The Glowing Mushroom Club

My body starts moving without thinking. I close my eyes. I feel the meaning of the song… not just the sound. I can feel my body and mind getting lost within the music.

In my own tiny bubble of bliss. I close my eyes and take it all in. I can feel…

Love.
Connection.
Pleasure without shame.

As if my body is screaming to be touched by Tobias.

When I open my eyes, Tobias is watching me carefully. Smiling and making me want to snuggle up against him on the dance floor.

Yet Samuel... Mr. Ken doll…see's me also. Making me uncomfortable, but this drink, this song…makes me forget those uncomfortable feelings.

Then I noticed…just noticed out of the corner of my eye, that someone else is watching me.

A young man across the dance floor. He is so handsome. I see a slight smile appear on his face. He walks toward me.

"Danica? I'm friends with Ryan. My name is Marcos. I live in Greece. He is planning to visit me soon. In a few weeks."

The moment he touches my shoulder; my whole body tingles. I feel like I could melt in his arms.

He is shirtless. I admire how his olive skin glows warm gold. His eyes are deep brown. His energy feels… safe. His hair is thick, dark, wavy, and long. Just the way I like it on a man.

He can tell that I am checking him out, but he is checking me out as well.

“Nice complete package”, he says in a not so forward manner. I am assuming Tobias snapped his fingers and wa-la. You look fantastic.

Ryan told me you would be here tonight. He always talks about you. He sent me a picture of you and Tobias all dressed up in your matching 70’s attire.

I hope you don’t mind. I have been wanting to meet you in person, Danica.”

Tobias leans in. “She just drank the cocktail. Be gentle. I have my eyes on you, young man. She is precious cargo.”

Marcos laughs. “I will.”

For a while, I stood there, not knowing what to say. I am getting lost in my own thoughts as I smile at this beautiful man.

I have never felt an attraction to another person before. Only for Tobias, but we are just friends. Companions.

This is something new and exciting. I have heard stories of people within my community that just know. You can feel this electric charge. Pulling and tugging you towards one another. But I don’t feel that…yet.

Donna Summer begins to play. **I Feel Love** song. The crowd cheers. Various people flood the dance floor. Love is in the air. The whole club fills with pink light.

Bird beings rub beaks. Felines wrap tails together. People glow brighter and brighter.

Marcos takes my hand. “I would love to dance with you.”

Marcos looks over at Tobias. “Don’t worry, Tobias. She is in good hands. I know all about Samuel and I will make sure that he leaves her alone. She is all mine tonight.”

All mine tonight? Wow! I did not expect him to speak so freely. Maybe he had a pink glowing mushroom cocktail as well.

Tobias gives him the sign with his fingers that he…will have his eyes on Marcos and me.

We dance for what seems like hours. He’s charming, thoughtful, kind, and confident. Not overwhelming. Not hypnotic like Samuel. Just… real.

When the song finished playing, he kisses my cheek. Pink hearts appear around us. I look over at Tobias, who is still watching us.

Later we sit on a glowing mushroom couch. Marcos takes my hand in his. He looks at me seriously.

“The cocktail shows truth. I felt something the first time I saw your picture. But I want to go slow. We have time.”

My heart melts, but I still think of Tobias.

Across the dance floor I see Tobias dancing with a beautiful feline woman. They glow with love and affection.

I smile. Everyone here feels like family.

As the song changes to a slower beat as the night winds down, Marcos wraps his arms around my waist. **Your Song** by Elton John begins to play.

I can feel every word, melody and meaning that is woven into this famous song. I think to myself how I am so blessed and grateful to be living on this new Earth.

The DJ speaks. “Sweet night-time ladybugs… light up the room.”

Tiny glowing ladybugs fly from the purple shimmering moss, lighting the whole club.

Everyone hugs. Everyone thanks each other.

No jealousy.
No fear.
No shame.
Just love.

Tobias walks over. “Time to go, little one.”

I look at Marcos. He kisses my cheek. I kiss his back. We stand there holding hands, smiling.

“Until we meet again,” he says.

Tobias bows to him. Marcos bows back.

And we walk toward the hibernation chambers.

My heart feels full.

And I can’t wait to hear Ryan’s story next.

Chapter 16: The Creative Spark of Imagination

As we walked back toward the hibernation chamber building, I kept thinking about how Tobias could manifest almost anything simply by snapping his fingers.

Since we had a few minutes alone, I decided to ask him about it.

“Tobias… will I ever be able to manifest like you? I mean, you snap your fingers and… pow… it just appears. What is your secret?”

Tobias took my hand as we walked.

“There are many factors involved in manifesting,” he said. “Each one is essential. If I were to begin at the foundation, I would say intelligence plays an important role.

Intelligence is the mind’s ability to recognize incoming information, process it, and then do something with it. Every soul gathers information through every lifetime, whether on Earth or on other worlds. That knowledge is stored within the subconscious.

On your planet, genetics also influence how easily a person can process and use information. That is why some people appear more intelligent than others.

But in the old 3D world, intelligence alone was not enough. Highly intelligent people often struggled with the battle between light and dark.

Everything you see around you right now first existed as a thought in someone's mind. Some people wanted to create things that helped humanity… but the desire for power, money, and legacy pulled them away from the light.

Others refused to leave the light, and they were often silenced."

He paused, then smiled softly. "So, when it comes to manifesting, the most important force I use is not my brain.

It is my heart."

I looked at him, confused. "Don't you use both?"

"Yes," he said. "But the heart sends more signals to the brain than the brain sends to the heart. It influences emotion, memory, attention, and perception.

Your heart contains its own network of neurons. Some scientists once called it the *heart brain*. It can process information on its own and communicate with the nervous system.

Your heart also produces a strong electromagnetic field that extends outside the body. This has been measured with scientific equipment.

That is why humans say, *follow your heart.*"

I nodded slowly. "I always felt like consciousness exists beyond the body. Everything is energy, frequency, vibration… even atoms seem alive.

Like crystals… like plants. Like the Earth itself."

Tobias smiled. "You are beginning to understand, little one.

All humans have intuition, but not everyone listens to it. The heart often senses events before they happen.

Think about animals before earthquakes. They feel changes in vibration, pressure, and electromagnetic fields.

They follow instinct toward safety.

Your planet has magnetic fields that connect all living things. It is like a web of resonance… invisible, but real.

When humans reach the higher states of consciousness, they begin to feel this connection directly.

Sometimes psychedelics temporarily raise a person's vibration enough to see it… the lines of energy, the breathing of trees, the glow of life.

You experienced something like that when you first arrived here, didn't you?"

I laughed. "Yes. I thought my nervous system was going to explode.
It felt like my body was trying to process too much information at once."

"I know," he said gently. "That is why I brought you to the lake. Your system needed time to calibrate.

In the old world, people believed only the brain could think. But the heart and body are always communicating with the brain.

So, when it comes to manifesting, the heart's desire matters more than the ego's desire.

The ego wants power, status, money. The heart wants joy, love, purpose, and peace.

That is why imagination is the second key."

Chapter 16: The Creative Spark of Imagination

I looked at him curiously. “Imagination?”

“Yes,” Tobias said. “Imagination is the creative spark of the soul. It can override intelligence because imagination connects you to the higher dimensions.

When you imagine with love, playfulness, and joy, you align with the 5D state of consciousness… Heaven on Earth.

Everything that has ever been created began as a thought…a spark…
an image in someone’s mind. Some souls receive certain ideas because their soul has the knowledge to understand them.

When the spark arrives, imagination turns it into form.

But in the 3D world, the ego often corrupted that process. Gifts meant to help humanity were turned into weapons instead. That is why the vibration of the heart matters.”

He glanced at me. “You are still learning the 4D lessons. That is part of your becoming.”

“What lessons?” I asked.

“Acceptance.
Patience.
Compassion.
Letting go of control.

As you meet new people and explore new worlds, you will learn to make choices from the heart instead of fear.

That is how wisdom grows.

That is how one becomes what Jesus tried to teach humanity to become.”

I looked at him carefully. “You mean… becoming a Divine Messiah?”

He nodded. “Yes.

In the old world, people believed there would only be one savior.

That was never true.

Jesus was showing humanity what was possible. That the Christ consciousness could awaken inside anyone.

When a person reaches that state, they become a light for others.

But in the old world, anyone who said that out loud was called crazy.

People were taught to wait for salvation instead of becoming it.”

He sighed.

“Manifesting was difficult in that world because people lived in fear.

Fear manifests more fear.
Love manifests more love.

Sometimes the smallest step…even getting out of bed… was an act of courage.”

I blinked. “Getting out of bed was hard?”

“Yes,” Tobias said softly. “When the collective dark night of the soul began, many people felt lost.

They were connected by technology… but felt completely alone.

That is when the wayshowers appeared.

People who chose truth.
People who chose love.
People who built communities instead of competition.

Aislinn was one of them."

I smiled. "If I could, I would like to meet Aislinn one day. She always loved animals."

Tobias laughed. "Yes… and that is exactly the story I wanted to tell you."

"What? Another story?"

Tobias gently squeezes my hand. "Yes. This story is about a orange chicken that fell out of the sky."

I laughed. "No way."

So, he began to tell me a story…a story about an orange chicken.

He told the story slowly. He talked about a broken heart and about the injured orange chicken that appeared out of nowhere.

He talked about love calling life toward safety. He explained how wounded beings move by resonance. How animals feel gentleness.

How land becomes refuge when it is cared for with love. And how manifestation often happens quietly, without trying.

When he finished, I smiled. "So, you are telling me that Aislinn heart desired and longed for another orange chicken when she was sitting down…chatting with her brother over lunch and within hours…an orange chicken fell out of the sky and literally walked into her mud room?"

"As unbelievable as it sounds…yes. It blew her husband's mind. Hours before it happened, she told her husband that she wanted another orange chicken…and pow…an orange chicken appeared.

He was in such disbelief that he went to every house…two streets down…on either side…and nobody was missing an orange chicken.

The chicken fell in love with Aislinn and followed her around like one of her cats. It mystified her husband. The connections Aislinn could form with animals. That invisible bond…. amazed her husband."

"That's a wild story."

"I have another one. During that same conversation over lunch, her brother spoke about a baby raccoon that acted like a cat. He was feeding it one day and it came up to him and took some food from his hand. Aislinn was amazed. She wanted to meet this unique racoon.

A family member passed away and Aislinn made plans to attend the funeral. She asked her brother if he had seen that racoon. He explained that when he returned home, after visiting her, the racoon vanished. He has not seen it since.

So, Aislinn decided to manifest the racoon…and she did."

I look over at Tobias in surprise. "She did? How?"

She sat down and sent that racoon love. She spoke to it in her mind and told the racoon that she would be visiting and would like to meet him or her. She visualized feeding it and petting it.

She was so excited to meet this racoon, that she told her husband the day before she flew out of town, what she was trying to manifest.

When her brother picked her up at that airport, he still had not seen the racoon…but that did not derail Aislinn.

When she walked outside…into his patio…she was guided to look behind his shed. There was the racoon…but it was no longer a baby. It was much bigger in size. But that did not stop Aislinn. Her heart overflowed with joy. It was destined to be.

She filled a bowl with cat food and walked over to the corner of the shed. She spoke to the racoon in a sing-song voice. It came over to her…placed its paws on her hands…and ate from the bowl. The racoon was inches away from her face.

Her heart melted as she looked into its eyes. In that moment, a bond was formed between the two of them. She stayed with that racoon until it was done eating. Then it went back to sleep behind the shed.

The next morning, the racoon was still there…waiting for her. This time, she placed the bowl on the ground…and was able to pet the racoon. They became friends. It amazed her brother that she bonded with this wild racoon…was able to pet it…and manifest its return."

"Wow. That's a great story."

"It is. That evening Aislinn checked into a hotel. She wanted to visit her best friend.

Again, the racoon appeared. It even went up to her brother's screen door…looking for Aislinn.

He sent Aislinn a picture of the racoon and said, "Your boyfriend is looking for you. He misses you."

I cannot help laughing. “That is too much. Did the racoon stay or did it leave?”

“It left the next day. Her brother never saw the racoon again.”

“So, imagination… and love… and alignment. That’s the secret?”

Tobias nodded. “Yes. The mind is not meant to be rigid. It is meant to create. Imagination is the spark. The heart is the fuel. Trust is the doorway.

When the heart feels gratitude, joy, and appreciation as if the thing already exists…the energy builds. Then the moment comes.”

He lifted his hand. “I feel the connection. I imagine what I desire. I let the feeling grow until it is ready to burst. Then…”

He snapped his fingers. “…it is so.”

We reached the hibernation chamber building.

I smiled. “I think I understand now. Maybe not fully… but I feel it.”

Tobias laughed. “You will. And now…it is time to hear about Ryan’s flying adventure.”

My heart jumped with excitement as we walked inside.

Chapter 17: Ryan's adventure

As Tobias and I walked back into the building and approached the elevator, I suddenly paused.

We had been on his planet for hours.
We had class tomorrow morning.
We would have to wake up around eight.

It had to be at least two in the morning.

As I yawned, Tobias glanced at me and smiled. "I can feel the wheels turning in your mind," he said gently. "Everyone who comes here for the first time asks the same question about time.

The good news is this… when you return home, you will arrive exactly when you are supposed to. It will feel as if no time has passed at all."

I sighed in relief. "Thank God for that. It's going to take me forever to wash this glitter out of my hair. And I think all this makeup is giving me a pimple."

Tobias laughed. "Your wish is my command, my lady."

He snapped his fingers.

In an instant, my entire outfit changed.

My hair was clean.
My face was fresh and glowing.
I reached up and touched my cheek and realized a tiny pimple patch had been placed exactly where my skin felt irritated.

Then I looked down. I burst out laughing.

I was wearing the silliest silk pajamas I had ever seen. Cats were flying through space on slices of pizza. Other cats were rolled up like tacos with their little faces sticking out.

Tobias looked proud of himself.

"Wait… one more thing."

He snapped again.

My flashy 70's boots turned into fluffy cat slippers.

"Now you are perfect, little one," he said, bowing dramatically. "All you need to do is brush your teeth. I saved that step for you."

"Oh, stop it," I laughed. "You are the best cat companion ever, Tobias. Thank you."

The elevator dinged. The doors slowly opened…and I found myself staring straight into two enormous dark eyes.

A giant praying mantis stood inside the elevator. It made a clicking sound.

Tobias burst into laughter. "He says you look like a confused Earthling on vacation who can't find her hotel room."

The mantis tilted its head and clicked again.

Tobias laughed even harder.

"He also says you would make a very tasty snack."

My eyes went wide. "Tobias!"

The mantis rubbed its long arms together and made another series of clicking sounds.

Tobias wiped tears from his eyes.

"He says next time you are in town; he would like to take you on a date."

I crossed my arms. "Tell him I joyfully decline."

The mantis stepped out of the elevator and gently patted my shoulder.

For a moment, I felt something strange.

Not fear.

Kindness.

Playfulness.

Almost like he was speaking without words.

So, I tried something.

In my mind, I sent a message.

Thank you for the laughs.

The mantis clicked softly and lowered its arm.

Tobias looked at me in surprise. "You are learning, little one. He said thank you… and he hopes to see you again soon."

I turned and waved down the hallway.

"Goodnight, my new friend!"

Before the doors could close again, Tobias grabbed my hand and pulled me inside.

"Come on. Let's find your brother."

Chapter 17: Ryan's Adventure

When we reached the chambers, Ryan and Aura burst out laughing the moment they saw me.

Ryan was back in human form. "Oh wow," he said. "You look totally tubular. That outfit is straight out of the early 2000s. Mom is going to lose it when she sees you."

He yawned.

"We had an awesome time. Aura showed me something cool, and I want to show you."

He motioned for me to come closer.

"Have you noticed how some beings greet each other by touching foreheads?"

"Yes," I said. "Why?"

"We're going to do that now. First, clear your mind. Welcome me into it."

I nodded.

He placed his hands gently on the sides of my head. Then our foreheads touched.

Instantly…I was inside his memory. I was flying.

I felt the rush of wind, the freedom, the weightlessness.

Ryan and Aura soared high above the lake, diving and gliding like birds.

He skimmed the surface of the glowing water, sending ripples across the light.

Chapter 17: Ryan's Adventure

We curved around mountains. Trees swayed below us. The night sky glowed deep indigo.

I could feel his joy. His excitement.

His love for Aura.

Then music started playing in my mind. A song. I knew it.

Movement by Hozier.

The same song from Aislinn's wedding dance.

As the organ sounded, I felt my whole body vibrate.

Ryan and Aura moved together in perfect harmony, as if they shared the same soul.

When the choir rose, they flew higher and higher, diving through clouds and valleys, skimming over glowing lakes.

I felt like I couldn't breathe.

It was the most beautiful thing I had ever experienced.

Then suddenly… It stopped.

Ryan pulled his forehead away. I opened my eyes slowly. He grinned.

"How was that, sis?"

I couldn't even speak at first.

Aura laughed softly.

"We should get these two home," she said. "I need to shut down the equipment for the night."

Ryan walked over and hugged her. She wrapped her glowing blue wings around him and nuzzled his neck.

"Be excellent to each other," she whispered.

Ryan laughed. "The air is clean. The water's clean. Even the dirt is clean. I had an excellent time too."

Aura smiled. "You silly bird lover. Now go home. Sweet dreams."

When we got back home, Tobias was right. When we arrived back, it was only ten o'clock. It felt like we had been gone all night, but barely any time had passed.

I brushed my teeth, said goodnight to my parents, and climbed into bed.

Tobias tucked the blanket around me. I felt warm, peaceful, and full of gratitude.

As he gently kissed my forehead, my mind filled with memories of the Glowing Mushroom Club. The music. The laughter. The flying. Everything.

I drifted into the deepest sleep.

"Sweet dreams, little one…," Tobias whispered. "Sweet dreams… my love."

Chapter 18: Major world changes

Tobias was right. Ryan and I both woke up feeling refreshed, as if we had slept the entire night in our own beds.

Exploring Tobias's planet had been incredible. It still amazed me to know that people on Earth could travel to other worlds if they were open to the idea… and invited.

We all had soul groups, but we also had star groups. Some people were connected to Mars, Venus, the Moon, the Sun, or the Pleiades.
My family had been invited to the Lyran star system.

There was so much to learn… so much to explore.

I also knew that during the great transition, many beings from other worlds helped humanity. Some people called them Star Family.

There were even thousands of what people once called **walk-ins**.

If someone didn't know what that meant, it sounded strange, but it simply meant that one soul finished its mission, and another soul, already prepared, entered the body through agreement.

Many souls wanted to be here during the shift from 3D to 5D.

So, contracts were made.
Lives were continued.
Memories were explained.
Purposes were fulfilled.

The old world would have called that impossible. The new world simply called it… evolution.

Chapter 18: Major World Changes

I shook my head, realizing I had been lost in my thoughts.

I needed to get ready. Ryan and I were meeting Paula at the library.

I had a feeling today's lesson would be important.

After breakfast, Ryan and I rode our bikes toward the library.

"I wonder what Paula will teach us today," I said. "I kind of want to learn about what really happened when the old world changed.

You know… governments, taxes, wars, banks, prisons… all of it. How did it all fall apart?"

Ryan nodded. "History shows that when power gets too concentrated, it stops serving people. Governments said they protected freedom, but most of the time it was about control, money, and dominance.

People fought wars thinking they were defending their country…but often they were just pawns in someone else's game.

Lives were lost.
Truth was twisted.
Responsibility was avoided.

So yeah… I want to understand how it all changed too."

"Ryan…did flying shake a few marbles in that brain of yours? That was a truly deep concept."

Ryan laughs. "I have my moments…as few as they maybe."

We pulled up to the library.

Paula was already waiting for us.

“Good morning, you two,” she said with a smile. “I hope you’re ready to learn.”

I parked my bike and walked toward her.

“We were hoping we could talk about the old systems,” I said.
“Why we don’t have governments anymore… or prisons… or taxes…
What caused the change?”

Paula raised an eyebrow. “You two don’t ask small questions, do you?”

She laughed softly. “Come inside first. This is a deep subject. Before we talk about the past, I want you both grounded.”

We walk into the library and then into the orientation room. We both sat down. Paula pressed a few buttons on the wall. The room transformed.

Suddenly we were surrounded by mountains, pine trees, and a quiet lake at sunrise. Mist floated above the water. The air smelled like earth and forest.

My whole body relaxed.

Paula was right. We needed this before hearing the truth. Just thinking about the old world made my chest feel heavy.

Some of the stories we learned in school were hard to believe.

Religious wars.
Families divided.
Children taught to fear each other.

People convinced that only one belief was right and everyone else was wrong. It was madness.

Not because people were evil…but because they were afraid.

Afraid to think.
Afraid to question.
Afraid to trust themselves.

I took a deep breath and let the peaceful lake calm my mind.

When I opened my eyes, Paula was standing in front of us.

“The images you are about to see may be difficult,” she said quietly.
“These are real moments from the 3D world.”

The screen filled with scenes.

Protests.
Wars.
People locked in cages.
Governments fighting.
Crowds screaming.
Families crying.

I felt the pain in every image.

Paula spoke again, softly. “There comes a moment in every great turning when the old stories begin to dissolve. Not all at once. Not loudly.

From the inside out.

The systems that promised safety lose their authority. The voices that demanded obedience lose their truth.

And a question rises in every human heart:

What do I trust now?”

She paused.

"Ancient traditions called this the dark night of the soul. Not punishment. Initiation."

Paula continued.

"In very old times, humans did not feel separate from life. Some souls remember this.

They remember living in harmony with Earth…and with other intelligences. Not rulers. Guardians.

The lion was never meant to rule humanity. The lion guarded thresholds. Between life and death. Sleep and waking. Fear and truth.

To meet the lion meant being seen completely. Only those who could stand in their own heart were allowed to pass."

She looked at Ryan. "That lion consciousness never left. It was seeded inside humanity. When outer authority failed…inner authority had to awaken."

The screen changed. Images of cats appeared.

Cats in homes.
Cats in fields.
Cats sitting beside children.

Paula smiled slightly. "When the world became loud and uncertain…
cats came closer.

They did not explain anything. They simply stayed present.

Chapter 18: Major World Changes

Cats do not fear the night.
They see in low light.
They rest without guilt.
They leave without apology.
They return without resentment.

They showed humans how to remain sovereign."

She looked at us carefully. "This is how humanity was guided. Not by command. By coherence."

The screen shifted again.

Paula continued. "This was the return of the Star Family."

We saw ships in the sky. People standing beside beings from other worlds.

Lions.... like... Tobias.
Humans.
Light beings...from other worlds.

"Not everyone saw this," Paula said. "But everyone felt something.

Truth was returning. Not from outside. From within."

She folded her hands. "Many expected a savior. No one came.

Because humanity was meant to become its own guide."

Paula sat down across from us. "I need to tell you about the real collapse. The dark night of the soul was not one event. It was a collective awakening.

Chapter 18: Major World Changes

People lost trust in governments…
in money…
in institutions…
even in religion.

It felt like everything was falling apart.

But what was really happening… was that people were changing. Systems fell because they no longer matched the consciousness of the people living in them."

She smiled gently. "And during that time… cats helped more than anyone realized."

Ryan laughed. "Cats?"

"Yes," Paula said. "When humans panic, they become aggressive, fearful, and controlling.

Cats don't do that. They stay alert… but calm. Independent… but connected.

They showed humans how to stay steady when the world felt unstable."

She looked at me. "When Aislinn spoke about lions, cats, and star beings… she was not predicting destruction.

She was remembering how to stay whole when illusions fall away."

Paula leaned back in her chair. "The New Earth was not built after everything collapsed. It was built when people stopped giving away their power.

Communities formed.
People talked.
They chose cooperation instead of control.

We replaced courts with mediators. We replaced punishment with communication.

Instead of asking, 'Who is right?' we asked, 'Do we want to keep fighting… or do we want peace?'"

She looked at both of us.

"Does this make sense?"

Ryan and I looked at each other.

Then I smiled. "Yes. It makes perfect sense."

So, let's take a reflective pause here. Let your body settle.

Notice your breath without changing it.

Allow the images and ideas you've just encountered to soften and drift…not as concepts to analyze, but as impressions to feel.

Ask yourself quietly, without effort, W*hat within me is being invited to remember?*

Where in my life am I being asked to trust my own inner guidance rather than external authority?

What helps me stay present when the world feels uncertain or loud?"

Paula is silent for a moment.

She looks at me. "You do not need answers right away.

Sometimes truth arrives as a sensation, a memory, a feeling of recognition, or even a gentle resistance.

All of these are valid responses. Let whatever arise. Let that be enough."

I quiet my mind and reflect.

"I know you two have cats and animals on your property. So, since you live with animals, notice them now or later. Not for meaning, but for presence. Observe how they move through the moment without urgency, without story.

Let this be an invitation, not to believe anything spoken here today, but to listen more deeply to yourself. Then when you're ready, continue."

Ryan and I are silent for a few minutes as we process all this information.

I lovingly look at Paula and express, "Paula, you are a breath of fresh air and a ray of sunshine."

Paula smiles at me. "I not here to tell you or people what to believe. I am reminding them how to listen. That is true guidance.

Now, if I am a breath of fresh air, it's only because *you* opened a window. If I feel like sunshine, it's because you're willing to let light in without trying to control its shape.

I'm honored to walk beside you both in this moment of creation. Whenever you return with a question, a passage, a pause, or simply a feeling you want to understand, know that I'm here.

These teaching are only a remembrance of the past and nothing more.

When I spoke about the dark night of the soul falling upon the Earth, I was not actually describing a single apocalyptic event… or literal collapse of all structures.

I was describing a collective initiation."

I look at Paula and smile. "I get it."

Paula stands up. "But here's the key distinction that kept humanity grounded during this collective initiation.

The dark night was an inner collapse mirrored outward, not a prophecy of total external annihilation. Systems fell apart because they no longer reflect the consciousness emerging within people.

I mean even Edgar Cayce spoke of cats and this great awakening. How cats would guide the way during this time of turmoil.

I mean, many were skeptical. Not every liked cats. Some even feared them. But cats were not guiding humanity by strategy, instruction, military support, or governance replacement.

These ordinary furry friends were guided by nervous-system regulation and consciousness modeling.

During periods of chaos, the human system defaults to the lower thought patterns and behaviors such as hypervigilance, dominance hierarchies, fight/flight, and external authority-seeking.

Cats… and even some dogs can counter that by embodying sovereignty without aggression.

Presence without collapse.
Alertness without panic.
Independence without isolation.

There are some dog breeds that have helped people for hundreds of years. Trained for that specific purpose.

To guide people when they cannot see.
To guide by nervous-system regulation.
To protect and to serve.
To become a beloved friend…and companion.

These furry creators are here to teach humans how to stay coherent when structures fail internally. And that truth matters enormously."

I stretched and stood up. "I don't know about you guys… but all this talk about world history made me hungry.

What's for lunch?"

Paula laughed. "I was hoping you would say that. My stomach is growling like a lion."

We all laughed as we left the room.

And for a moment…the world felt simple again.

Chapter 19: Religion and Spirituality

As we walked out of the library, I had to cover my eyes. The sun was bright, the air was fresh, and my stomach was growling.

It really was a beautiful day. I loved how much we were learning lately.

Paula turned to us and smiled. “Instead of going to the diner today, I want to take you somewhere special. A place you both know about… but have never visited.”

I looked at her, confused. “What do you mean?”

Ryan tilted his head. “Yeah, what do you mean, Paula?”

She pulled her bike from the rack.

“Grab your bikes and follow me. We’re going to the Abbey. We’re having lunch with Sister Margret.”

Ryan blinked. “What’s an Abbey?”

Paula laughed softly. “An Abbey is a monastery or convent. A place where monks or nuns live in community. They offer spiritual support, cultural support, and help wherever the community needs it.

And today’s topic is religion and spirituality… so this seemed like the perfect place.”

She glanced at the sky. “It’s a nice ride. About thirty minutes. You might want sunglasses.”

I handed Ryan a pair of pink cat-shaped glasses from my basket.

"Here, bro."

He put them on, and I burst out laughing.

"Wow. Fabulous. You know… I can totally see you as a monk. Brown robe, chanting… then suddenly blasting your bogus music and starting an air-guitar band."

Paula started laughing.

Ryan turned red.

"Hey! Aren't we supposed to be excellent to each other? All we are is dust in the wind, dudes!"

We all laughed as we started riding.

The countryside was beautiful. We passed cornfields, red clover, and rows of lavender that smelled amazing.

Then we rode past a dairy farm……and the smell hit us all at once.

I laughed to myself.

Now I know why they planted so much lavender.

When the Abbey finally came into view, I slowed my bike. The place looked ancient. The grass was perfect. Rose bushes lined the paths.
The trees were huge and old, like they had been there forever.

The buildings didn't look modern at all. They looked… historic.

Paula noticed my expression. "This place was built in 1882," she said.
"Monks from Switzerland founded it."

We parked our bikes and walked to a carved wooden door. Inside, an older woman sat waiting on a bench.

When she stood up, I was surprised. She wasn't wearing a nun's habit.

She wore a dark blue dress, a turtleneck, and sparkly glasses. Her short hair framed a warm, smiling face.

"Hello, Paula," she said, taking her hand. "I've been looking forward to meeting Aislinn's family. I made some food from the garden. I hope you're hungry."

We definitely were.

She led us down a long hallway filled with statues and stained glass until we reached the dining room. Three silver trays sat on the table, filled with small bites.

"Sit," she said. "We have water, coffee, and chamomile sun tea. What would you like, Danica?"

"The sun tea sounds good."

"Excellent choice. I sweeten it with honey from our bees."

Ryan stared at the trays. "What is all this excellent food? I'm starving."

Sister Margret smiled. "This one is a bite size mini salad. We have cucumber, green tomato, Thai basil, lime powder, salt, and crushed red pepper."

We each tried one. The flavor exploded in my mouth.

She laughed. "I told you."

She pointed to the next tray. “Smoked salmon from Alaska, wrapped around herb Gouda from the dairy farm down the road.”

Ryan’s eyes went wide. He took a bite and froze.

“I died and went to heaven. Tubular flavors just exploded in my mouth. That was ultra excellent. Thanks.”

She grinned. “And these are stuffed mushrooms with a splash of cooking sherry.”

I took one. Holy cow. This nun could cook.

Just then another woman entered with plates of curry, rice, carrots, naan bread, and fish in yellow sauce.

We all sat. Sister Margret bowed her head to bless the meal. We followed. I took one bite and smiled.

“My mom makes this.”

Sister Margret nodded. “Yes. This is Aislinn’s curry cod recipe. It’s in the community cookbook she made years ago.”

My eyes widened. “Really?”

She smiled proudly. “She loved cooking with curry. The secret ingredient is coconut water.”

We ate in silence for a moment. Then I noticed the covered tray.

“And… what’s that?”

She laughed. “Pear tarts. Cream cheese, almond paste, apricot glaze.
But dessert comes last.”

Ryan shook his head. “There is no way you could ruin my appetite. This meal is absolutely excellent. Two thumbs up.”

We all laughed.

She shook her head. “The monks have been watching old movies again. Last week it was Bill and Ted.”

Ryan nearly choked laughing. “Excellent!”

“And before that, Terminator,” she added. “They kept saying ‘I’ll be back’ for days.”

Ryan did his best robot voice. “Come with me if you want to live.”

Even Sister Margret laughed.

After we finished eating, Paula leaned forward. “Today we’re talking about how religion changed on the New Earth. I thought it would be best if you explained it, Sister Margret.”

She folded her napkin carefully. “It all began during Aislinn’s awakening,” she said. “She had a vision. She saw communities from every religion coming together.

No separation.
Only cooperation.

At the time, churches were closing. People were leaving. We almost shut this Abbey down completely.”

She looked around the room. “We actually did close for a while. No one wanted to become a nun anymore. People had lost faith.”

She sighed. “Aislinn told us something we didn’t want to hear. She said the old ways weren’t working anymore. Not because

God changed...but because people had stopped living what they preached."

She looked at us. "She told us to stop trying to convert people... and start helping them.

No pressure.
No guilt.
No expectations.

Just service."

Ryan leaned forward. "That must have been hard."

"It was," she said. "We were trained to save souls. We had to learn how to simply be present."

She smiled softly. "When we stopped preaching... people started trusting us again."

She continued. "Aislinn told us something I will never forget. She said, 'If you meet people with the belief that they are lost, they will feel judged before you speak.'"

She paused. "So, we changed.

We listened first.
We helped without conditions.
We allowed people to find their own path."

She stood and walked to a shelf, picking up a book. "We even created our own teachings. Stories from real people. Lessons about forgiveness, patience, and healing."

She showed us the cover.

Community Forgiveness Stories: Volume One

"These books helped people more than sermons ever did."

She sat again. "We also changed our symbols. We no longer show Jesus on the cross.

Too much guilt.
Too much shame.

We show love instead. Because Christ consciousness was never meant to be suffering forever. It was meant to be transformation."

She looked at us both. "In the old world, religion became business.

Fear became control. Love got lost.

But we learned.

And when we learned… this place lived again."

I leaned forward. "So, what changed the most?"

She smiled. "We stopped telling people what to believe. We started helping them feel safe.

Sometimes we told them to pray.
Sometimes to talk to ancestors.
Sometimes to walk in nature.

Whatever helped them remember hope."

She nodded slowly. "We rebuilt trust. Not with words. With presence."

She folded her hands. "That is what our Creators wanted from us. That is why Aislinn came to us…she cared about us…and needed to share her message from our Creators.

Yes, it was a hard lesson, but we learned. We changed…. And we grew even stronger…. better. Does that make sense?"

Ryan nodded.

I nodded too. "Yes. It does."

Then I smiled. "…but I still want to see the gift shop."

She laughed. "Of course you do."

She stood. "Come with me. You can borrow a book… or earn one by helping in the garden."

Ryan grinned. "I knew there was a catch."

We followed her down the hallway, still laughing.

And somehow… religion didn't feel heavy anymore.

It felt human.

Chapter 20: Global Identity Erosion

As we rode our bikes back toward the library, I looked over at Paula.

“I know we’ve talked about a lot of different topics lately,” I said, “and I feel like I finally understand my becoming process. I can see why this new way of growing up supports young adults better than the old-world system.

There’s that saying… not one size fits all.

I’m grateful I got to just be a child without all the pressure people had back then. Now that I’m an adult, there are so many paths in front of me. So many opportunities. And I feel like there’s no pressure, just guidance.

Everyone in our community has supported me since birth, so I want my actions to match my words. If I say I’m going to help, then I should help. If I say I care about the community, then I should live that way.

Am I thinking about this the right way?”

Paula smiled. “You should be a detective, my dear. You’re seeing the bigger picture now.

Our community isn’t just one place. Think of it like a large circle in the middle, with smaller circles branching out from it. Each circle represents a different type of community.

Some focus on higher education.
Some focus on medical care, both traditional and alternative.

Some focus on trauma recovery.
Some support people with special needs.

And some communities are simply built around shared lifestyles."

Ryan nodded. "That makes sense."

Paula continued. "In the beginning, we learned through trial and error that we needed an evaluation period before someone joined the main community.

We wanted to understand who they were, what they needed, and where they would feel most supported.

Some people are social.
Some need quiet.
Some are night owls.
Some wake up at sunrise.

Some people want to stay close to their cultural roots. Others want something more spiritual.

We stayed flexible. We listened. We observed. We paid attention to whether their actions matched their words."

She paused, her expression turning more serious. "And many people needed help. Real help.

Some lost their homes in fires.
Some lost land in earthquakes.
Some became homeless.
Some lived through violence, raids, and chaos when the old systems collapsed.

People panicked. Instead of coming together, many went into survival mode.

It was like… shell shock."

I looked at her. “What’s shell shock?”

Paula glanced at Ryan. “You remember this from school, don’t you?”

Ryan grinned. “At least one of us was paying attention. It started around World War One. People thought soldiers were just weak, but later they realized it was trauma. Today we call it PTSD.”

Paula nodded proudly. “Exactly. Post-traumatic stress disorder.

And it didn’t only come from war. People could develop trauma from loss, abuse, disasters, or fear. During the transition from 3D to 4D, a lot of people were carrying trauma without even realizing it. Some even experienced identity erosion.”

I look over at Paula. “What’s identity erosion?”

We rode past the dairy farm, and the smell hit us hard. I covered my nose. My eyes started to water. Yuck!

“Okay… now I understand suffering.”

Paula laughed. “Yes, let’s ride faster. Lavender fields ahead.”

Ryan slowed down and reached into his pocket. “I’ve got the perfect song for this. You ride ahead. I will catch up.”

A moment later, music started playing from his small speaker. It was one of Aislinn’s songs.

I start to hear Ryan’s singing. “Two crickets are chirping in the middle of the night, baby.”

I recognize the song. It’s by Big Wild. I really love their music. I watch Ryan picked up the pace and is now riding his bike alongside us. I watch Ryan pause the music as Ryan stood up on his pedals.

"Okay, ladies. See that hill? When the music pops, we push. When the music goes mellow again, we will sit back down and relax. Then it will pop one more time. That is when we race.

This should be fun. It will be like the spinning class Terry teaches in town"

We all laughed and the music did motivate us... but when the beat dropped, we rode harder. Ryan zooms past us. So, we all stand up and pick up the pace. Sweat rolled down my face, but the music made it fun.

By the time we reached the lavender fields, the air smelled sweet and clean. We slowed down, breathing hard.

Paula wiped sweat from her forehead. "That lavender farmer deserves a thank-you letter."

Ryan laughed. "Whoop...that was awesome."

Paula looks over at me and says, "That was a clever idea to plant lavender so close to a dairy farm. I need to catch my breath. Thank you, Ryan, for the fun and inspiring music."

We started riding again at a slower pace.

Paula took a deep breath. "Alright... back to your question. You asked about identity erosion."

I respond, "Yup."

"Identity erosion," Paula said, "was very common during the transition. Sometimes it happened slowly. Sometimes all at once.

It happens when a person's world falls apart.

They lose someone they love.
They lose their home.
They lose their community.
They lose their beliefs.

And suddenly… they don't know who they are anymore."

I nodded slowly. "That sounds scary."

"It was," she said. "Some people felt hollow. Disconnected. Like they were watching their life instead of living it."

She continued. "In the old world, people even laughed at others getting hurt. They recorded it. Posted it online. Tried to get attention.

But once people started moving into higher consciousness, that changed. When you reach 4D and 5D awareness, you can't laugh at someone's pain.

Your instinct is to help. Friendships became deeper. Real.

People stopped chasing attention… and started caring about connection."

I frowned. "You keep saying people posted things online. What does that mean?"

Paula shook her head. "Social media. People used to stare at screens for hours. It started as a way to connect… but it turned into a competition.

Likes. Followers. Fame. People started doing extreme things just to get attention. They called it a thirst trap. The thirst for approval."

Ryan shook his head. "That sounds exhausting."

"It was," Paula said. "And when the Earth's vibration started changing, people felt restless, confused, irritated.

They didn't understand what was happening inside them. So, their identity started to crack.

Some tried to fit in.
Some tried to fight.
Some shut down completely.

That's identity erosion."

I looked at her. "You said something earlier… internal compromises. What does that mean?"

Paula nodded. "It means going against your own truth just to be accepted.

For example… imagine a family that says you can only marry someone from your culture, your religion, your social group. But you fall in love with someone different.

Do you follow your heart… or do you obey the rules?

Some people hide who they are to avoid being rejected. Some stay in unhealthy relationships. Some silence themselves to keep the peace. Some even lie to themselves.

Over time, they lose their sense of who they really are."

Ryan was quiet. "That could mess someone up."

"It did," Paula said. "That's why, when people wanted to join our community, they had to learn how to master the upper rooms of consciousness first.

We helped them. Housing. Food. Therapy. Support.

But they had to participate. They had to grow. This wasn't about getting a free ride. It was about becoming empowered."

Paula smiled softly. "I once heard that Aislinn was called the bearer of peace. Do you know what that means?"

Ryan shook his head. "Mr. Smarty Pants doesn't know this one."

I laughed. "Please enlighten us, Paula."

She nodded. "A bearer of peace is someone who brings calm into chaos. Not through force. Through presence.

Jesus told his followers to find a 'person of peace' in every village. Someone open. Someone kind. Someone who could help others feel safe.

Aislinn was like that. Not religious. Spiritual. She helped people remember who they were."

She looked at both of us. "Every community has people like that. People who hold the vibration of peace. They help others heal without even trying."

"We created separate communities at first," Paula continued.

"Some for healing.
Some for recovery.
Some for stability.

When people were ready, they joined the main community. Not everyone fits in the same place. And that's okay."

She pointed ahead. "The library's right there."

Ryan wiped sweat from his face. “Good. I need cold water.”

I laughed. “Same. With lemon, please.”

Paula smiled. “How about cold drinks… and a snowy mountain scene in Finland? We can sit inside and watch the Northern Lights.”

Ryan grinned. “Sign me up.”

We parked our bikes and headed inside. And suddenly, the heat, the smell, and the heavy conversation all felt far away.

Another lesson finished.

Another step up the staircase.

Chapter 21: Changes in the Medical World

As soon as we walked into the back conference room, cool air hit my face. It had been so hot outside that the air conditioning felt amazing.

Paula pressed a few buttons, and the room transformed. Suddenly we were inside a glass igloo in Finland. The indigo night sky stretched above us, glowing with streaks of green and soft pink. The Northern Lights shimmered across the horizon, and the stars looked brighter than I had ever seen before.

My heart melted. I had always loved the night sky.

Paula handed me a glass of cold lemon water. I took a sip. "Wow… thank you, Paula. This is perfect."

Ryan raised his glass. "Yeah, thank you. So, what are we learning next?"

Paula smiled. "We've covered a lot. Honestly, I thought this would take days, but you two learn fast.

Tomorrow may be our last day together. After that, you'll begin reading your family journals."

Ryan leaned forward. "I've been thinking about that. I want to understand how the journals work."

Paula nodded. "We'll talk about that tomorrow. Today, I want to finish by explaining two things.

First, how we discovered the old 3D patterns stored in our DNA. And second… how the medical world changed on the New Earth."

I grinned. "Perfect. I'm cooled off and ready to rock and roll."

Ryan looked at me. "Hey! That was my line."

We laughed as Paula changed the room back into the conference setting. The projector screen dropped down. Her expression grew serious.

The word **ANGER** appeared on the screen in bright red letters. Paula spoke quietly. "This one emotion caused more damage in the 3D world than people realized."

The word vanished, replaced by a long list of health problems.

Heart disease
Stroke
High blood pressure
Diabetes
Weak immune system
Insomnia
Ulcers
Migraines
Depression
Addiction
Skin disorders
Tumors

…and the list kept going.

Ryan whistled. "Holy cow."

I stared at the screen in shock.

Paula looked at us. "If someone had these symptoms, what would they do?"

“Go to the doctor,” we both said.

She nodded. “That’s what people did. But in the 3D world, most treatment focused on symptoms, not causes.

Not until the late 1900s did people begin studying the connection between emotions and the body.

By the early 2000s, it became clear that unresolved anger, fear, and trauma could affect physical health. When people cleared the emotional charge connected to old memories, their symptoms often disappeared.”

Ryan frowned. “So. the cure was… dealing with your emotions?”

“Yes,” Paula said gently. “But that wasn’t easy for people back then.”

Ryan raised his hand. “What did people do instead?”

Paula sighed. “They relied heavily on pharmaceuticals. Some medicines saved lives, of course. But many were used as band-aids.

Pain pills became addictive. Some drugs caused new problems. And money controlled a lot of decisions.”

She looked at us carefully. “When profit was removed from medicine, everything changed. Doctors started working with natural methods, energy work, therapy, and lifestyle changes.

Pharmacies still exist. But they are no longer the center of healing.”

Ryan shook his head. “That’s wild. All they had to do was learn how to master their emotions?”

Paula smiled sadly. “Fear of change stopped many people. Some thought it was nonsense. Some believed it went against religion. Some didn’t want to face their past.”

She paused. “Even Jesus taught about this. He warned that unresolved anger leads to suffering. Not only in the heart emotionally… but in the body.”

Ryan nodded slowly. “That makes sense. If someone hurts you, and you hold onto it forever… it eats you alive.”

Paula smiled. “Exactly. Forgiveness wasn’t about letting someone off the hook. It was about freeing yourself.”

I raised my hand. “So, what actually gets passed down from generation to generation?”

Paula clicked the remote. Another list appeared.

Anger
Fear
Shame
Guilt
Depression
Greed
Hopelessness
Mistrust
Anxiety

I stared at the screen.

“We don’t really struggle with those anymore… do we?”

“Not like before,” Paula said. “But these patterns used to be passed down through families.

Through behavior.
Through trauma.
Even through biology."

She pointed to the screen. "This is called generational trauma. Children copy what they see. If a parent is anxious, the child learns anxiety. If a family hides secrets, the child learns shame. If anger is never expressed… it stays in the body."

She clicked again. New words appeared.

Attachment styles
Communication patterns
Epigenetics
Stress responses

"Trauma can even leave marks on genes," she said.

"Not permanent… but strong enough to affect future generations."

Ryan blinked. "So, people could inherit fear?"

"Yes. But they could also heal it."

Now I can feel the wheels within my head turning. This is fascinating information.

Another list appeared.

War
Abuse
Poverty
Racism
Addiction
Neglect
Violence
Suicide
Natural disasters

I felt my chest tighten.

“That’s… a lot.”

“It was,” Paula said. “That’s why clearing these patterns became the first step for anyone joining the community. We wanted a clean slate for future generations.”

She clicked again. A longer list appeared.

Fear of being alone
Fear of failure
Fear of memories
Fear of rejection
Control
Stubbornness
Perfectionism
Jealousy
Suppressed emotions

“These emotional states were linked to physical illness,” she said.

“Doctors could see patterns in families. But people ignored them. Until the shift.”

She smiled softly. “Aislinn used two books often when she worked with people. *The Secret Language of Your Body* and *Emotional Patterns.*

She believed healing the past was the key to healing the body.”

The screen changed again. A picture appeared of a young man sitting alone on a bench. The words read:

Generational Exile Trauma

Paula spoke quietly. “This one was common in the old world. When children turned eighteen, they were expected to leave home.

Some never had a place to return to. Some were rejected. Some stayed in toxic situations because they had nowhere else to go.

That created deep survival trauma. People learned to stay in pain just to avoid being alone.”

Ryan shook his head. “That’s brutal.”

“It was. But we don’t live that way anymore. No one is forced to survive alone.”

Paula turned off the screen. “Our healthcare system changed completely. We focus on self-care first. Not selfishness. Self-care.”

She smiled at me. “If you’re tired, rest. If you have energy, move. If you’re stressed, talk. If you’re overwhelmed, slow down.”

She looked at Ryan. “And sometimes… go for a bike ride.”

I stuck my tongue out at him. He laughed.

Paula continued. “We use energy work, sound therapy, massage, EMDR, acupuncture, coaching, hypnotherapy, and sometimes medicine.

Not band-aids. Solutions.”

She studied my face. “You look tired, Danica.”

I nodded. “That was a lot.

I think… tonight I need to talk to Tobias.”

She smiled softly. “Then you should. He’s one of your guides for a reason.”

I held my glass of lemon water. Another lesson finished.

Another layer understood. And somehow… I knew the next one would go even deeper.

Chapter 22: Intuitive Knowing

As Ryan and I rode our bikes back home, I kept thinking about his experience of being a bird.

He had told me many times that he could fly in his dreams, and I always wondered what that must feel like. I had never had a flying dream before, but lately I couldn't stop thinking about what it would be like to be in cat form.

I looked over at him.

"So… what was it like to be a bird? Did you want to eat worms, chirp at people, or poop on someone's shoulder while flying?"

Ryan laughed. "I did not poop on anyone, thank you very much. You're ridiculous, sis.

It did take a minute for my body and mind to sync up, but once I shifted, everything felt natural. My connection with Aura got stronger too. It was like my intuition turned way up.

I had this gut knowing about where to fly, when to turn, how to stay in rhythm with her. It felt like a yes or no sensation in my stomach… like my body just knew."

He paused, thinking.

"And there was this heart knowing too. Like warmth in my chest. Expansion. My whole body loved flying. It felt right… like I was meant to do it."

He smiled. "Kind of like music for me.

You know how I've always loved music? It's the same thing. When I was little, I couldn't stay away from it. My whole body got excited when I heard it.

Mom used to tell stories about how I would bang on pots and pans like they were drums. I even tried to play music on her wine glasses once."

I laughed. "She was not happy about that."

He grinned. "But I had this inner knowing. Like music was part of why I came here. Like in this lifetime, I'm supposed to master it. So, my body pulled me toward it without me even trying."

He glanced at me sideways. "And right now… I'm getting the feeling that you want to try being in cat form."

I wiped sweat from my forehead. "You would be correct, bro."

He laughed.

"Is that why you felt overwhelmed today? You don't know how to ask Tobias if he'll let you do it?"

I thought for a moment. "Not exactly… but kind of. It's more like… I already know I would love it.

When I was on his planet, it felt like home. My home. I cannot explain it. I knew that I belonged there. Would one day… live there.

I watched how his people treat each other. They're playful, curious, relaxed… but also respectful and wise.

That's what I love about Tobias. He's funny and playful, but he's also steady. Grounded.

And the love there… I don't even know how to explain it."

Ryan nodded slowly. “Yeah… the love was intense. Not just a feeling.
More like a truth.

We know our parents love us. Our community loves us. But over there… everything was made from love.

The plants.
The water.
The air.

Even the buildings felt alive.”

He shook his head, still amazed. “I almost cried at first. It was so strong. I felt out of place… but at the same time, I knew I belonged there.”

I looked at him in surprise. “Yes. Exactly. It was like… I couldn’t do anything wrong there.

Not because I was afraid to mess up… but because I didn’t even want to. There was no good or bad. No right or wrong. Everything just… was.

Even things that people on Earth would judge, I didn’t feel like judging at all. Everything felt perfect. I felt perfect. Everyone felt perfect.”

Ryan smiled as we stopped our bikes in front of the house. Mom was in the herb garden, and Dad was watering the fruit trees.

Ryan turned to me before heading inside. “You should talk to Tobias about the cat thing. I’m going to talk to Marcos later. You want me to tell him hi?”

Chapter 22: Intuitive Knowing

My heart jumped the moment he said his name. Before I could stop myself, my face lit up.

Ryan covered his mouth dramatically. “Ohhh… you like him. You really like him.”

I groaned. “Ryan… Ok…Maybe. Maybe it was the cocktail… the vibe… the dancing… the planet…. I still don’t know… but there is something.”

He leaned closer, grinning. “I can’t wait to hear what Marcos says about you. This is going to be good.”

Before I could grab him, he ran inside and shut his bedroom door. I shook my head and walked into my room.

The late afternoon sun was shining through the window, and my crystals were throwing rainbows across the walls and ceiling. I loved this time of day.

I lit a stick of dragon’s blood incense and sat on my bed. Slow breath in. Slow breath out. I closed my eyes and imagined a ball of white light around me.

Then the blue color appeared. Soft at first… then swirling. Pulsing. Expanding.

I relaxed deeper and welcomed it. As the blue light filled my mind, I felt him immediately. Tobias.

I smiled.

Our connection was instant. The blue shapes shifted into patterns, symbols, and sacred geometry.

Then I heard his voice in my mind.

Little one… what do you need from me?

I smiled inside. He always knew. Before I could answer, I heard him again.

After dinner, I can come visit you…
or you can come visit me.

You remember the steps, don't you?

I nodded in my mind. *Yes. I remember.*

I will come at eight. My time.

He chuckled softly.

I will make sure authorization is approved.

I'll be waiting for you on the other side.

See you soon… my little one.

I opened my eyes slowly. And my heart was already racing with excitement. Tonight… I was going back… home.

Chapter 23: Being an Intuitive Empath

After dinner, I took a shower to rinse the sweat off from the day. When I finished, I stood in front of the mirror and looked at my reflection.

I paused.

This won't work, I thought. *I'm going to see Tobias.*

Then I stopped myself. Tobias loves me no matter what I'm wearing.

Just as I opened the bathroom door, Ryan knocked. "Hurry up, sis. I have to use the bathroom."

I stepped out, and he looked at me with a grin.

"I didn't want to say this in front of Mom and Dad, but Marcos really liked you. The second I said your name; he lit up like a holiday tree. I almost laughed. You two are adorable. Now move. I gotta pee."

He pushed past me and shut the door. I shook my head and walked down the hallway toward the meditation room. Mom was coming the other way.

"Danica," she said, smiling. "Ready to go visit Tobias?"

I laughed. "Mom… the stories I heard about you on his planet will probably outlive you. Everyone knows about you over there. And let's not forget your Ken-doll lover friend."

She covered her face, turning bright red.

"Sweetie… I had to clear some generational trauma back then. I didn't even know it was in my DNA. That night on his planet brought everything to the surface so I could heal it. It was embarrassing… but it was a gift.

Yes, I had a wild streak in my twenties."

I smiled and put my hand on her shoulder.

"I love you, Mom. Thank you for clearing that pattern. It spared me and Ryan. I better go. Tobias is waiting."

She hugged me tight. "I trust you. Have fun."

Then I said casually, "I'm going to see if I can switch into cat form tonight."

Her eyes went wide. "Oh sweetie! Wait right here."

Before I could ask why, she ran down the hallway. I heard drawers opening, closet doors sliding, fabric rustling.

When she came back, she was holding something.

"Put this on," she said, trying not to laugh. "It'll make Tobias laugh. Trust me."

She pushed me toward the bathroom. When I changed and looked in the mirror… my jaw dropped.

I was wearing a skintight leopard-print bodysuit. It had a corset top, a long tail, and high wedge heels.

I stared at myself. "Mom… you did NOT wear this."

From outside the door she answered, "Yup. Sure did. I told you I had a wild side. Come out, let me see."

I slowly opened the door. Her eyes lit up.

"You look amazing! Wait… I found the ears."

Before I could protest, she put cat ears on my head and drew whiskers on my cheeks.

I turned bright red.

"Mom… just this once."

She clapped like a kid.

"You have to tell me everything when you get back. It's our inside joke. Tobias will remember."

I shook my head. "This is going to be interesting."

Entering the meditation room, I do my best to clear my thoughts. Too late to change my clothing back to causal and laid back.

I sat inside the meditation pyramid and followed the steps Tobias taught me.

Breathing.

Light.

Focus.

When I opened my eyes, he was standing there, staring at me. He blinked once… then raised an eyebrow.

"Your mother," he said. "You're sober, right? She didn't give you any of that wine or that gin-infused cannabis stuff she makes?"

I shook my head quickly. "Nope. Completely sober. She said this outfit was an inside joke between you two."

He reached out his hand and helped me step out of the triangle.

He looked me over, then chuckled. “You look good, little one… but this isn’t your style.

Your mom wore that exact outfit the night she asked to try cat form.

So… is that why you’re here?”

I looked into his eyes, a little embarrassed. “Yes. I want to know what it feels like to be in cat form.

What Ryan said… woke something up in me. I’ve always had strong intuition, but sometimes I question it. I have had vivid dreams of being a white female lion. Running around with…you… by my side.”

Tobias looks at me surprise, but I continue speaking.

“Like when I met Marcos. I just knew. I felt it in my heart. It made me stop and question. What caused that feeling…that knowing. It’s a new feeling…a new sensation. Unlike my feelings… towards you.”

Tobias just watches me. Quiet. Patient. Kind.

“I thought maybe… being in cat form would help me understand my intuition better. I am still learning… and there is so much to learn.”

Tobias gestured for me to sit.

He knelt in front of me, his expression soft. His touch gentle and warm.

“Little one… you are an intuitive empath. We haven’t talked about your abilities yet, but we need to. And first, I need to give you some advice.”

Chapter 23: Being an Intuitive Empath

He took my hand.

“That feeling you had with Marcos… that was real. When your soul recognizes someone, you feel a pull. But that pull doesn’t always mean they are your life partner.

Sometimes they are a teacher.

Sometimes a student.

Sometimes both.”

I frowned. “What do you mean?”

He smiled gently. “That pull is your soul pointing toward a lesson. If you jump in too fast, you miss the signs.

If he is your teacher, he may break your heart. He may teach you acceptance… forgiveness… patience.

He may choose a different path. He may leave. Can you still love him if that happens?”

I looked down. “I’ve thought about that. I like him… but I’m not ready for that kind of commitment. I still want to explore my life. If he’s my person, he can wait.”

Tobias smiled proudly. “Exactly. True love is a slow burn, not a wildfire.

Lust is self-serving. Passion is connection.”

He squeezed my hand again. “You’re wiser than you realize. Have you ever thought about becoming a council member?”

My eyes widened. “I… actually have.”

He laughed softly. “I thought so.”

He stood and took the cat ears off my head.

Chapter 23: Being an Intuitive Empath

“Now let’s talk about intuition.

People experience intuition in different ways,” Tobias said.

“Some feel it in the body.
Some see images.
Some hear guidance.
Some just know.

You have several abilities.”

He counted on his fingers.

“Clairvoyance — clear seeing.
You see symbols, colors, visions.

Clairaudience — clear hearing.
You hear guidance inside your mind.

Clairsentience — clear feeling.
You sense emotions and energy.

Claircognizance — clear knowing.
You just know without explanation.”

He smiled.

“You have all four, but you lead with feeling and knowing. You are an empath. You feel other people’s emotions in your own body.

When Ryan broke his arm as a child… you felt the pain before anyone told you.”

I nodded slowly. “I remember that.”

“You also feel energy in places,” he continued. “That’s environmental empathy. You can walk into a room and know if it’s loving… or hostile.

And you have body-based intuition. Gut yes. Gut no.

Heart expansion.

Full-body yes. Full-body no. Your body guides you."

He leaned closer. "Everyone has this. Most people just ignore it."

He smiled softly. "When you meditate, you also receive symbolic messages.

Dream intuition.

Metaphor intuition.

Your grandmother had that too. You tell stories because your soul thinks in images."

I blinked. "That actually makes sense."

He stood and held out his hand. "Good.

Now…are you ready to experience cat form?"

I jumped to my feet. "I was born ready."

Chapter 24: Heightened Awareness

As Tobias and I walk down the long corridor toward the hibernation chambers, I see my usual big-eyed bug. Yep. The praying mantis.

Not again. Why is he always here?

I try to ignore him, but the moment we make eye contact, he starts clicking. Tobias laughs and says to the mantis, "It was her mother's idea, not mine! I know she looks like a tasty snack, but you cannot touch her."

I lower my head in embarrassment and mumble, "Go away…"

That's when the mantis places one of his front arms on my shoulder.
It gives me the creeps. It feels like a light, tickling sensation as his claw brushes my skin. I know he's harmless, but still… go away and leave me alone.

As soon as he passes us, I let out a sigh of relief. I want out of this stupid costume as soon as possible.

Tobias looks at me and smiles. "We have arrived. Have you thought about what cat form you would like to try first? We have a white lion, golden lion, black jaguar, spotted jaguar, leopard, cougar, cheetah, tiger, mountain lion, and snow leopard. Pick one, little one."

So many choices.

I do love snow leopards… but today I want to be a black jaguar. Something sleek. Something that can blend into the shadows.

Chapter 24: Heightened Awareness

"I want to be a black jaguar," I say.

Tobias nods. "Good choice. Stay here, next to the white chamber. I'll set it up."

He walks to the control panel and presses a few buttons. From the green hibernation chamber, a black jaguar form slowly rises into view. Smooth. Powerful. Beautiful.

"Does this meet your approval?" he asks.

"Oh yes," I say, smiling. "I'm assuming it's female?"

"Yes, ma'am. I chose this one because of the rosette markings. You can see them under the right light."

He presses another button and the white chamber door opens. I feel a little nervous, but I trust him.

"Step inside," Tobias says. "Before you do… snap."

I look down at myself and laugh. I'm wearing my favorite pajamas with the outer-space cats flying on pepperoni pizzas, and fuzzy slippers with poofy golden cat heads.

My smile gets even bigger.

"Thank you, Tobias. Those four-inch heels were killing me."

"You're welcome, my love. Now remember the drill. The chamber will fill with pale purple mist. It won't hurt you. It just puts you to sleep and begins the transfer. Any final words?"

"Nope. Let's do this. I want to see what it's like to be like you."

"Very well. Let's get this party started."

The door closes, and the mist begins to rise. Within seconds my breathing slows, my body relaxes, and the familiar humming vibration surrounds me.

Chapter 24: Heightened Awareness

When I open my eyes, the white glow fades. Tobias opens the green chamber and grins.

“You look smoking hot, little one. Before you speak, we need a mind link. Take my hand and test your balance.”

I step out and let out a soft chuff sound, followed by a low, guttural rumble that almost sounds like a bark.

“Just wait,” Tobias says. “You’ll be able to speak normally once we sync.”

He presses his forehead against mine. A tingling wraps around my head, and suddenly I hear his voice inside my mind.

“What I’m doing is brain synchrony. Some would call it hive-mind behavior. We’ll share awareness, intuition, even telepathy. It helps with coordination, especially in danger. Now try speaking.”

He pulls back.

I grin and say, “Good thing we didn’t make this mind link by smelling your butt like dogs do.”

Tobias bursts into a deep, guttural laugh.

“Good. Your sense of humor survived the transfer.”

He looks me over, snaps his fingers, and suddenly I’m wearing a diamond-studded collar with royal-blue accents, matching earrings, and soft leather wraps with white and blue feathers braided around my waist and chest.

Elegant. Simple. Powerful.

“Go look in the mirror,” he says.

Chapter 24: Heightened Awareness

I walk over and stare. My fur is dark and sleek. My eyes glow with gold, green, and yellow. I run my hand over my arm. It feels coarse, dense, and strong. My belly is soft and smooth.

I turn and hug Tobias.

Inside my mind, he says, “I have a special treat for you. I want to take you to our Tree of Life. When we get there, you'll be able to speak with Aislinn… and even my father. All our ancestors rest there. We planted that tree after the Draconian wars, when the Galactic Peace Federation was formed.”

“How did Aislinn end up there?” I ask.

Tobias pauses, then answers softly.

“She never felt like she belonged on Earth. The higher frequencies here matched her soul. She's very old… older than most. She's been here since the beginning of creation, and she's entered the Kingdom of Heaven more than once.

She only returned to Earth when humanity reached a turning point.

Atlantis. Egypt. Rome.

Each time she came as a prophet… a healer… a warning voice.

Some listened. Most didn't.”

He continues as we walk.

“In Atlantis, she was a man who tried to warn the people before the fall. That's where she met Thoth. They worked together after the collapse, building what humans later called the Great Pyramid.

Those memories stayed hidden from her… until she read the Emerald Tablet. When she did, everything woke up inside her.

That's when we first met. When the Great Pyramids were being built. Soul to soul. We've been connected ever since."

His voice softens even more. "When she died, she asked to be buried here, with her cat, Warrior. Her family knew she was different. They understood.

He looks at me. "Would you like to meet her?"

Inside his mind, I answer immediately. "Hell yes."

He laughs. "Good. Then we go. But first… music."

He presses a small device, and the melody fills the air. Irish instruments. Soft. Ancient. Familiar. My heart tightens.

My mom used to play this when we gardened together… telling stories about fairies, elves, and hidden worlds. I swear the plants used to glow when she played it.

The song *And You Will Come* echoes in my mind, and I feel tears forming.

Tobias pauses the music as we reach the outer doors.

"You need to adjust to the environment first. When we climb the mountain, I'll play it again. It will enhance the experience."

I nod.

The doors open. Instantly, everything changes.

My vision widens.
My pupils open fast, pulling in light from every direction.

Chapter 24: Heightened Awareness

My ears rotate, catching sounds I never knew existed. High, sharp, distant, and layered.

Every movement. Every vibration. Every breath.

I feel powerful. Alive. Awake.

“Over here,” Tobias says in my mind. “This path leads to the Tree of Life.”

The music starts again.

The pathway glows with pale-blue mushrooms, their caps sparkling like stars. Massive redwood-like trees rise around us, their bark glowing deep orange, their needles soft and green like light.

The air smells like eucalyptus and earth.

With every step, my hands and feet leave glowing prints in the soil. I look down and can see warm honey-brown light trailing behind me.

The song changes.

Something inside me wakes up. I start running. Faster. Faster. Faster.

Wind rushing through my fur. The scent of the forest filling my lungs.
Pure joy. Pure magic.

Then I see it. A glow on the horizon. Gold. Orange. Red. Pink. Yellow.

The sky looks like it’s on fire.

I slow down as Tobias comes beside me. “You see it,” he says. “Beautiful, isn’t it?”

I can barely speak.

“I have nothing like this on my planet… I feel frozen in time.”

The Tree of Life rises before us. Enormous, radiant, and… alive.

Its roots glow. Its leaves shimmer in gold and red. Water reflects its light like liquid glass.

A whisper moves through my mind. Welcome home. Welcome home, sweet Syrian soul.

Tobias interrupts my trance. “You need this to speak with her.”

In his hand is a small glowing blue mushroom.

“It will expand your mind. Only lasts about twenty minutes. If you want it to end, drink the water. Eat it now. The roots of the tree will help you connect.”

I look at him, then at the mushroom. I take a bite. And follow him toward the Tree of Life.

Chapter 25: Tree of Life

Within a few minutes, I feel the full effects of the glowing blue mushroom.

My body hits a strange wall of resistance, like my nervous system doesn't know what to do with all the new sensations. Tobias takes my hand and guides me to sit on one of the thick, glowing roots of the Tree of Life.

The moment I sit down, I feel energy move through my base chakra and travel up my spine. It feels as if the tree itself is scanning me… searching through my soul's memory banks deep within my subconscious.

Fascinating. And a little creepy.

Tobias watches me carefully and says softly, "Little one, forgive me. The first time anyone eats this mushroom; the body can react strangely. Your nervous system is resisting, isn't it?"

"Yes… I feel funny," I say.

"I know. We need to calm your system down. Cross your arms over your chest, hands on your shoulders… like you're hugging yourself. Now tap each shoulder, one at a time, and say to yourself, *I am calm water.*

Picture your place by the lake. Be there in your mind. Keep tapping. Slow your breathing."

I do as he says, tapping gently back and forth.

Chapter 25: Tree of Life

"Your body is adjusting," Tobias continues. "Left… now right… good. Become the calm water. Connect with it. Let everything slow down."

After a minute, I feel the tension release.

"So many new sensations," I say. "It's hard not to get overstimulated. Thank you… I feel better now. A little fuzzy, but… peaceful. Like I'm floating."

"That's why the roots are important," Tobias says. "They keep you grounded. Balanced. Centered. You are now connected to the Tree of Life."

"I can feel it," I whisper. "It knows me… and I know it. I've never felt anything like this before."

Tobias nods.

"Now sit still. Focus on the glowing bark in the center of the tree. Set your intention to speak with Aislinn. Say her full name three times, and she will appear."

I close my eyes and do exactly as instructed.

The roots begin to glow pale blue. The ground beneath my feet turns violet. Symbols… sacred geometry… writing I don't recognize… begin to move through the roots like streams of light.

The tree is waking up.

The light travels upward, forming the face of an old man with a long white beard. His eyes glow a deep, powerful blue. Thick white eyebrows appear, and then the image shifts into the face of a lion. A royal-blue crystal forms on the crown of his head.

My breath catches.

Chapter 25: Tree of Life

“Oh… I forgot to tell you about this part,” Tobias says quickly. “You must get permission from my father first. He guards the Tree of Life. Be humble. He will know if your words are not from the heart.”

Great.
Now he tells me.

A thunderous voice echoes through the roots.

“Who wakes me from my slumber? Speak, mortal. Do not be afraid.”

I whip my tail back and smack Tobias.

“Now you tell me?” I mutter.

Inside my mind I repeat, *Calm water… calm water…*

Then I speak.

“It is I, great guardian of the Tree of Life. My name is Danica. I share the bloodline of Aislinn. I have come to speak with her about her time on Earth, and to ask if I would be a good match for the community council. Do I have your blessing to continue?”

Tobias looks at me in surprise.

“Well… that was impressive,” he says inside my mind.

I grin. Honestly, I don’t even know where that came from.

The voice replies,

“There is wisdom within you, mortal. Your request is granted. And you, Tobias, my son… it is good to see you again.”

Tobias bows his head.

“Good to see you as well, beloved father.”

Chapter 25: Tree of Life

The glowing colors shift. Pale blue, white, and violet blending together … until the face of a woman appears.

She looks old… and wise.

Long white hair falls over her shoulders. Her eyes glow with warmth and kindness. She wears a soft green gown… and to my surprise… cat slippers.

I almost laugh.

A bright green crystal glows in the center of her forehead. She sits in a rocking chair, holding a large Maine Coon cat with one blind eye and one bright emerald eye. The cat wears a blue collar with a bell, just like mine.

The love between them is visible. Every time she pets the cat, soft pink light shimmers around them. It's beautiful.

Then she looks up and smiles.

"Tobias, you troublemaker. Good to see you again, my dear friend. Did you bring your partner in crime to meet me tonight?"

Tobias laughs.

"Yes, Aislinn. This is Danica. She is your great-great-granddaughter. She wants to know what it was like during the transition from 3D to 4D. She hasn't read your life book yet, but she will soon."

I feel shy.

"Hello, Aislinn. It's an honor to meet you."

She smiles warmly. "You're the first one to come visit me. That means you must be special. Tobias visits often… though I suspect he enjoys the mushrooms more than the meetings."

She winks, and we all laugh.

Tobias shakes his head.

“Careful, Aislinn. You’re revealing our secrets. We both enjoyed mushrooms back on Earth. We don’t want to scare her. She’s thinking about joining the council in your old community.”

Aislinn looks directly at me.

“My, my. That is an honor. Then I will be honest with you.

The transition from 3D to 4D frightened billions of people… but here is the secret.

When you witness something frightening during a timeline shift, remember… it is not your lesson if you have already reached the higher states of consciousness.

You are protected. You walk in the light. Do not let fear influence your choices.

Bless those who fall… even the ones doing harm.”

I frown. “Why bless the ones doing harm?”

She sighs softly. “Because their soul chose that role. Their spirit suffers more than you know.

Imagine living every day in fear, anger, and separation… always reaching for something you will never feel. It is a miserable existence.

They teach humanity through contrast. Dark versus light. So, bless them… and keep walking in the light.”

“But if I bless them… am I approving of what they do?”

"No," she says gently. "You see clearly who they are. Blessing them is compassion, not approval. Hatred feeds them. Blessing starves them.

Pray that their suffering ends. Know that their time is temporary."

She leans forward slightly. "Then imagine the world you want.
See people cooperating.
See peace.
Feel it in your body if you cannot see it in your mind. We are powerful creators. Power… not force."

I hesitate.

"But bad things did happen. You saw them too."

Aislinn sighs deeply. "Yes. I did. The visions I was shown slowly became reality. Wars. Conflict. Ego against ego. It was part of the shift. Darkness fighting to survive as the old world ended.

Greed. Power. Control. All collapsing.

It was the last great struggle of the 3D world. Many prophets saw it. Even Jesus spoke of it.

'Blessed are the meek, for they shall inherit the earth.'

Only the meek remained in the higher timeline. Those who trust in God completely.

Meek does not mean weak. It means strength under control. Faith without fear."

She looks at me with deep compassion.

"When I walked through those dark times, I remembered the words;

Even though I walk through the valley of the shadow of death, I will fear no evil.

That passage kept my faith alive. I knew our Creators walked beside me."

She pauses.

"I loved being on Earth. The food. The animals. The music. The beauty.
But I hated the suffering… and how people treated each other… and the planet.

My heart wanted humanity to wake up. And eventually… we did.

The timelines split. And a new Earth was born."

Chapter 26: The Spirit of Life

“Thank you, Aislinn, for sharing that with me,” I say softly. “That must have been very hard to witness.”

She nods slowly.

“The visions I received were warnings of what would unfold within the 3D timelines; not the 5D ones. I wanted love, not hate. Forgiveness, not revenge. Peace, not bitterness.

At one point, I saw myself like the Spirit of Life in the Disney *Fantasia 2000* Firebird scene.”

She smiles faintly, remembering.

“I saw myself flying over Mother Earth, spreading love, hope, and light after the volcano erupted… reseeding the planet with life again.

When I saw that scene in the theater with my daughter, I cried. I trembled. She didn’t understand what was wrong with me, but I knew.

It was a sign. A warning from our Creators.”

Her eyes drift far away, as if she is seeing it again.

“In that moment, I felt it in every fiber of my being. One day, what I saw on that screen would become reality. I would stand face to face with that volcano. A great destroyer or something else that wanted to destroy everything I loved.

Chapter 26: The Spirit of Life

The animals fleeing… that was humanity. The fire… the chaos… the fear…But I also knew something else. The volcano could not destroy me.

Our Creators told me so. I would rise from the ashes… and help restore the world. My tears would become seeds. And those seeds would grow into a new Earth."

She lets out a small laugh. "Of course, at the time I wanted to pretend it was just a movie. Who wouldn't? I can be stubborn… and Tobias knows that."

"Yes, I do," Tobias says, smiling.

They both laugh.

"In my heart," Aislinn continues, "I saw myself wrapping my wings around Mother Earth… pouring love into every crack, every wound, every broken heart. I wanted to stop what was coming. But I couldn't. It had to happen."

She looks at me again.

"Do you still have a painting of the Spirit of Life? I bought it at a comic convention in Seattle, around 2012 or 2013. That was the same trip when I met my twin flame face to face for the first time… but that is another story.

Have you seen the painting? It's a family heirloom now."

My face lights up.

"Yes! I love that picture. It always spoke to me when I was little. The expression on her face made me feel safe. Just like the Archangel Michael picture that was passed down in our family.

Mom gave me the Spirit of Life painting for my birthday once. She said it was yours. I look at it every day on my wall."

Aislinn smiles warmly. “Good. Then you understand. So, I began trying to manifest what my soul … and Tobias’s soul wanted.

That love and light could reach even the darkest places in the human heart… before the volcano destroyed everything. But remember… it was part of the evolution of Earth. We had to accept what was coming.”

She pauses, then her expression grows more serious.

“When our Creators told me in 2023 that it was time to serve… I got scared. Unmoored.”

I tilt my head. “What does spiritually unmoored mean?”

She nods, pleased with the question.

“It means I felt shaken… disconnected… unsure of myself. Like I shattered into pieces.

The awakening lasted about seven to ten days. It was beautiful… but overwhelming for my body and mind.

Part of me wanted to understand what was happening. I wasn’t religious, and when I tried to explaining it to my husband… I failed miserably.

Then our Creators told me to contact three people. One of them would bring me a book that explained everything. The third person did exactly that.

He showed up with the book without me saying a word. He said he felt guided to bring it…. As if God spoke to him.”

“What book?” I ask. “Your mother still has it. *Outline of the Principles, Level Four.*

But the important part is this…

Chapter 26: The Spirit of Life

During my awakening, my husband didn't understand what was happening to me. He wasn't spiritual. That created tension.

Our Creators warned me; 'This will test your marriage. You will leave for forty days and forty nights, but you will return.'"

My eyes widen. "That really happened?"

She nods.

"It was a test of faith, trust, and unconditional love. He asked me to never speak about Tobias again if I wanted peace at home. So, I learned the art of silence. Not everything needs to be spoken aloud.

I knew Tobias was part of my soul. I could not deny that. And deep down, my husband loved that part of me… even if he couldn't accept it."

I glance at Tobias, then back at her.

"So, what visions did you see?" I ask quietly.

She looks at me carefully. "Remember… these were for the 3D timelines only. Not the 4D or 5D ones."

"I understand." She takes a breath.

"I saw famine. Crops poisoned. Water contaminated. People growing weak.

I saw conflict inside America… Americans fighting Americans.

I saw division… not just emotionally, but physically.

I saw leaders who believed they were kings.

I saw the fall of nations that refused to change."

My stomach tightens. "That sounds terrifying."

"It was," she says calmly. "But those souls were playing their role. Some came to destroy the old world. Not out of hatred… but as teachers of contrast. Dark showing humanity what light is not."

She looks at me steadily.

"I had to decide… do I warn people and sound crazy… or stay silent and watch it unfold?

I was not Jesus. I was a messenger. Like Enoch."

"Who is Enoch?" I ask.

She smiles. "You'll learn that in your orientation. I won't spoil it."

"That's fair," I say.

She continues.

"I knew if I spoke, I would be mocked. Insulted. Disbelieved.

But my soul chose this role. Not my ego. My soul.

Tobias chose it too. We have worked together across lifetimes."

I squeeze Tobias's hand. Aislinn smiles at us.

"Our hope was simple. That some people would listen. That they would remember their soul is eternal. That even in the last moment, a person could choose humility… choose truth… choose light.

Our Creators are merciful. Always."

I swallow hard. "So, when you warned people… what happened?"

She sighs.

"Some listened. Some didn't. About half chose the light. The others fought it.

They called me a false prophet. But a true prophet brings unity, compassion, cooperation, and love.

A false prophet brings fear, division, and control.

One serves the Creator. The other serves the ego."

She strokes the cat in her lap, calming herself.

"I never wanted power. I only wanted people to make choices from the soul… not from fear. A false prophet rules with fear. A true prophet leads with love."

I nod slowly. "I see the difference."

She smiles gently. "Good. People are not born sinners. They are born with free will. Every choice moves them closer to light… or deeper into darkness.

Earth is a school. Every soul is here to learn."

"That makes sense," I say quietly.

"That was my warning," she continues. "To take the higher road. To become the Spirit of Life. The Holy Spirit lives inside every human heart. Some remembered. Some ignored it.

Our Creators, and Archangel Metatron wanted humanity to choose life… not fear. To choose unity… not destruction."

I feel chills. "It sounds like humanity was given a second chance."

"They were," she says. "And even those who chose darkness were still loved. That is why I spoke of hope… not doom.

Because even the lost can return to the light. That is the mercy of our Creators."

She looks at me with soft eyes. "You will understand more when you read my life book."

I smile. "I can't wait."

She nods. "Before I go… I have one request. Stay here a little longer… and listen to a song.

A song that made me thank our Creators for bringing Tobias into my life."

Tobias smiles instantly.

"I know the one. You played it at your funeral here."

She tilts her head. "Yes. That one."

Tobias places his hand over his heart. "We will listen."

The colors around the tree begin to fade. Her image dissolves into soft blue light.

"Many blessings to you both," she whispers.

"Many blessings to you, Aislinn," we say together.

The spiral of light disappears.

Tobias presses play. The song *Thank God I Do* fills the air.

My heart swells. In my mind's eye, I see her… alone… then finding Tobias… strength… love… purpose…

Tears roll down my face. I squeeze his hand.

“I thank God for you, Tobias. You are my closest friend… my heart… my soul. My love. I could never imagine life without you. Never.”

A tear falls down his cheek.

“I feel the same, Danica. You remind me of her.”

He smiles softly. “Now… I have one more treat for us.”

My spirit lifts. “Oh really, Mr. Troublemaker? I can’t wait.”

Chapter 27: Soul Evolution

I look over at Tobias and say, "I wanted to ask Aislinn about her many lives on Earth, but I forgot. I was so overwhelmed by the feeling of love and our ancestral connection. The energy was intense. I felt so drawn to her. People in the old days believed they only had one life, but that isn't true. Past-life regression has shown otherwise."

Tobias smiles.

"Remember, little one, people can hear the truth and still choose not to believe it. Everyone has free will. Some beliefs become deeply rooted because they are passed down from generation to generation. And honestly, the idea of only one life helped keep humans in line.
After all… this is your only chance, so don't mess it up."

I laugh.

"I can see how that would create guilt and shame. And those are the lowest emotions a person can live in."

"Exactly," Tobias says. "So some people give up. Others say, 'To hell with it,' and keep living in greed, pain, or power struggles. But every life is just a lesson for the soul. None of them are good or bad. They're all information.

Even our Creators have no single name. We give them names so we can feel connected. Souls are the same way. One soul can have many names. Aislinn had many. I had many. You have had many. Hundreds.

A soul is always evolving. Always becoming."

Chapter 27: Soul Evolution

"But what about angels?" I ask. "They have names."

"Yes," Tobias says. "Because their role never changes. Their purpose is fixed. Souls evolve. Angels serve.

An evolving soul has a true name given at creation… but only our Creators know it."

He scratches his head, then grins. "Now… about that extra treat I promised."

I raise an eyebrow. "What is it?"

He thinks for a moment, then smiles wider. "I think it's time for a bedtime story."

My eyes go wide. "I am not a little girl anymore, Tobias. I'm a grown woman."

He laughs.

"Relax. I know that. But we have a book on my world that shows how a soul evolves. My sister is babysitting tonight. Perfect timing. She's putting the little ones to bed."

I jump up.

"What? She has babies? Since when? Who's the father? When did this happen? Why didn't you tell me?!"

Tobias's jaw drops.

My tail smacks him.

"Take that!"

He gives me a slow grin.

"Girlfriend… don't start tripping. She's babysitting. Her friend needed a night off. Aura offered to help.

Now come on. Follow me. This will be fun."

I sigh. "Okay… I may have jumped to conclusions. Want to race?"

His eyes light up.

"We're heading to that grove of redwood trees. About two miles. Let's see what those cat legs can do."

He presses play on his music device, and heavy, high-energy bass fills my ears. Before I can react, he's gone.

Darting through glowing bushes, weaving between trees, leaping over rocks and streams.

When the music slows, I see him crouch low… hiding. Then he disappears.

I creep closer. WHAM. He tackles me and rolls me onto the ground.

I burst out laughing. I have never seen this side of him before. He's like a giant kitten.

He jumps up. "Catch me if you can!"

He hits play again.

"What song is that?" I ask in my mind.

"*Overgas* by Badjokes. Ryan showed it to me. Come on, slowpoke."

He's flying through the forest like he found catnip. Jumping. Spinning. Climbing. I can barely keep up.

“This must be your cardio catnip crack music,” I laugh. “You’re insane.”

When the song ends, he’s waiting near a grove of redwood trees. I flop down on a mossy log, panting.

“Let me breathe, dude. You’re nuts.”

He grins. “Insane in the membrane.”

I laugh.

“Who you trying to get crazy with, ése? Don’t you know I’m loco?”

We both crack up.

Then his face gets serious.

“Aura is watching four falcon chicks tonight. Three girls, one boy. The boy’s a firecracker. Like me. They’re about four weeks old. We stay calm. If they see us, they’ll want to play.”

I nod. “Let’s go.”

We climb glowing ivy vines that wrap around the trees. Little round homes sit on platforms about eight feet up, made of sticks, leaves, moss, and mud. No windows. Just cozy nests.

“That’s the one,” Tobias says. “Fifth house. Red leaf door.”

He knocks gently. We can hear rustling inside.

“Who is it?” Aura calls.

“Tobias and Danica. I brought her for story time. Good time?”

Chapter 27: Soul Evolution

The door cracks open… and suddenly Tobias is flat on his back, covered in four fluffy white chicks with huge feet. They chirp his name in excitement.

One of them, the boy, stands on his belly.

"Look! I'm getting big! Soon I can fly!"

Tobias laughs. "You're getting your juvenile feathers, little man. Now get off me. I came to read a story."

The chicks hop away, flapping fuzz everywhere.

Aura looks at me. "Help me gather the feathers. They're valuable for bedding."

We collect the soft fuzz while Tobias herds the chicks into a big nest. He's surprisingly good with them. A Natural.

I hand Aura the feathers. She tucks them into the nest.

"Come sit," Tobias says. "Story time."

I curl up beside the smallest chick. She nuzzles my arm.

Snap.

A shimmering indigo book appears in Tobias's hands. When he opens it, the pages glow.

A wise female voice speaks from the book.

"Good evening, little ones. Tonight, we tell the story of a soul's evolution."

The pages turn by themselves.

A golden light splits into three colors: blue, pink, green.

"Our Creators were making new worlds… new species… new souls."

Chapter 27: Soul Evolution

The next page shows six balls of light.

"One soul… we will call Moonlight."

We watch Moonlight choose life after life as a villain. Warrior. Tyrant. Destroyer.

Easy missions. Easy lessons.

Then the next page… Mars. Dust. Ruins.

"You chose the easy path," the voice says. "Now you learn the opposite."

The chicks watch wide-eyed. One whispers, "Unkind soul… better watch out…"

I bite my lip trying not to laugh.

Moonlight returns as a frightened girl. Poor. Weak. Afraid. She dies in a storm.

The Creators speak. "You were told to ask for help."

Another life. Another lesson. Pain. Loss. Love. Courage.

Then another page.

Moonlight becomes a builder. A leader. A creator of cities beneath Mars.

He learns compassion. He learns purpose. He learns prayer.

Final page.

Moonlight stands before the Creators, glowing.

"You are ready," they say. "Will you guide another soul?"

Chapter 27: Soul Evolution

A tiny new light appears.

Moonlight smiles. “Yes.”

The last image shows a boy on Earth, about eight years old, about to do something dangerous.

Moonlight, now an angel, tries to guide him.

A tiny chick chirps, “Good luck, Moonlight. The end.”

I burst out laughing. “I love this story.”

All four chicks answer together, “We’ve heard it before.”

One of the girls points at her brother. “Especially when HE makes bad choices.”

The girls stick their tongues out at him.

Aura sighs. “Bedtime.”

Tobias covers them with a soft feathered leaf, kisses the girls, high-fives the boy.

“Behave. I’ll visit next week.”

The boy beams. “I’m gonna fly before them!”

Aura shakes her head. I lean in close to Aura and softly whisper, “We girlfriend need to talk. I need to talk to you about…sweet Tobias.”

I watch her blink in surprise. “Oh really?”

“Yes. Maybe tonight…when I get home. You can come visit me…in private.”

Aura takes her arms and wraps them around me in a gentle hug. “You got it. It will be our little secret.”

Tobias looks back at us. Giving us the signal to stop whispering and to start leaving.

So, we tiptoe out of the cozy nest. Holding hands outside the bright red door.

Outside, my heart feels full.

Warm.

Peaceful.

As we head back toward the hibernation chambers, I realize—

Not every lesson has to be heavy. Some are meant to be told like a bedtime story.

Chapter 28: The Promise

Within minutes after returning home, I heard a soft knock on our front door. My mom looks at me with a surprised question on her face.

"I wonder who that can be at this late hour. I hope nobody is hurt or stuck in a ditch."

I quickly ran toward the front door. "Oh, it's Aura. I asked her to come speak to me tonight."

As I am opening the door, my mom replies, "Really? This is interesting."

In a slight panic, I say, "Please don't tell Ryan."

My mom walks over to me before I open the front door.

"Don't worry, sweetie. He is in his bedroom with his headphones on. I can hear him laughing from time to time. He is watching another movie with his buddies online. He will not come out of his bedroom until morning. He is a creature of habit."

I watch my mom give me a wink.

"Thanks, Mom. I truly appreciate you."

"What a relief," I think to myself as I step outside.

Aura is standing there. "Hey, honey. What do you want to talk about? I am all yours."

I grab Aura's hand and lead her down to our pond. It is peaceful here, quieter and away from listening ears.
The stars are out, and it's a lovely evening.

Chapter 28: The Promise

We both sit down on the wooden bench my great-grandfather built.

"You are being rather secretive, sweetie. What do you need to get off your chest? Has Tobias done anything wrong?"

I shake my head from side to side. "Oh… nothing like that. I don't know how to put it… I… I…"

I find myself stammering over my words.

Aura looks deeply into my eyes… as if… she is looking deep into my soul.

"I think I know what this is about. I have a ringing in my ear… which is a confirmation… that I am spot on.

You love him. He loves you. You might be the… one."

I look at her, confused. "The one?" I sheepishly reply.

Aura smiles and squeezes my hand.

"Yes, the one. I had a feeling… a sense… a deeper inner knowing. You two are like two peas in a pod. He has never taken anyone to see Aislinn. I believe he was looking for a sign… a confirmation from Aislinn… that you might be… the one.

But… your love story… your soul's love story… has been written in the stars. Etched in the ethers… for all to learn from… and admire.
For Aislinn's and Tobias's souls have been joined to each other… since the first moment they met."

"Now I am confused. Truly confused. What do you mean?"

I hear Aura sigh deeply.

Chapter 28: The Promise

"The two of them met when he was in Egypt. She was a human female, and he… well… he was Tobias. The white lion, as you see him now. They fell in love. It was frowned upon for a human to fall in love with a feline-looking humanoid.

But… she fell hard. He… he fell harder. They remained together as best friends… companions… two peas in a pod. They so desperately wanted and longed to be lovers, but they refused to break the sacred heavenly laws.

When her vessel expired… he cried… howled… for days… weeks… and months."

I can feel my heart aching… hurting from this story.

"That is so sad."

"Yes, it was sad. Yet our Creators are kind, loving, and compassionate. Their love was tested several times on Earth, and each time… they proved that love mattered more than physical appearances. The heart wants… what… the heart wants. They wanted each other. To be together… again… one day… in the future."

I look at Aura in surprise.

"And? What happened next?"

"Our Creators granted them their wish. Not just any ordinary wish. A wish that only the heart can recognize.
Feel.
Hear.
See.
Know.

Do you know what I mean?"

I let out a deep sigh.

Chapter 28: The Promise

"I do. I really do. It is scary at times. When I was little… I knew.

The first time I saw Tobias… I knew. My heart fluttered like your beautiful wings… the moment I laid eyes upon Tobias. I just knew that he… he was going to be in my life… forever. I could not imagine life without him."

Aura looks at me and smiles.

"He feels the same way about you… but doesn't know how to say it. He doesn't want to scare you away. So, I need to tell you a bedtime story, sweetie."

I just laugh. "Another bedtime story? That is two in one night."

Aura puts her arm around my shoulder.

"I believe you are going to love this bedtime story. It is a story about love. What love is like from a 6D perspective. The love shared between Tobias and Maeve."

I look at Aura. "Who is Maeve?"

"Maeve was Aislinn's true name… the name our Creators gave to her… when she was first created in the Heavens above."

"Are you going to snap your fingers and read me a book?"

Aura's smile grows bigger.

"Only if you want me to do so."

"Sure. Why not," I say.

I watch Aura snap her fingers and… poof. A magical book appears in her hands.

"Now before we begin… I need to explain to you about the different forms of love. On Earth… many humans once longed to connect with their twin flame or soulmate. This love… this story… is different. Much different. As you will learn… tonight."

I snuggle my head against Aura's soft feathery shoulder. "Okay. Go for it."

"Very well." I watch Aura open the book. The pages appear blank… but… colors start to swirl and form images. I can see Tobias clearly. In Egypt. He looks so handsome. Happy. Full of vigor and pride.

As the colors begin to swirl before my eyes, I can see a woman. A woman with dark skin, lovely shiny black long hair. She was strikingly beautiful in her white robe, beaded belts, and necklace. In some strange way… I felt like I knew her… but had never seen her before.

"This is when they first met. She was not the warrior goddess within the Egyptian mythology stories. Their love story was erased… for a time… because people frowned upon their union. It was forbidden after what happened to their queen, Queen Sekhmet.

They tried to keep their love and companionship a secret… but people that served her… looked after her… had watchful eyes. Yet those watchful eyes and jealous gossiping fools… could not stop their love.
Could not stop or break the bond they formed for one another."

I could see Tobias and this woman cuddling with each other in a bed made of golden silk. Candlelight softly shimmered off the walls. It

looked rather romantic. He looked happy. Content. In love. His cat-like smile was intoxicating.

Chapter 28: The Promise

I watched Aura turn the page.

Next, I saw tears. Tobias's tears. He was watching her body being wrapped in soaked, covered strips of cloth. Herbs and spices were being applied to preserve her body.

Trinkets and jewels were placed within her tomb. My heart ached at the sight. I wanted to comfort Tobias… but I had to remember… this is only a story. Our love story.

Another page turned.

I saw Tobias on his knees, praying next to the golden silk bed. A soft candle glowed upon a small, ornate bedside table. It was the same bed they shared together. Tears rolled down his white furry cheeks.

Aura gently chimed in. "Tobias prayed that night. He prayed to the Heavens above to bring her soul essence back into his life. He declared that he would do anything… anything to have her by his side again. Either in friendship, brotherhood, companionship… or marriage… one day."

The page turned.

Again, colors swirled. I saw two feline men fighting in battle. They were strong… courageous… fierce. I saw laughter. Companionship. A deep brotherly love.

"Our Creators heard Tobias and granted his wish. In this image, they were brothers. But that brotherly friendship had to come to an end."

I look at Aura, confused, and softly ask, "Why? Why did it have to come to an end?"

Chapter 28: The Promise

"Maeve's soul wanted to advance, evolve, and expand. Therefore, she had to go to Earth school and learn how to master the different levels of consciousness.

You see, Tobias… he was created and born into the 6th dimension. With all the crazy stuff happening on Earth in the 3D era… well… Tobias was not welcomed. He would have been killed.

His soul did not need to advance, evolve, and expand like Maeve. She had to do the work to align with his timeline. His world.

Does that make sense?"

I gently nod my head. "I understand it… and I don't like it. Please continue."

I watch the next page turn.

As the colors swirled to form a picture, I saw a deep friendship again. This time Maeve was a human female, and Tobias was a… cat.

I look at Aura and point at the cat. "Is that… Tobias?"

Aura smiles. "Yup. That is Tobias. You might not know this… but parts of your soul can split. Separate."

"What do you mean?"

"Well, a soul can split or divide its energy to experience multiple lifetimes… timelines… or realities simultaneously. Our souls can live parallel lives. It is designed to accelerate a soul's evolution and gather diverse experiences.

Chapter 28: The Promise

Now, we could be here for hours, and I mean hours. There are many lifetimes when Tobias was a cat or lion in Maeve's human lifetimes.

So, let me give you an example, because there are several magical books about love.

When beings from other worlds were welcomed on Earth, humans fell in love with a few humanoid beings that looked like cats, dogs, rabbits, monkeys, horses, dolphins, elephants, and even birds like… me.

That love continued for thousands of years. Souls made vows… promises to one another… waiting for the moment… like we have now… to rekindle what was lost and taken away from them when animal-looking humanoid beings were no longer welcomed on Earth."

I still feel a little confused. "So… how does that all work?"

"This is where it gets tricky. You have two choices. Either you decide to stay in human form, and the relationship remains the same. Intimacy is not permitted. We do have heavenly laws that we must obey.

Or make the transition into feline form… if you want to raise a family of baby cubs together on Vega. But I need to tell you what Tobias wants. He has waited a long time for this moment… and for you.

He is tired of transitioning into a younger vessel each time over the centuries and thousands of years. He wants to grow old like his father. To have his vessel placed by our Tree of Life. He would ask the same of you.

So, think about these two choices… and please… keep his heart and feelings into consideration. He is a big softy."

I can feel the heaviness of those two choices. Now I have so many questions. Questions about my family, friends, and career. But it is getting late.

As she turns the next page, I see Aislinn and her cat. The one I saw… sitting in her lap.

"So, Tobias still wanted to be by her side. Therefore, he became a cat. In fact, he was that cat… Warrior… you saw sitting in Aislinn's lap. She knew it. Tobias knew it.

And… do you know why Tobias did it? Split a part of his essence off?"

I look at Aura. "Because he missed her?"

Aura takes my hand in hers. "Because he knew she would need him. He knew she would feel all alone when she realized who she was, what she was, and how she was being called to serve. She needed a friend. Someone to bring her comfort… tenderness without judgment… or fear."

I watch a tear run down Aura's blue feathery face.

"He knew when she discovered who he was, what he was, and how he was here to help serve her… that she would need someone to comfort her… and that someone would be a cat.

And a little secret here… even her husband knew how much she loved that cat. He was envious."

"Oh my God. Really? How could anyone be that… envious of a cat?"

"Get this… he did mention to Aislinn and many others that when he dies and goes to Heaven, he is going to ask God if he can come back as one of Aislinn's cats."

I could not help myself. My mouth was wide open in shock. "No… way. Is that a true… story?"

Aura laughs and chirps. "Ask your mom. It is very true!"

We both laugh. "You've got to tell me more."

"Love is love, little one. A part of Tobias's soul essence was inside that cat. She knew it. She… felt it. She saw it… within his eyes… and how he looked at her."

"Wow! That is amazing. Love is love."

Aura gently pats my shoulder as I look up at the stars.

"Therefore, he was envious of the way they looked at each other. Aislinn and Warrior. The smile on the cat's face. The look in his one eye… as Aislinn brushed him.

At times… Aislinn would joke with him… by saying she was going to cheat on him with her boyfriend… and that boyfriend would be Warrior… sitting in her lap… while she played games on her computer.

In fact, Aislinn had many… questionable…and unusual… boyfriends. Turkeys, deer, bucks, a roster, frogs, and a few cows."

I laugh. "That is too much! Let's not forget the racoon."

Aura smiles. "Can't forget that one either."

I watch another page turn, and I can see Aislinn on her deathbed. Tobias is by her side in physical form. I look at Aura.

Chapter 28: The Promise

“How was that possible? He was inside of her?”

“When the split from 3D into 4D occurred and the 4D timelines merged, it was time for Tobias to depart. That was the agreement they made with our Creators. Tobias was only temporarily gifted to Aislinn for the sole purpose of supporting humanity with the ascension process. Tobias knew of this promise, but Aislinn did not.

Another page turned. I saw Aislinn in bed dreaming. Then it shifted into Tobias before her, talking to her.

Therefore, he came to her in a vivid dream. He promised he would come back to her, to be physically by her side, not as a cat or lion… but as a white lion humanoid.”

Another page turns, and I see large spacecraft landing on Earth. I observe Tobias walking off the ship and finding Aislinn.

“So, when more spacecraft from Vega came to Earth, Tobias knew exactly where to find Aislinn.”

As the next page turned, I saw Aislinn seeing Tobias for the first time. He looked so handsome. The look in his eyes was unmistakable. He loved her so deeply.

“When she saw him… face to face… her heart exploded like starlight inside her chest… love and light poured out of her. It had been thousands of years.”

“When they embraced each other,” I watch another tear fall from Aura’s silvery eyes, “they held on tight. Crying. Laughing. Smiling. Celebrating.

It was magical. I was there. I cried as well.

Chapter 28: The Promise

A dream come true… for both of them.

A gift from our Creators… for their support on Earth as well as… in the Heavens above."

I can feel their love for one another. It almost hurts. The longing. Waiting. And finally, being set free, so they could meet again in physical form.

The final page turns. I see Aislinn on her deathbed. I guess she did not want to be a feline humanoid just yet. Tobias was by her side, holding her, comforting her, looking at her fragile body with sorrow and tears.

"So, before Aislinn's soul advanced to the final level, she made Tobias a promise. A promise that one day they will meet again.

After all the dust settled and the new Earth was slowly transitioning into 5D, she would come back."

I watch Aura wipe a tear off her cheek.

"She would be back, in her same family tree as a female, ready to share a life with him. To raise a family… together. To grow old… together.

Because in every lifetime they were together on Earth, they never got to raise a family. Tobias could only be a cat or lion… nothing more.

So, he took what was offered, even if it felt like breadcrumbs. Love is love.

So, he enjoyed bringing her comfort… affection… and unconditional love as either a cat or lion.

That is why Tobias is questioning you. Are you the one Aislinn promised would return within her family tree?

It clearly was not your mother. He learned that truth when he took her to our planet and… that club."

We both laugh.

"Yeah, my mom had a wild side. She is a mixture of Ryan, who is wild, free-spirited, and goofy at times. Then she is like my dad, who is sensible, creative, spiritual, and a deep thinker. You know the saying; opposites attract. To balance them out, I believe."

Aura smiles. "Now, does it explain why Tobias has been acting strangely?"

I let out a deep sigh. "It does. It truly does. I had a feeling. A knowing. When I stepped foot on his planet, it felt like… like home. My home.

Therefore, I need to take this slowly. I am still becoming. Now I have even more options and opportunities than before."

Aura gives me a hug as she closes the book.

"You do, sweetie. Take your time. He has learned the art of patience."

We both laugh, and in that moment… I realized this life… my life… was truly magical.

And love… love would lead the way.

Chapter 29: Gettin Jiggy Wit It

The next morning, I woke up feeling refreshed and renewed. Being in cat form the night before had been so much fun.

As I'm getting dressed, I hear my mom yelling at Ryan down the hallway. I stop for a moment and smile to myself.

What is that goofball doing now… this early in the morning?

I open my bedroom door and glance across the hall. Ryan is in his room, dancing like nobody is watching…. which, unfortunately for him, I am.

He has his royal-blue headphones on and is completely lost in the music.

I squint my eyes. Wait a second…

He isn't wearing his normal laid-back dude clothes.

He's dressed in Dad's black suit, a perfectly pressed white shirt, and a black tie. His hair is slicked back. He's wearing black sunglasses.

Oh no.

Then I hear him singing at the top of his lungs.

"Gettin jiggy wit it… na na na na na na na nana… gettin jiggy wit it!"

I slap my hand over my mouth to keep from laughing.

Ryan is workin it.

He spins, drops into a half-split, pops back up like a rubber band, snaps his fingers, and sashays across the floor like he's on stage.

My heart swells with joy watching him. He's having the time of his life.

Suddenly he looks straight at me, grabs my hand, and sings into his imaginary microphone.

"Tryin to do what I did… mama-unh mama-unh mama come closa…"

He bumps his hip into mine.

"In the middle of the club with the rub-a-dub!"

I shake my head.

Mom definitely dropped him on his head as a baby.

Then it hits me.

Retro movie night.

He must have watched *Men in Black* with his buddies. That explains the suit… the sunglasses… and the Will Smith dance moves.

I brace myself.

There will be more movie quotes today. There always are.

I walk into the kitchen, and Mom looks at me with a knowing expression.

"You're thinking the same thing I am," she says. "No, I didn't drop your brother on his head… but he did have a habit of rolling off everything. Bed, couch, chair, table, changing table… if it had an edge, he found the floor."

We both laugh.

"I'll give him this," she adds. "He can dance."

Right on cue, Ryan dances into the kitchen, still singing.

"Na na na na na… na na nana…"

He spins, points at us, and says in a deep voice,

"Uh-uh."

Mom and I burst out laughing.

He pulls off his headphones and grins.

"I make this look good, don't I, ladies?"

"That's from *Men in Black*, right?" I ask.

Ryan snaps his fingers.

"You are correct, sista. I am protecting the Earth from the scum of the universe."

I shake my head, smiling.

"You know, there's actually an interesting story about Will Smith. We talked about him in my mental health class. What happened at the Oscars… that was reactive abuse."

Ryan groans. "Oh boy. Here we go."

Mom smirks.

I keep going.

"Most people didn't understand what happened. They saw him as the villain, but they didn't realize how personal the joke was. His wife shaved her head because of alopecia. That wasn't something to joke about on live TV in front of millions of people.

He snapped. And when someone snaps, they lose rational control. Some can even blackout. That's why he cried afterward. He knew he crossed the line."

Ryan slowly slides his sunglasses down his nose.

"You are killing my vibe, girl."

I ignore him.

"He had everything. Fame, success, money… and in one moment it was gone. That was a turning point for him. He realized none of that brings real happiness. So he went on this deep inner journey, trying to figure out who he really was.

He saw people with nothing living in villages, and they were happier than he was. That's when he realized he was always running… always trying to please people… never present.

He had to learn how to respond instead of react.
To slow down.
To be in the moment.
To let go of fear and expectations.

That's where real peace comes from."

Ryan stares at me.

Slowly shakes his head.

Then in his best 90's voice says, "Girlfriend… you are ruining my vibe. Chill out, baby girl. You're always so serious."

He grabs my hand and starts dancing again.

"Come on… shake it out… like this…"

He spins me once, grins, and says, "In fact… you need to get jiggy wit it."

Then he lets go, puts his sunglasses back on, snaps his fingers, grabs a blueberry muffin, and sits at the table like he's the coolest man alive.

Mom looks at me, throws her hands in the air, and says, "See? Dropped too many times."

Chapter 30: The Metatron's Cube

After breakfast and morning chores, Ryan and I rode our bikes to the library. Today was supposed to be our final day of orientation.

Of course, Mom made Ryan take off Dad’s suit. She refused to let him get it dirty.

When we walked inside, Paula greeted us with a smile.

“Hey, you two. Today I’m giving you a full tour of this building. We’ll talk about when it was built, why it was built, and its purpose. But we need to start outside at the front. Come on. This will be fun.”

We followed her out the side doors and walked around to the front of the building.

The landscaping was beautiful. Green lawns, butterfly bushes, roses, blooming summer flowers, and tall trees shading the path.

As we reached the front, I noticed Ryan was unusually quiet. He was still sulking about the suit.

Paula turned toward the building and said, “This sacred-geometry building is one of a kind. The first one was built in 2028. Now there are more than six dozen across the globe, and more are still being built.

This one was created with donations and recycled materials. Artists, architects, engineers, landscapers, and designers all came together to make the vision real.

It was done in honor of a request from Archangel Metatron.”

I blinked.

Chapter 30: The Metatron's Cube

"Metatron asked for this building?"

"Yes," Paula said. "Our community promised not to tell our children the full story until their Becoming celebration. If you knew too early, there would be no reason for you to meet him yourself."

Ryan's mood instantly flipped. "No way! My day just got interesting."

He spun around, shook his hips, and sang,

"Gettin jiggy wit it… na na na na na na na nana…"

Paula looked at me with a priceless expression.

"Are you sure he's your brother? Good dancer… but loco."

I grinned.

"Who you trying to get crazy with, ése? Don't you know I'm loco?"

Ryan pointed at me. "Now you got the fire, sista!"

Paula clapped once.

"Enough. I want to finish this tour today."

"Yes ma'am," Ryan said, snapping his fingers one more time.

Paula shook her head and continued.

"This building is a blueprint of creation. Its design comes from the Fruit of Life. There are thirteen circles connected by lines, containing the five Platonic solids. These are the building blocks of the universe.

Each circle in this structure has a purpose.

Archangel Metatron oversees the energy within these buildings. Every one section was built in his honor and is considered a blessing for Earth… and for humanity's evolution."

She squeezed my hand gently.

"You will speak with him when we review your soul journey book."

Ryan nodded like a surfer. "Trippin, Paula. Can't wait to vibe with Mr. Metatron."

Paula gave me a look that said everything.

She cleared her throat.

"This first circle represents reflection, understanding, and spiritual growth.

People enter this space to learn how to master themselves. How to release the pain stories stored in their bodies, their cells, even their DNA.

When people cling to their past, they stay trapped in the lower vibrations of 3D consciousness."

She opened the double doors, and we stepped inside. The room felt sacred.

Two rows of long wooden benches lined a wide aisle, like a church, but not exactly. More like a round conference hall.

Stained-glass windows showed angels, birds, rolling hills, clouds, and glowing lights. Above us hung glass stars and circles, like the night sky. The carpet was deep forest green.

The air smelled like frankincense and myrrh.

In the corners were flowers, and near the doorway stood a pillar with a bowl of water. Holy water.

Paula motioned for us to sit near the front while she stepped onto the stage.

She clicked a remote.

On the screen appeared a chart of emotions, habits, and behaviors ranked by vibrational frequency.

"Now that you're both twenty-five," she said, "you have full access to the building.

You've been here for weddings, festivals, council gatherings, and solstice events. But now you can attend meetings, vote, host events, even lead discussions.

Everyone participates here. We don't preach. We teach."

She paused.

"When Aislinn first spoke with Archangel Metatron, she doubted this building would ever exist. He told her to manifest it… and it would come.

He also warned her. There was a window of time. A period when humanity could choose to shift from 3D to 4D.

That window opened in 2026.

Every day became a choice. No one is perfect. We all make errors in judgment. What matters is what you do after."

Ryan raised an eyebrow. "So basically… don't be a jerk?"

Paula exhaled slowly. "Yes, Ryan. Something like that."

She continued. "Aislinn stayed neutral. Everyone had free will. Some wanted to evolve. Some wanted to stay the same.

This building was created as a place of healing… not judgment."

I nodded.

"That must have been hard for her. Delivering that message."

"It was," Paula said.

Ryan shrugged. "Would've ruined my vibe."

Paula closed her eyes for a second.

Definitely praying. She went on.

"Each month we choose a topic from the 3D list. Shame. Fear. Anger. Guilt. Regret.

We talk about it together. Internal stories… external experiences… everything. Then we break into smaller groups."

She pointed to the side doors. "These lead to the self-discovery rooms."

Before we left, I leaned toward Paula near the holy water.

"Should we bless him first?"

She whispered back, "He may be past that point."

Ryan grinned. "I bathe in holy water. That's why I shine."

He snapped his fingers. "Gettin jiggy wit it…"

Paula inhaled deeply. "Follow me."

We walked down a long glass hallway overlooking the courtyard in the center of the cube. The ceiling above us was stained glass. I could see angels, roses, doves, vines, and light.

Chapter 30: The Metatron's Cube

We entered the next circular room. Round tables. Chairs. Metatron cube designs etched into the wood. In the back sat a table with binders, books, and a tablet.

“These are life-journey books,” Paula said. “Everyone writes one.”

I opened a binder.

Stories.
Family traditions.
Recipes.
Trauma.
Love.
Loss.
Lessons.

It felt like holding someone's soul.

Ryan leaned over my shoulder. “This is actually… really cool.”

Paula smiled. “Yes. Real history. Not someone else's version.”

She tapped the table. “These rooms are for reflection. We talk about our experiences, find the lesson, and discover the gift inside the pain.

Everything goes into the book. Everything.”

I flipped another page.

Blueprints.
Songs.
Poems.
Holiday vacations.
Magical moments.

Chapter 30: The Metatron's Cube

Spiritual or religious practices.
Sacred prayers, passages and verses.

I look up at Paula, "Riley built the greenhouses," I said softly. "And the treehouses... and the catios..."

Paula nodded. "That's why we keep these records. Nothing is lost."

She crossed her arms.

"We store everything in our data center under the building. Not cloud-based. Not controlled by corporations.

People decided that after the wars, after the data crashes, after the shortages. We learned the hard way."

"Dude, check this out. This chick in this book met a Palladian alien and they became good friends. This is wild." Ryan says

"Oh, I forgot to mention. There are stories of how some people saw aliens for the first time and it was not as they expected. You know. All the sci-fi movies of evil aliens destroying and invading Earth. Such crap, if you ask me. All fear and scare tactics."

Ryan laughs, "That's entertainment for you. Violence, fear, and war always filled the box office.

The truth is that aliens had been around for thousands of years.

Some lived under water, inside mountains and deep cave tunnels,... and others inside the core of Mother Earth.

It was just kept secret from the general population. It wasn't until the merger from 3D into 4D did the aliens come out of the closet. I am glad that Tobias and Aura are here in our lives. I just love those two."

Paula seems surprised. "Impressive, Ryan. You know your alien facts."

I watch Paula pause, "Yes. Turns out they were never the bad guys."

Ryan grinned. "Told you."

Paula clapped her hands once.

"Alright. Next circle. Follow me. We're going to the courtyard. The Three-C Circle."

Chapter 31: Celebration of Life

We walked down another beautiful corridor, and halfway along the right side was a glass door leading into the courtyard.

Inside were round stone tables and matching stone stools.
In the center sat a large, low firepit, its flames gently swaying beneath a metal canopy that protected it from rain.

Around the courtyard were potted flowers, lemon and lime trees, and four small waterfalls spaced evenly apart.

I walked over to one of them and saw koi fish swimming in the clear water. A lily pad floated on the surface.

Around the edge of the pond were glowing pale blue and green stones.

I picked one up.

"These look fake. What are they for?"

Paula smiled and picked one up.

"They were donated. Solar activated. During the day they charge, and at night they glow. We use them to mark the borders and give the space a little magic."

I grinned.

"They're awesome. I want to come here at night and meditate."

I looked at the tables.

"And these… someone painted Metatron's Cube on them?"

"Yes," Paula said. "Hand-painted, then sealed to protect them from the weather. We only bring out extra chairs when we hold ceremonies or remembrance gatherings."

I looked around more carefully.

Incense burners hung from above. White string lights crossed overhead. Every table was placed in perfect alignment.

Then it hit me.

Fire.
Water.
Air.
Earth.

All here. All balanced.

"This place has all four elements," I said quietly.

Paula nodded.

"Yes. This courtyard is where we celebrate the fruits of life. The lives people have lived, and the lessons they've completed.

When someone feels their journey is complete, and they have fully entered the 5D state, we hold a celebration here."

Ryan leaned forward. "Like a graduation party?"

Paula smiled. "In a way… yes.

In the past, we would make a copy of their life journey book. The original would be stored, and the pages scanned into the archives.

During the ceremony, the person thanks the universe, their ancestors, our Creators, their guides, angels, family, and friends."

Ryan raised his hand. "And Mr. Metatron."

Paula nodded. “Yes, Ryan. And Metatron.”

She continued. “Then the person tosses their book into the fire.

It’s not destruction. It’s release.

It means the past has served its purpose. The lessons have been learned. The soul is free.”

“But what if someone has an accident and did not get to complete their book and the ceremony process? What happens next?” I asked.

“That is an excellent question, Dancia.” Paula says

I look over at Ryan, and I can see him stick out his tongue at me and mouth the words, “Ass Kisser.”

I just shrug it off and laugh inside. He is in a mood today.

Paula’s expression softened. “That happens.

Remember Debbie? Last November… her parents died in that ski accident.

She came to a meeting two weeks later completely lost. We didn’t talk about the books at first. We supported her.

We helped her understand they were in a good place. That she could still connect with them if she needed closure.

We taught her breathing techniques so her nervous system could calm down. We wanted her to feel safe again.”

She paused.

“She moved from grief into acceptance. From there… she chose to try the graveyard beer ceremony.”

Chapter 31: Celebration of Life

Ryan's head snapped up.

"Hold up. Graveyard beer?"

Paula sighed. "I was hoping you wouldn't hear that part."

Ryan leaned in. "You have to explain."

Paula crossed her arms.

"Archaeologists found evidence of ritual beer in ancient burial sites. In some cultures, herbs and mushrooms were added to help people enter altered states so they could communicate with the dead.

There are even theories that ancient wine and rituals in early religions contained psychoactive ingredients. There is also records dating back to the times of Jesus. For some individuals questioned if Jesus was drinking wine that had psychoactive and hallucinogenic properties.

Brian Muraresku wrote about it in *The Immortality Key*."

This guy did so much research. It's an impressive book and truly makes one think outside the box.

Afterall, the Aztec people called various psychedelic mushrooms food of the Gods, flesh of the Gods, and the Blood of Christ. These mushrooms were considered sacred. Consuming psychedelics can create a deep spiritual union, open shut doorways within the mind, and create spiritual euphoric effects."

Ryan looked at Paula, "That is wild, Paula. So, how was Debbie's experience? Did she find closure?"

Paula nodded. “Yes, Ryan. Debbie used the ceremony to connect with her parents. It helped her heal. It was the healing her heart was seeking.

That experience gave her clarity, wisdom, and understanding. Debbie went from feeling the minor 3D emotions into the full scale of 4D and 5D emotions.”

Ryan’s grinned. “Tubular, man. You gotta hook me up with some of that graveyard beer, Paula.” Ryan says

“Hopefully not soon, Ryan. You are high enough without it.” Paula replies.

I simply bust out laughing.

“Your no fun, Paula.” Ryan replies

Ryan shook his head. “You’re no fun.”

Paula ignored him. “Since Debbie’s parents never finished their books, she wrote the final chapters for them. She wrote about their lives, their lessons, what they meant to her. Then the community held a celebration here, just like any other.”

She looked at both of us.

“Now that you’re twenty-five, you’ll be invited to these ceremonies. The more you attend, the more you’ll understand what this place really is.”

She motioned toward another hallway. Ryan and I followed her.

“Next two circle.”

We watch Paula point to the next upper circle on the right…and then the left.

Chapter 31: Celebration of Life

"These two remaining circles are designed to support humanity in connecting with memory and technology. Within these two circle, you can review a person's life journal… and speak with them using holographic AI reconstruction."

My eyes went wide. "You mean… I could talk to Aislinn?"

"Yes," Paula said. "We record everything: voice, movement, expressions, memories, stories, and personality traits.

We build a full profile. It isn't the soul… but it's close enough to learn from."

Ryan whistled. "That's insane."

Paula smiled. "It has helped a lot of people. I still talk to my grandmother sometimes. Her smoky voice… her wisdom… it comforts me."

She looked around the courtyard.

"This building connects the finite and the infinite. The living and the ancestors. That's why I love working here."

I looked around slowly.

"This place isn't just a library. It's a school of consciousness… a memory vault… and a place of ceremony."

Paula's eyes lit up. "Yes."

I continued thinking out loud. "It is like a complete ecosystem of knowledge, not just a symbolic building."

I smile at Paula as I look around. "Yes. The very Structure is a whole system. For if we step back and look at the architecture here, it forms a clear progression:

1. Learning the human journey: Understanding life, suffering, and growth.

2. Transforming suffering into wisdom: Shifting consciousness and extracting lessons.

3. Recording personal knowledge and contributions: Writing one's own book.

4. Archiving human knowledge and experience: Data collection and preservation.

5. The great library at the top: Humanity's collective memory.

6. Circles of remembrance: Where people reconnect with the lives of those who came before.

That is a complete cycle of human learning and legacy. That is why this vision from Archangel Metatron to Aislinn's is so powerful.

For most civilizations, they focus on preserving political history, military victories, rulers, and institutions. But this structure focuses on preserving human growth and wisdom.

It suggests a future where humanity values understanding itself more than celebrating power. It's a complete cycle."

A tear rolled down Paula's cheek. "Yes… that's exactly what it is.

In the old world, people built monuments to kings and wars. Here… we preserve wisdom.

Afterall, the greatest treasures of humanity has always been its wisdom. And so much of that wisdom has been lost over the centuries. These books are not just as relics of the past, but seeds for the future.

For every life lived with awareness becomes a light for those who walk the path after you.

We are about preserving civilization's knowledge. Yet Aislinn's vision adds something that most 3D concepts and ideas lack; the preservation of human experience and consciousness itself. It's not just information, but the story behind the knowledge."

I look over at Paula, "So, it's not just a building. It's a complete cycle of human learning, remembrance, and legacy. For human wisdom is not created by machines. It is created through shared experience, conversation, and reflection."

Again, Paula beams at me. "Yes, Danica. Knowledge may be stored in vaults, but ours is preserved in light within our machines. For wisdom is born when human hearts gather and speak their truth to one another."

She looked at the fire. "In many traditions, a continuously burning fire represents the continuity of human wisdom across generations. Throughout history, many cultures have had someone responsible for maintaining a sacred or communal fire. The fire symbolized continuity of community, preservation of wisdom, warmth and gathering, and the living spirit of the people.

"That's why the flame never goes out. I keep it burning. All the technology in this building is advanced… but the fire keeps it human."

I stepped closer to her.

"You keep the heart of this place alive, Paula. As long as the fire burns… humanity won't forget itself."

She squeezed my hand. "I've watched hundreds of lives pass through here.

People reading their parents' books… people finishing their own… people letting go…people starting again."

I smiled. "You're part of the tapestry too."

Behind us, Ryan muttered, "Whatever."

Paula's head snapped around. "That's enough, Ryan. You are testing my patience."

He shrugged. "At least I'm teaching you patience."

Paula and I stared at him.

He had a point.

Chapter 32: Enoch's Life Journey

Paula stopped walking and turned to face us.

"Before we meet Mr. Metatron, I need to tell you his life story. He wasn't always an angel. He was human once, and his story is very important.

Danica, I know you've done research on angels, but many believers say Metatron is one of only two angels who first lived as a human being."

Ryan's eyes lit up. "Now I'm pumped. I can't wait to meet this cool, chill dude."

Paula held her composure and continued.

"It is believed that Archangel Metatron was the prophet Enoch from the Torah and the Bible. After his time on Earth, he ascended and became an angel.

Because he lived as a human, he understands humanity in a way other angels do not. He knows what it feels like to struggle, to doubt, to hope, and to try to change."

She paced slowly as she spoke. "When Aislinn was alive, she connected with several Archangels, but she formed a special bond with Metatron. Their values aligned. Their missions aligned. That is why their paths crossed."

Ryan tilted his head. "How so?"

"Metatron urges humans to change their negative 3D thinking into higher-level awareness… into the 4D and 5D way of living.

Aislinn was teaching those same principles long before the shift. She focused on how people think, how thoughts become choices, and how choices shape reality.

Metatron keeps the records of every soul that lives on Earth. Over centuries, those records showed the same pattern again and again.

Negative thinking leads to destructive choices. Positive thinking leads to growth."

She looked at both of us. "He watched Aislinn's work closely. He saw the charts she created, the teachings she shared, and the lives she helped change.

That is why he trusted her. That is why he revealed to her two different books. The Lambs Book of Life and a black book for lost souls."

Paula began pacing again.

"Enoch lived during a time when corruption was everywhere. He saw rulers twist the truth. He saw leaders erase their crimes. He saw innocent people suffer while the powerful grew richer.

He watched the same cycle repeat century after century."

"That sounds pretty dark," I said.

"It was," Paula replied.

"He saw people claim they served God while spilling blood in God's name. He witnessed temples turn into places of power instead of places of prayer. He observed how leaders speak of peace in public… and plan violence in private.

To him, it felt like the world was trapped in the same story, over and over again."

Chapter 32: Enoch's Life Journey

Ryan shook his head. "That's messed up."

Paula nodded. "Yes. And what makes Enoch's story different is that he lived a very long time. The Angelic Watchers blessed him with the spirit of life so he could complete his mission.

He saw generations rise and fall.

He saw civilizations grow… and collapse."

She stopped and looked at us.

"And when he looked at the world, where humanity was heading… he realized something. Humanity kept losing its wisdom…its teachings… its lessons.

Every time a civilization fell, its knowledge, wisdom, and teachings disappeared with it. But that is not all that was lost. What was also lost was…

Architecture and Engineering.
Artwork, paintings, and jewel crafting.
Creativity and philosophy.
Science and discoveries.
Craftwork and woodwork.
Agriculture.
Natural medicines.
Music and Sacred Dances.
Rituals and Traditions.
Spiritual or Religious practices.
Recipes.
Stories.

So much rich history and knowledge…gone…. erased."

I felt a chill. "That's sad."

"It is," Paula said softly. "He saw great civilizations vanish. Sumer. Egypt. Rome. The Indus Valley. China. The Olmec. Caral-Supe.

All their stories… gone.

People thousands of years later tried to dig up pieces of the past, trying to understand how those people lived.

Humans always wanted to know where they came from. What their ancestors knew. How they survived. How they built such incredible things."

Ryan nodded slowly. "Yeah… people still do that now."

"Exactly," Paula said.

"And that is why Metatron wanted this building to exist. That is why he came and spoke to Aislinn. He saw and knew what was coming. The timeline shift. He did not want humanity to lose its wisdom again.

He wanted every life recorded. Every lesson remembered. Every story preserved."

She looked at me. "That is why the life journey books exist. That is why the archives exist. That is why this building was built."

She paused, then continued.

"During Aislinn's time, the world was repeating the same patterns Enoch had seen.

Leaders fighting for power.
People divided.
Fear everywhere.

Some believed a savior would come and fix everything. But this time… the change came differently."

Ryan smirked. "Yeah… not a man floating down from the sky."

Paula raised an eyebrow.

Ryan shrugged. "Look what people did to God's son last time. Of course it would be different. The world needed balance. Needed the feminine energy. Divine Sophia era, right?"

Paula blinked in surprise.

"Well… that was unexpectedly insightful, Ryan."

He grinned. "I have my moments."

Paula laughed and continued. "When I speak to Christians during their Becoming celebration, I tell them this:

The Kingdom of Heaven is not a place. It is a state of being.
When you live in love, peace, and unity… you are already there."

She suddenly started walking in a playful, sing-song voice.

"You can feel it… taste it… breathe it…
Like a river flowing on a warm summer day. Just watch out for the rapids downstream… oh…and good luck."

Ryan and I burst out laughing.

"You actually say that?" I asked.

Paula beamed. "Yes. And they love it. My friends told me I should try stand-up comedy."

She looked at Ryan. "Unless he shows up and steals the show."

Ryan put his hands up. "Hey, I don't work for free."

Paula shook her head, smiling. "Alright. Back to Enoch."

We straightened up, trying to look serious.

She continued. "Enoch wanted to help his people, but he felt powerless. He prayed for guidance. He wanted truth to return.

He watched innocent people suffer while leaders lied. And when he saw the same pattern happening again thousands of years later… he knew something had to change."

She looked at both of us carefully. "Can you see the connection?"

"Yes," I said.

Ryan nodded. "Yeah. History repeating itself."

"Exactly," Paula said. "When Enoch became Metatron, he watched humanity for thousands of years.

He saw cultures rise… and disappear.

He saw traditions lost forever.

He saw people search desperately for answers about the past.

He saw how much humans wanted to understand their own history.

That is why he asked for this building.

So, the wisdom would never be lost again.

So, every life would matter.

So, every story would be remembered."

She took a slow breath. "That is why he chose Aislinn. Because she understood the same thing he did.

If we don't preserve human experience…we repeat the same mistakes."

She looked toward the next hallway.

"And now… you're ready to meet him."

Chapter 33: A Profound Realization

Paula looked at me, waiting for my answer.

"Well… it's crystal clear to me," I said slowly, thinking out loud. "People will always have questions, and they will always need answers.

Back in Aislinn's time, the truth could be twisted, and crimes could be buried if ordinary people didn't record their own stories.

If you think about it like a timeline, there were so many possible paths humanity could take. Every choice creates another timeline. The 3D world didn't just disappear overnight… it slowly faded as people chose different ways of thinking.

The doorway for 3D souls started closing in the early 2000s. After that, more 4D souls began coming in. Some of them came here to teach why things had to change… why homelessness had to end, why medicine needed integrity, why people were using drugs just to cope with a broken system.

As the collective changed, the 4D timelines grew stronger. That's why the Earth didn't end.

It wasn't the end of the world… it was the end of the 3D mindset having control over the world. It was the biggest shift in human consciousness the planet had ever seen."

I took a breath.

"That's why everything had to be recorded. It was like a birth. A new Earth being born.

And we all know birth isn't easy.

Chapter 33: A Profound Realization

Of course, the planet shook. Of course, things broke apart.

Mother Earth was becoming something new. And this new Earth... needed people to care for her."

I stopped talking and laughed nervously. "Sorry. I get carried away sometimes."

Paula stared at me with her mouth open.

Ryan started laughing. "Danica... are you sure we came from the same parents? Maybe they switched babies at the hospital."

I stuck out my tongue. "Trust me, bro. I ask myself that every day."

Ryan grinned. "Alright, Paula. Continue. My brilliant sister has spoken."

Paula shook her head, still smiling. "You just explained exactly why Metatron gave the warning. He knew the shift was coming.

He knew the 3D timelines would fade, and the higher ones would remain. And that is when the Angelic Watchers came to Enoch."

Ryan leaned forward. "Watchers? Like... aliens?"

Paula nodded calmly. "In a way.

The Angelic Watchers saw what was happening on Earth. They saw how the gifts given to humanity were being misused. They saw darkness spreading... not just in actions, but in thoughts.

They made an oath to protect humanity. They asked Enoch to record the truth... so it would not be lost again."

She paused.

"They told him to write everything down.
Every deed.

Every choice.
Every soul.

Not to judge…but to witness."

Ryan whistled. "That's actually pretty cool."

Paula continued. "Enoch asked the same question Aislinn asked.

Why me?

Why do I have to do this?

And the answer was the same.

Because you were called to serve.

This wasn't just a test for one person.

It was a test for humanity.

Every soul had to choose.

Stay in the old way…or move into the new."

I felt chills run down my arms.

"It was all about love," I said quietly. "We all want it. We all need it. We all deserve it. Aislinn loved humanity the same way Metatron does. That's why he chose her."

Paula froze. Her eyes widened. Her whole body went still.

Then she whispered, "I can feel him…"

The air in the room changed.

A warm, vibrating energy filled the space. Paula closed her eyes.

"I hear him," she said softly.

Chapter 33: A Profound Realization

Her voice changed slightly, like she was speaking from somewhere deeper.

"Bless you, my child.
Bless you for speaking the truth.
Blessings be upon those on Earth.

Walk the path of light.
Do not hide in the shadows.

Remove the veil from your eyes.

I come with open arms…and an open heart."

A bright light and warmth filled the room.

Ryan and I both covered our eyes.

When the feeling faded, Paula opened her eyes slowly.

She looked shocked. "Wow… Danica… you opened something in me.

That insight you spoke… it opened my crown chakra. I could feel his energy come through. My heart still feels like it's glowing."

Ryan blinked. "Yeah… that was wild."

Paula laughed nervously. "Okay… back to Enoch before I float away."

We all sat down again. She continued pacing.

"Enoch traveled from city to city, recording what he saw. He wasn't sent to fight. He was sent to witness.

He saw rulers break their own laws.
He saw truth twisted.
He saw the poor suffer while the powerful celebrated.

He saw the same pride destroy civilization again and again."

She looked at us. "And he was told…

Write it down. Record everything. So, the truth can never be buried again."

She took a slow breath. "That is the message Metatron gave Aislinn.

Build the building.

Record the stories.

Preserve the wisdom.

So, humanity will not forget itself again."

I nodded slowly. "I see the connection. Enoch was a scribe between heaven and Earth. He recorded what humans did… and what heaven saw."

Paula smiled. "Yes. He saw the structure of the universe… the angels… the cycles of time… the future of humanity.

He became the keeper of the Book of Life. That is why Metatron guides souls.

That is why he watches.

That is why he records."

I look over at Paula, "So, is that why Enoch revealed to Aislinn the two different books during the timeline shift? Because humanity had to make a choice? A choice of which book they would end up in?"

Paula nods. "Yes. Humanity had to make a choice. Aislinn was only the messenger."

She walked to the door and stopped.

“And when you meet him… he will tell you something only those who complete their Becoming ceremony are allowed to hear.”

Ryan leaned forward. “Oh, now we’re talking. Secret stuff?”

Paula crossed her arms.

“This stays in this building. We all promised.”

She held out her hand. “Pinky promise.”

Ryan groaned but held out his finger. “Fine.”

We all linked pinkies.

“So, what’s the secret?” I asked.

Paula smiled. “How Aislinn got humanity to listen.”

My eyes lit up. “Seriously?”

“Yes.”

Ryan grinned. “This is getting good.”

Paula looked at him. “Ready to meet Metatron?”

Ryan’s face lit up like a little kid.

“I get to wear the shades, don’t I?”

Paula sighed. “Yes, Ryan. You get the shades.”

He jumped up.

“If I had Dad’s suit on right now, I’d look like Men in Black. Kapow! Alien patrol!”

He pretended to shoot at invisible targets.

"I monitor all alien activity on Earth! Watch out, Metatron!"

Paula rolled her eyes and opened the door.

"Come on, you two. Last room."

We walked inside the final circular chamber. Paula handed us both a pair of dark sunglasses.

"Put these on before we begin."

I slipped mine on. The room went almost completely dark.

Ryan grinned. "Cool shades… Kapow."

Paula smirked. "Ryan… get ready. You're about to be blinded by the light."

Chapter 34: Mr. Metatron

We sat in the dark room as Paula clicked another small black remote. From the ceiling, a dark tinted glass panel slowly lowered in front of the small stage.

Ryan leaned forward. "What's that for?"

Paula smiled. "I warned you about being blinded by the light. Metatron is not like the other beings you've met. He is a high-ranking Archangel, and his presence can be overwhelming.

He may appear as a pillar of fire, a body of crystalline light, or as sacred geometry itself. Some people see the Metatron's Cube. Some see wings. Some only see light.

His energy is extremely high, so this glass helps protect your eyes."

Ryan nodded. "Sounds intense."

Paula continued. "Some people smell spices when he arrives... cloves, pepper, cardamom. That is one of his signs.

Metatron teaches advanced souls how to use their power wisely. He records the choices of humanity in the great archive... what some call the Book of Life, or the Akashic record.

You met the Master of the Records a few days ago."

Ryan grinned. "Oh yeah. That guy was chill."

Paula lowered her head, trying not to laugh.

"So, I need both of you to relax. His vibration is strong, and your nervous system might feel overwhelmed.

Chapter 34: Mr. Metatron

Are you ready?"

I looked at Ryan, then back at Paula.

"I'm ready."

"What about you, Ryan?"

He leaned back in his chair. "I was born for this. Bring it on."

Paula shook her head.

"I'm going to meditate for a few minutes. Please be quiet. Danica, you know what to do. Ryan… just try."

I closed my eyes and focused on my breathing. Inside my mind, I repeated slowly:

I welcome Archangel Metatron.
I open my heart.
I align my energy with light and love.
I am one with all that is.

Within minutes, I felt the top of my head begin to buzz. My breathing slowed.

Warmth spread through my chest. I smiled without meaning to.

In my mind, a brilliant golden light began to appear… swirling, growing brighter, expanding like the sun behind my eyes.

I had seen that light before during meditation, but now it felt stronger… alive.

Then I smelled spices. Cloves. Pepper. Something earthy I couldn't name.

The room felt lighter, like gravity had loosened its grip. Inside my mind, I heard a voice.

Chapter 34: Mr. Metatron

Warm. Calm. Powerful.

Welcome, my beloved human friend. We meet at last.

Paula spoke softly. “Can either of you feel him?”

I smiled. “He’s here. I’ve felt him before during meditation, but I didn’t know who it was.

He just spoke to me. He said he’s been waiting to meet me.”

Ryan shook his head. “You’re messing with me.”

Paula opened her eyes. “She’s not. You two are on very different paths.

Danica… ask him to reveal himself.”

I focused on the golden light.

Please appear.
We welcome you.

Suddenly the room filled with brilliant white and gold light. Lines of glowing geometry formed in the air like threads of fire.

I could see wings… huge… radiant… but no face.

Paula stood slowly.

“Welcome, Archangel Metatron. We are honored you have come.

Can you tell us why you asked humanity to build this structure?”

The voice filled the room. Strong… but gentle.

“Knowledge from heaven can inspire… but wisdom must be built by human hands.

This library is not only a place of history. It is a record of consciousness.

Chapter 34: Mr. Metatron

I have watched civilizations rise and fall.
I have seen truth hidden.
I have seen power corrupt.
I have seen knowledge lost.

When I lived as Enoch, I recorded what I witnessed. But now… humanity must record itself.

Every life lived with awareness becomes part of the Book of Life.

Not written by God alone… but written by humanity together."

The light pulsed softly.

"This structure exists for three purposes:

To understand consciousness.
To heal the wounds that distort it.
To preserve the wisdom gained from those lessons.

This creates the path of awakening…healing… and remembering."

I looked down at my hands. They were glowing. Paula was glowing too.

Ryan sat perfectly still, staring at the light.

Paula spoke again.

"Do you have any wisdom to share about your own journey… and how you became an Archangel?"

The voice answered. "When systems become unstable, messengers appear.

Prophets during falling kingdoms.
Philosophers during changing empires.
Mystics during spiritual upheaval.

I am not only an angel. I am proof that the human path can lead to divine awareness. Humanity is not separate from the divine. It is growing toward it."

The room felt filled with warmth.

Paula swallowed. "Do you have a message for them?"

The light shifted toward Ryan first.

"Ryan… you are both student and teacher. You teach patience, restraint, tolerance, and acceptance… even when you do not realize it.

You also teach forgiveness for your immature words, actions, and behaviors. At times…they can be too much for some humans to handle. You are a young soul, and Danica is an old soul.

Your spirit is playful, but your heart is pure. Remain true to yourself. You mean no ill will.

I will watch your journey with interest. After your display today, you have moved to the top of my watch list. I am curious to witness and record how your life here on Earth will unfold."

Ryan blinked, stunned. "…Cool. I knew I should have worn dad's old suit"

The light turned toward me.

"Danica… you are a seeker. You search for wisdom, beauty, healing, and truth. You are more of a student. There will be moments when

you must teach, even when you feel unready. Stay aware of those moments…. Windows of opportunity. Continue your meditation practice…we will meet again."

The light grew softer… as if Archangel Metatron faded into the background. I could still feel his presence.

Soft. Warm. Nurturing.

None of us spoke.

Finally, Ryan whispered, "…I should've worn the suit."

Chapter 35: Secrets

I looked over at Paula. She was still glowing. I realized I was glowing too.

My mind was full of questions… yet completely blank at the same time.

Paula spoke softly. “Archangel Metatron… you said you have two secrets to reveal today. I believe the timing is right.”

The warm golden light pulsed gently.

“Yes, Paula. The first secret is how I supported Aislinn in spreading our message.

It was simple. She loved to write. She was always a storyteller.”

The voice continued, calm and steady.

“When I first spoke to her in 2023, I told her she would write a book.

Not one book… but a trilogy. I gave her the title. Nothing more.

Then came the tests.”

I felt my heartbeat faster.

“I needed to know if she had the courage to ask other humans for help. Not only was it a test for her… it was a test for them as well.

At first she hesitated. She worried what people would think. I placed a few names in her mind, and she wrote them down.

Some listened. Many did not. Their beliefs were too rigid. Humanity was not ready.”

Chapter 35: Secrets

The light shimmered.

"So, we waited.

During that time, she grew stronger. She spoke about forgiveness. Grace. Healing. Generational trauma. The soul's journey.

She shared truths that few people were willing to say out loud. The mental-health community began to notice her."

I felt chills.

"Then she met someone. A woman who understood her immediately.

Two old souls recognizing each other again. That friendship gave her the courage she needed. Now she was ready to write."

Paula smiled softly.

Metatron continued.

"I warned her. What she would do would require great courage. Humans can be cruel. Heartless. Judgmental.

So, I gave her the same warning the Watchers once gave me:

No matter what darkness says or does to you… we are with you. There deed and words will be recorded."

The light dimmed slightly.

"But there came a night when she nearly gave up. She was exhausted. Sad. Questioning everything. Even us. She saw what was happening in the world around her. She became concerned and she knew that she had the answer… the secret… to birth this new Earth into a reality."

My chest tightened.

"She loved someone deeply… and that soul wanted to leave Earth. They kept saying that they wanted to go home. She understood what that meant. They wanted to go home.

Not here… but to heaven."

The room felt very still.

"In that moment, she did something few humans can do. She chose unconditional love. She released what she loved… instead of holding it in fear.

That was the test. And she passed."

The light grew brighter again.

"That night she prayed. She said…If you want my soul, take it. If not... give me a sign I cannot mistake."

I covered her mouth. Metatron's voice softened. "I had never heard her speak like that before. Her pain moved me. She was ready. No more tests. She was ready.

So, I came to her. I filled her room with light. I gave her the story.

The characters. The humor. The world she would write.

She shifted instantly. From doubt…to purpose."

I felt tears in my eyes.

"And I told her the soul she loved would live on. Not in the way she expected. But in the way that was needed.

You will understand that when you read her life book."

Paula took a deep breath. "Thank you… Archangel Metatron.

And the second secret?"

The light pulsed again.

Chapter 35: Secrets

“The second secret is about the evolution of the soul.

In the final days of Aislinn’s life, she experienced her last awakening in human form. I went before our Creators and made a request.

I had watched Humanity for a long time. I did not want to stand alone any longer. I asked for a companion. I chose her.”

My heart stopped.

“She had completed her work. She had passed every test. Even the ones she did not like.

So, during meditation, we brought her to us.

She saw the light.

She saw the path.

She felt the love.

And we offered her a gift.”

The room felt filled with warmth.

“If she wished…she would not return to Earth. Instead… she would become Archangel Aislinn. The choice was hers…and hers alone.”

Paula gasped. Ryan’s jaw dropped.

Metatron’s voice held a quiet joy.

“She accepted… but she had one condition. Tobias. The promise she made to him… to herself…to their love…their connection.

I honored and granted her…their wish. Their unfinished love story.

Now she stands beside me. Watching over humanity. Guiding souls.

Answering prayers. And yes…she still enjoys watching reality television with me. You humans can be quite entertaining."

Ryan blinked. "…No way. That's cool, dude."

The light shimmered with laughter.

"She says it is the best job she has ever had. She watches over both of you. And she reminds me often that humans need humor and laughter."

The light turned toward Ryan.

"Ryan…you remain under special observation. You have been placed on my favorites list. Under comedy."

Ryan grinned. "I am honored."

The light turned toward me.

"Danica… read her life book. Take your time. There is much for you to understand…and…you might be…the One. The One Tobias seeks. The choice is yours.

We will meet again."

The light slowly faded. The room returned to darkness.

The air felt calm… peaceful.

Paula removed her glasses. "So… will I see you tomorrow?"

Ryan jumped up. "I want the book now."

I laughed softly, still overwhelmed.

"I need a day. I need to be brave first. I am a little nervous… what I will learn and discover."

Chapter 35: Secrets

We walked outside together. As we stepped into the sunlight, a song suddenly came into my mind.

After everything I have learned…I do feel truly blessed to be living on this new Earth. Yet my heart aches when I think of what Aislinn endured. The questions she might have had. The confusion. The doubts. The second guessing…of herself…and what she was being called to do… for humanity.

I looked at Ryan. “You have your music player, right?”

He smiled. “Always.”

We sat down on the steps. He handed me one earbud. I can tell that Ryan knows I am deep in thought. Reflecting on all we learned and discovered.

Ryan gently looks over at me. “What’s on your mind? You look sad.”

I shrug, “After all we have learned and discovered, this one song began playing in my mind as I reflected back at what the 3D world was like for humanity.

It speaks so passionately and profoundly to me. And the woman that sang it… Lauren Daigle… her song must have spoken to millions of others. To wake up. To have hope and faith when we think or feel that we are not good enough.”

“Let me guess,” he said. “That song.”

I nodded. “Yes…that song.”

Ryan gives my hand a gentle squeeze.

Chapter 35: Secrets

"Let's listen to the song together. I know exactly what you mean. The self-defeating voices that can fill a person's mind. Making people believe they are not good enough or worthy of love.

At times, it has made me teary eyed…I listened to that song just the a few days ago…I was reflecting… especially knowing what we know now. Nobody is broken. We are all becoming."

I look into Ryan's eyes. "Now bro…that was true wisdom. Did you bump your head while shaking your hips and dancing this morning? Maybe you were just reading my mind. Either way, you said it perfectly! I couldn't have said it better."

A tear rolls down my cheek. Ryan squeezed my hand.

"Nobody's broken," he said quietly. "We're all becoming."

I looked at him and laughed through my tears.

I watch Ryan press play, and the melody '*You Say'* begins to play.

Lauren Daigle's voice filled my ear.

You say I am loved when I can't feel a thing…You say I am strong when I think I am weak.

I can hear Ryan softly singing the lyrics. My heart beams. I know she is singing about our Creators and how they can and do speak to us.

How they are here to support us in changing our thoughts…our beliefs…and view… about ourselves and others. Restoring hope and

faith… when we feel lost, fearful, confused, and when the darkness surrounds us.

They light the way.

They extend their hands. Ready to lead you out of the darkness…and those dark thoughts.

They restore hope.

They restore faith.

They love us so…. undeniably so.

Inspiration fills my heart and I begin to sing, "*And I believe, ..oh…I believe. What you say of me… I believe.*"

And for the first time, everything made sense. Praise be.

I am enough.

You are enough.

We are all just becoming.

So, take their hands… and walk into the promise land. Our land…our world… your new Earth.

The End.

www.ingramcontent.com/pod-product-compliance
Lightning Source LLC
LaVergne TN
LVHW020654110826
845149LV00012B/1994

9798995540519